DARK WATERS

DARK WATERS

BOOK ONE OF
THE LONELY ISLAND SERIES

MAGGIE ALLDER

Matador
Unit E2 Airfield Business Park,
Harrison Road, Market Harborough,
Leicestershire. LE16 7UL
Tel: 0116 2792299
Email: books@troubador.co.uk
Web: www.troubador.co.uk/matador
Twitter: @matadorbooks

ISBN 978 1803135 298

British Library Cataloguing in Publication Data.
A catalogue record for this book is available from the British Library.

Printed on FSC accredited paper
Printed and bound in Great Britain by 4edge Limited
Typeset in 11pt Aldine401 BT by Troubador Publishing Ltd, Leicester, UK

Matador is an imprint of Troubador Publishing Ltd

To all my friends in Arizona and Texas, who have become such an important part of my life.

ABOUT THE AUTHOR

Maggie Allder was born and brought up in Gamlingay in Cambridgeshire, the second daughter of a village police officer. She studied at King Alfred's College, Winchester (now the University of Winchester), in Richmond, Virginia, and later at Reading University. She taught for thirty-six years in a Hampshire comprehensive school. After exploring more orthodox forms of Christianity, Maggie became a Quaker, and is happy and settled in the Quaker community in Winchester. She has previously written three novels which form a trilogy of sorts: *Courting Rendition*, *Living with the Leopard* and *A Vision Softly Creeping*. The fourth and fifth novels, *The Song of the Lost Boy*, and *Beyond the Water Meadows*, each stand alone. All these first five novels take place in and around Winchester, where Maggie still lives. Maggie volunteers for a not-for-profit organisation, Human Writes, which aims to provide friendship to prisoners on death row in the United States.

PROLOGUE

I am sitting in the corner of the Meeting House. Under my feet I can feel the gentle warmth of the heating coming up through the floor and through the soles of my warm winter boots. The boots are only two years old, heavily embroidered in bright colours in traditional En-Somi patterns, passed down by the *bondii*, or peasants, for generations – centuries, perhaps. The room is warm and, on this winter morning, full of shadows despite the wall lamps. People are still arriving. I can hear the gentle greetings of the welcomers in the strong stone porch, murmuring their "Good mornings" and their "*Goddi Morgoni*", which is island dialect, and more familiar, kindlier than the English.

I am one of the older ones. The children call me "*Mori-mori*", which means "Grandmother", but I have no grandchildren here. Soon I will have another one on the mainland, so I am told, but how easily Duncan will be able to bring his family to visit me, I cannot tell. I don't suppose I'll ever be able to see him, my only son, and his family, in their home. Travel is not so easy nowadays. Still, the children here call me *Mori-mori*, as they do all the old ladies. I am *Mori-mori Marie*, greeted with exuberance or shyly, depending on the child, and every time I hear those words my heart is delighted. Small children are a gift, whoever they belong with.

The room is becoming quite full, despite the strong northerly wind and the sleet outside, which you would have thought would be enough to keep anyone at home. We have no cars on the island. Almost everyone here will have braved the cold bluster to walk to Meeting, when the warmth of their hearths must have been so pleasant, inviting people to stay where they were. I am feeling peaceful and almost ready to settle into worship, only first I need one more thing to happen – or rather, one more person to arrive. We enter into the Light alone. It is for each of us individually to choose to worship or not to worship; no priest or pastor, no ceremony or ritual, can take us there. Yet we are all part of a group, a community. We are each alone, but not alone, linked to one another by something strong and intangible, linked also to the sleet and the northerly wind and the stones from which this Meeting House is built, and to the children who call me *Morimori Marie* and who believe that I am as old as the hills, older than they will ever be.

Ah! This is who I have been waiting for! Malcolm has come in, smiling from some brief exchange in the porch. He is unzipping his jacket, taking off his gloves, looking around the room. Our eyes meet and he gives a little nod of acknowledgement. I see that he is wearing that thick winter *gensi* which I knitted for him years ago. He likes the colours, the warm reds and greens and the natural beige of the undyed wool. I would like to knit him a new one, but he wouldn't wear it, so instead I darn the elbows every autumn and take pleasure in a man who takes pleasure in the gifts I give him.

Malcolm will sit by the door. More times than I can count, he has been summonsed out of Meeting by someone needing his help. The whole length of the room is between us, but even so, now that he has arrived, I feel complete. I look at the table in the centre, with its few books and the little pile of rocks which represent all of creation, then down at my embroidered boots, and then I close my eyes. It is good to be here, good to be worshipping in the silence, good to be old, with all my adventures behind me. I feel nothing but thankfulness.

I went to the Mediterranean once, years ago when I was young and the world was a very different place. I was with Xander, whose parents came from that part of Europe. We stayed in a small house down by the water's edge, where all the living accommodation was on the first floor to avoid the dust in the summer and the sea spray in the winter. We slept with the balcony doors open and I could hear the waves lapping against the shore whenever I turned over. It was spring, the year I finished my Highers, before Granny died. I remember thinking that the weather there was a friend to the local people. The sun browned their skin and ripened the olives and the oranges that grew in groves above the village. Even that early in the summer, the sea was warm enough to swim in, and in the evenings, even when it was dark, we could sit outside on our balcony and watch the fisherman putter home on their small, blue-painted boats. I didn't wear a jacket the whole time we were there.

Here, the weather is not our friend. Don't misunderstand me, it's not our enemy either. How can I describe it? The weather here is like a boisterous animal that has never quite been domesticated. It pulls and tugs at us, it controls us, even though we like to think that we are in control. It's unpredictable, in a very predictable sort of way. It causes us few surprises, but we never know what it'll do next. Even the old men sitting by the fire in the *fi'ilsted* don't try to predict the weather, the way farmers and seamen are supposed to do. The *fi'ilsted* is the small building which would be known as a pub on the mainland, but which is called a 'fish hearth' here, from the days when only the men were welcome there, and every grown male was a fisherman, at least for a part of the year. The old men sit around the fire, which is sometimes peat but usually driftwood, and discuss endlessly what the weather might do next. They claim no expertise or insight; their speculations are mere guesswork, as if the weather were a pack of cards and there was no knowing the hand you might be dealt next.

I am remembering a time way back, I suppose it must have been thirty years ago, or maybe even more. I tend to lose track of time nowadays. Duncan was already at school on Shetland, and I was alone in my bothy, the little crofter's cottage where I still live. It was dark and the wind was howling around my low chimneys, the wind turbine was whirling and creaking, charging the batteries that fuelled my home, a strange chorus of ancient and modern. From my windows, which face west, I could feel rather than see the dark churning of the sea below. There were no lights on the ocean. It would have been insane to go out on the water on a night such as that.

Inside, I was warm and comfortable. It was quite late. I recall that I was wearing pyjamas and a thick *gensi* that had passed its best, which I wore around the bothy for years after I had decided it was too worn to be seen out in. The bothy hasn't changed very much since then. It is built of stone, consisting basically of one room, with chimneys at both ends. The stove at the south end of the room is the cooking stove, made to look like the black iron range it replaced, but actually conforming to mainland regulations, fuelled by the En-Somi gales, harvested by the turbines. There is an alcove at the opposite end to the kitchen beside the second fireplace, an alcove with sliding doors across it and a bed behind the sliding doors, positioned so that the occupant, when there is one, sleeps with his feet towards the warm stones of the chimney, where we placed the ground-heat boiler. Duncan always insisted that he had his own bedroom, but he didn't really. Like many of the children here on En-Somi, he slept in a cupboard, comfortably close to any adults who might be sitting by the range and, when the Wi-Fi was working, watching television. Our children, here on the island, don't live

2

lives separate from the adults, the way so many did when I was growing up on the mainland, hundreds of miles away.

In the summers we have long, light evenings, but at the time I am remembering it was autumn and already dark. I was more or less happy to be living on my own, and since I had raised Duncan on the island, I felt very much at home, although back then I suppose I was still sometimes seen as an *un-fed*, or outsider. It is only recently that I have been sure that I am accepted as an *En-Som-in-Fedi*, or islander.

When I arrived on En-Somi, the pregnant partner of Bjorn, I was viewed with some suspicion. It was understandable, I know. The islands, even those that are less remote than En-Somi, suffered from unwelcome immigration. Things were hard on the mainland and too many people suddenly saw the benefits of the simple life, thinking that they could just make the transition from crowded cities to remote island life, although they brought no survival skills with them, and didn't begin to understand how to live out here in the roaring North Atlantic. If I hadn't had Bjorn with me, I don't suppose I would have lasted one winter, living in this little bothy on the edge of a slope so steep that it is really a grass-covered cliff, looking out over the fierce sea.

For nearly five years, though, I did have Bjorn with me. We renovated the little bothy, building the cupboard where Duncan slept and a sleeping platform to be our marital bed. I think we were happy. At any rate, I was. I know now that I wasn't in love with Bjorn, not as I was later to experience being in love, but I was fond of him and I liked the life. I enjoyed being a mother to Duncan, I took pleasure in putting hot meals on the table for my family every evening, and probably more than anything, I relished being away from the endless troubles of the world. I remember I liked it best when the Wi-Fi was down and we were completely cut off, not only from the mainland, but from the other islands. Not for nothing is this small patch of rock and turf called 'En-Somi', the Lonely Island.

So that evening I suppose I was just pottering around, the way I did after dark, after eating. Bjorn had long gone, and even Duncan was away, pursuing an education. I was alone and the wind was howling in the two squat chimneys, the turbines were swishing, and everything was all quite normal. And then I heard a sound.

It surprises me, looking back all these years later, that I heard anything. Many, many nights since then I have sat by my hearth and heard the sounds of an autumn storm and the whirling and straining of the turbine and wondered how it could have been possible to hear anything other than those wild winter noises, but I did. I heard it. I heard it distinctly enough to put on a jacket and my boots, and to grab a torch, and to leave the dimly lit bothy for the wind-torn night and the steep, rocky path down to the shore and the crashing waves.

As if I were an islander born and bred, I was always comfortable in the dark. No, I should correct myself. I don't think I was any more comfortable than any other sensible young woman, in the dark streets of Edinburgh or Melrose or Oslo, in the days of the troubles. I stayed inside and I stayed safe. Yet, from the moment I set foot on En-Somi, night-time fears left me. It was impossible to imagine pestilence or evil stalking those bleak, clean-swept cliffs or moors. The darkness was different from the day, but no more threatening, no less a part of the whole of life on the island. I took a torch because the steep path down to the shore was uneven, though goodness knows, I must have been familiar enough with it by then, and because I wanted to investigate that noise, a noise that should not have been there.

My bothy faces west, and that rocky western shore is only partly sheltered from the huge Atlantic rollers by a small peninsula of rock and two majestic stacks which jut up out of the water and seem to guard our little bay. I rounded the corner where once there had been another crofter's cottage, now ruined and useful only for sheep to shelter in on stormy nights. I could feel the spray from the waves on my face. There was a rush and

4

heave in the air and in the sea, a crashing of breakers on rocks and the gurgle of receding water, rushing back to the churning ocean.

I think I stood there, my feet firmly on the flat, rounded pebbles of the beach, looking out into the darkness, straining my ears, struggling to remember what I had heard. There was a myriad of sounds, a whole symphony of roaring and swishing, of howling and moaning, but it was all in tune, a concerto of rough, wild weather. Where was that discord I had heard when I was in my bothy? What was it that had brought me here?

★ ★ ★

I shone my torch across the beach. The storm and the incoming tide had washed fresh driftwood into a pile at its northern end. In the morning, I would come back and collect it up and take it to the *fi'ilsted*, where I would exchange it for fresh fish – Atlantic Cod, perhaps, or even crab. I had no need for traditional fuel, but anything and everything that was deposited on our shores was of value to someone. There are only twenty or so small trees on En-Somi, and they are squat, sheltered by stone walls in an attempt to protect them from the worst of the weather. Back then, they must have been no more than saplings. Perhaps they hadn't even been planted. It's hard to remember the order of things when the days and the seasons circle round and round. Anyhow, driftwood was valuable. It has never ceased to surprise me how much of it there must be in the sea, washing up on our remote shores.

Probably I would have ventured no further. The noise I had heard had stopped, or was being completely drowned out by, the swish and crash of the water and the air. I was beginning to think it must have been some trick of the wind in the steel ropes that anchored my wind turbine to the hill behind the bothy, or maybe some wild animal in distress. I was about to turn and climb the steep path back up to my glowing range and some hot tea and my bed, when something stopped me.

5

It is not quite that I saw something, more that I somehow became aware that I was not alone. Perhaps when you live for years in a wild open landscape, where there are more sheep than people, and more seabirds than either, a person develops a second sense, an awareness that another human being is close by. I remember standing there, all my senses alert, trying to feel, rather than to listen for, that alien sound.

And there it was. Not the call that I had heard from my bothy, but a moan, somewhere between a sigh and a groan, only a few feet beyond me.

I shone my torch south. A pile of rocks and loose stones was heaped against the bigger boulders that marked the edge of the beach. I could see something white. A sheep, maybe, caught below the high-tideline? They are not sensible animals, but every sheep belongs to a neighbour and every animal has value. I picked my way across to investigate. A wave, larger even than its predecessors, crashed onto the shore and the surf foamed round my boots. The thing moaned again. Not a sheep, I knew that now. I shone my torch over towards the stones.

It was a child.

She was wearing almost nothing – some sort of pale-coloured dress, maybe, and her white arms were stretched out as if she had been trying to hold on to something. She was lying crookedly on her side, her face towards me, the water swirling round one ankle, the other leg drawn up beneath her, as if she had been trying to crawl up the beach.

"Hold on!" I called. "I'm here. It's all right! I've got you!"

I doubt if she heard me. I stumbled in my hurry to cross those last few steps towards her, and the next rush of surf reached the child at the same time as I did. It would only have been a matter of minutes before the tide would have claimed her again, dragging her back into the sea.

I thrust my torch into my pocket and reached for the girl clumsily. I was sure she must be injured, that I might do her further harm as I grabbed her awkwardly and lifted her from the stony beach, but I had no choice. Even as I stood, the child in my arms, another wave rushed up the beach, the water topping my boots, tugging at my pyjama legs. I took a step backwards, almost fell, and then regained my footing. I took a deep breath to calm myself.

"It's all right now," I said, although whether I was speaking to the unconscious child or to myself, I'm not sure.

She was cold to the touch but breathing. I took a few steps up the path and around the first bend and lay her on the turf while I took off my jacket. Wrapping her in it, I lifted her again and staggered on up the path. I could see the bothy lights from there, I was almost home.

"Nearly there," I assured the child, or myself, "only a few steps more."

Then we were passing the old coal shed where I stored imperishable goods in neat rows on shelves that Bjorn had built, and at last I was pushing at the door, managing to lift the old iron latch, and then we burst into the calm warmth with more urgency than elegance.

★ ★ ★

The few bits and pieces I had left of Duncan's clothes were too big for such a waif of a child. He had been a sturdy boy, more like his father than me in stature, and the things he had worn when he was little had long since been passed to neighbours or traded. The wet rags which clung to the body of the child were useless. I stripped them from her easily, and lay her on the settle, the long, upholstered seat that all those years ago Bjorn had built against the east wall of the bothy. I rooted around in the chest where I stored my clothes, and found the soft pink shirt I had brought with me from the mainland. It swamped the girl, but it would be warm at least, and gentle against her skin.

7

I had to decide what action to take. We all had phones, of course, but at the best of times they only worked intermittently. The mast was at the other end of the island, not built for the *bondii*, the common folk who live out on the moors. It had been erected, some years earlier, to serve the wealthier people who lived in the area called Floirean's Cnoc. The signal where I lived, where I still live, was weak, blocked by the bulk of Fyrtarn Fjell, which is Beacon Hill in English. The Wi-Fi was down because of the storm. It was a twenty-minute walk, at least, to the Kullanders' place over the hill. And what could they do that I couldn't do?

I turned the range up two notches, so that the deep and reassuring orange glowed out more brightly from the glass panel at its centre. I switched on the kettle, feeling that perhaps I ought to make the strange child some warm tea. How did I expect her to drink anything? Her eyelashes fluttered a little and she moaned, but she was still unconscious. Her stick-thin arms were cold to the touch. I made the tea for me instead, and while it brewed, I stripped off my own soaking pyjamas and *gensi* and dressed in my thick, warm day-clothes. This was going to be no night for sleeping.

The *nasyonii*, the island police, would have to be told, I realised, as soon as possible. Somewhere there must be parents frightened half to death about their missing daughter. I didn't know the child. She wasn't from this side of the island. Was she even from En-Somi at all? But surely, she must be! We were fifty miles at least from Liten Stein, which is 'Little Rock' in English, and there was nobody living there anymore, and then another thirty or so miles after that to the Shetlands. Could she have fallen overboard from some trawler caught in the storm? But no; no child would be dressed like that on a boat.

The poor wee mite was moaning softly. Her lips were cracked and dry. I took a cloth and gently wiped some water onto them, and she stilled. Her limbs were cold to the touch. She needed to warm up, or she wouldn't survive. I pulled my rocking chair up to the hearth and took the girl onto my lap. I wrapped my arms around her as I had with Duncan all those years ago, when he was just a wee lad, and I hummed a song softly under my breath, '*Hush little baby, don't you cry*', and I rocked gently back and forth. And the wind howled, and the waves crashed against the rocks, and the steel ropes anchoring the turbine strained, and the blades whirled.

And sometime in the night, while I rocked gently, half asleep, the spirit of that little girl left her body.

★ ★ ★

I'm not sure when I realised that she had died. It was still dark, but of course sunrise isn't until nearly nine in the morning at that time of year. I was staring into the orange glowing window of the range, which so successfully mimicked a real fire, and I wasn't thinking about anything in particular. Then it seemed to me as if the body of the child grew suddenly lighter. I looked down at her face, and it was the same, but different. It was, I would say, a face at rest. I knew she had gone at once. I have thought about that so often since. Does the soul have a weight? An actual, physical heaviness, so that a person becomes lighter when they die?

So I placed her back on the settle and fetched the patchwork blanket from Duncan's bed to cover her, and I made myself some breakfast. And I found that I was still humming, '*Hush little baby, don't you cry*', and I found that I was weeping.

W hen Bjorn and I had first moved into the bothy, the simple business of leaving it, even to walk to the Kullanders' place, involved quite a lot of activity. The wind turbine wasn't erected nor was the ground-heat pump installed for more than two years, so we lived as his grandparents had lived. We never let the range go out, summer or winter. The fire in the north hearth was kept alight, too, from late September until May at least. If we were both going to be away from home at the same time, both heat sources had to be tended, the fires banked down and the flues adjusted so that the peat didn't burn too quickly. If the day was still and the chickens were out, pecking around the flattened earth east of the bothy, then before we left, we needed to usher them back into their coop. We learnt that the hard way, when a storm blew up while we were away, and we lost two hens and our prize cockerel. They must have been blown away.

The hens, of course, were safe in their coop, and I no longer had fires to worry about. I closed the shutters and checked one last time on the little girl. I knew she was dead, but it didn't seem right not to tuck her in more securely under Duncan's patchwork blanket, and to stroke her hair away from her cold face, and to tell her that I wouldn't be gone long.

The gale, when I left the shelter of my bothy, was blowing from the north. There was sleet in the wind. It stung my cheeks, and I pulled my scarf up over my mouth to protect as much of my face as I could. For a moment, I wished I had a dog. He would have been company for this wild walk, but the only dog we had ever owned had been Bjorn's, and had left with his owner. I took the old, heavy staff that had belonged to Bjorn's grandfather, and headed up the hill, away from the sea.

On calm days there seem to be sheep everywhere on these hillsides, but that morning there were none to be seen. Sheep, even our moorland breed, are stupid creatures, but they know how to hunker down during a storm. When my path joined the larger cart track heading for the Kullanders', the hillside seemed almost bare, just deep green grass and rock, but as I walked, I did occasionally spot dirty white wool in the lee of rocky outcrops and in grassy hollows. Overhead, the great black-backed gulls were wheeling and screeching, riding the blustering air, looking for carrion, for creatures that had not survived the night.

I was facing into the north wind for most of that walk. It was hard work, uphill all the way until I reached Oda's Corner, where to this day there is a small broken shrine to the saint, which nobody tends any more. Then the path turned south again, and became steeper, until I topped the hill and saw the Kullanders' house, a welcoming, dark-red, two-storey building with deep, overhanging eves.

The Kullanders were, like me, like all of us living on the west coast of the island, *bondii*, or peasants. It isn't a good translation. Peasants, in France or Russia, were hardly free; as far as I understand it their lives were governed by the whims of the wealthy. *Bondii*, on the other hand, have always been fiercely independent. Some say that we are directly descended from the Vikings who called at En-Somi on their way to Iceland. Others claim that it is the other way round, that the *bondii* of En-Somi once invaded the coasts of Norway, that the Norwegians are descended from our ancestors.

The Kullanders came from ancient island stock. They had once been wealthy, back when oil was respectable. An earlier generation had replaced the old stone bothy with the house which was there at the time I am telling you about, and which still stands there to the present day, looking westward, braving the Atlantic, backing into the moorland behind it. Lights shone from every window. It was a welcome sight.

I opened the door, which was rarely locked, and a blast of warmth seemed to rush out to greet me.

"Alf!" I called out. "Fiona? Anyone home?"

Fiona came out from the kitchen, drying her hands on a towel.

"*Morgoni*," she replied, a slight frown creasing her forehead. "You're out and about early on this stormy morning! Is everything all right? Come into the kitchen. I was just going to make tea."

As I took my boots off and propped them on the rack, alongside lots of other boots and shoes belonging to the family, Fiona was calling upstairs, "Alf! Marie's here. And I'm making tea."

Alf called down, "Be right down."

I followed Fiona into their wide, warm kitchen. Their house could hardly be more different from my cosy little bothy. It had once been the height of contemporary fashion, rather full of stainless steel and shiny work surfaces, but that was years ago, and now all the brashness had worn off. At different times various alterations had been made: the place had been heated by oil, which used to be stored in a huge underground tank behind the house. When they were forced by law to change to sustainable fuel, some pipes had been taken out, others introduced, and holes patched. Now the room had that comfortable, slightly scruffy appearance of a much-loved and lived-in room. There were children's drawings fixed to the fridge with magnets in the shape of letters of the alphabet, and a calendar hanging slightly crookedly next to the window, still showing October, although it was November by then.

"Sit down! Sit down!" bustled Fiona, pulling out a chair and wiping the wooden table in front of me with a grey rag. "Is everything all right at your place? Now let me see, you don't take sugar, do you…"

She had her back to me, pouring tea into three mismatched mugs. Just then, Alf came in.

"*Morgoni!*" he greeted me, just as Fiona had. "Blustery morning for a social visit. What's occurring?" He pulled out the chair opposite me. "I'm guessing this is not just a social call? Storm done some damage?"

Fiona put our mugs down in front of us, opened a tin of home-made biscuits, and then sat down herself.

I blurted it out. "I found a dead child on the beach."

Alf was just sipping his tea. He spluttered, coughed, and wiped his hand over his mouth. "You *what?*" he exclaimed.

Fiona was holding her mug halfway to her mouth, looking at me with shocked eyes.

"I heard a noise," I explained. "I went down to the beach to investigate. I found a little girl. She was still alive then. I brought her back up to the bothy, but she died in the night."

They were both silent for a moment, stunned. Fiona slowly returned her mug to the table.

Alf said, "And it was a wild night. Our internet's still down. You couldn't contact anyone." It was a statement of fact, an acknowledgement of what it was like to live in such a remote place. "And she's still in your house?"

"It felt cruel to leave her alone," I admitted.

Fiona put her warm hand over mine. "Who is she?" she asked.

"I don't know. She's not from around here."

"My God," sighed Alf. "Somewhere there's some frantic parents… and no way to contact them." He sipped his tea.

Fiona took her phone, which was sitting next to a pair of scales on the work surface. She swiped it on and looked hopelessly at the screen. "Still no signal," she said.

Alf was thinking aloud. "We need to contact the *nasyonii*," he said, referring to the island police. "I'd better walk up to the village." He gulped his tea and stood, putting his mug in the sink.

Fiona said, "I'll come down to your bothy, Marie. This is no time to be on your own." Then she went to the foot of the stairs and called up. Andy still lived at home back then, a gangling boy of about thirteen, being home-educated until his parents thought he was ready to go to the boarding school in Lerwick.

"We're both going out for a while, Andy," she shouted. "We don't know when we'll be back. There's cold chicken in the fridge for lunch!"

"Right, Mam!" Andy called down. "See you later." Then he came to the top of the stairs. "Can I have cake, too?"

"Just one slice!" Fiona admonished. Then, turning to me, "That boy's going to eat us out of house and home one of these days!"

★ ★ ★

It was a shock, going out into that northerly wind. From the Kullanders' house you could see for miles, over the roof of my bothy, which was hidden from sight by the slope of the hill, and out to sea. The ocean was grey, flecked with white. The sky seemed low and heavy. The storm pulled at our coats but seemed to push us down that first slope of the path, until we reached the corner, then we were halfway there. It was definitely easier going downhill!

My bothy was still and quiet. We tugged at our woolly hats, pulled off our boots, and hung our jackets on the hooks by the door. Fiona walked over at once to the settle and looked down at the little girl.

"She just looks as if she's sleeping," she murmured.

I went over and stood by her side. "I couldn't bear to pull the blanket up over her head," I explained. "It just felt so final – so uncaring."

"You're right, though," agreed Fiona. "She's not from around here. How old would you say?"

"Seven?" I guessed. "She's as thin as a rake. Undernourished, I would say."

"Some bairns are like that," said Fiona. "They run around all the while." She patted the shoulder of the child, as if comforting her. "It's heartbreaking, isn't it? I wonder what happened?"

★ ★ ★

14

We knew, Fiona and I, that nothing would happen in a hurry. Alf would walk up to the village. We all had mountain bikes, but nobody tried to use them in weather like that, and as you will know, it is one of the characteristics of the island that there are no motor vehicles. It has always been this way. Even when the world moved to electric cars, only a few *un-fedii*, outsiders, wanted to introduce them here. We are, I suppose, a conservative community, but there was more to it than that. Back in those days the islands were attracting a lot of interest and we were swamped with incomers. A small workshop had been built just outside our one small town, something to do with micro-electronics and the new technologies, and the owners wanted to showcase their creations where only carts drawn by ponies had previously been. The real *En-Som-in-Fedii*, or islanders, were never going to change their customs for a bunch of mainlanders and their foreign ways!

There was mud on the stone flags from when I had stumbled in with wet and dirty boots the night before, carrying the wee girl. Fiona found my long-handled broom and started sweeping, while I put the kettle back on the hob. I suddenly felt very weary, and Fiona must have noticed.

"Sit yourself down," she suggested. "There's nothing to be done now." She looked across at my blank router, housed on a shelf high up by the roof beams in an attempt to catch some sort of signal. It showed no lights. "We'll just have to wait until they get here."

I sat by the range and took out my knitting. Fiona pulled up the other rocker, and she, too, sat with her feet on the fender. Outside, the wind hummed in the steel ropes of the turbine and the sleet battered at the shutters. I could feel myself nodding off. I was glad Fiona was there. That poor wee child…

And then there was banging on the door, and a sudden cold draught, and I was awake, and Alf was standing in the open door with Lyle standing behind him. Both men had sprinklings of snow on their shoulders and on their woollen hats. Behind them in the open door, I could see that it was dark again.

"My God!" exclaimed Alf, taking off his jacket and shaking the snow off it, before hanging it over the jackets that were already on the hooks. "It's turned to snow!"

Lyle was a huge man. He was only young back then, perhaps in his late twenties. He had been a teenager when I had first arrived, some sort of cousin of Bjorn's, so I had seen him growing up. By the time all this happened, this business I am remembering here, he was a good six and a half feet tall, and big with it. He had a mass of ginger-blond hair and a beard, every inch a Norseman. He looked a little like Bjorn, to tell you the truth. He was quiet, too, the sort of man who seemed to think carefully before he spoke. He was the only *nasyoni,* or police officer, on this side of the island.

Fiona was making tea. Both men came over to the range in their stockinged feet, holding their hands towards the warmth. I saw Lyle glance towards the child, now looking icy white, with her dark hair spread out on the pillow behind her.

"It isn't wise to keep her in the warm," he said. "Poor lassie."

Fiona asked, "So you don't recognise her, Lyle? We didn't."

"*Nei.*" Lyle left his place by the range and stepped over to the child, looking down at her with a sort of gentle perplexity on his face. "She's just a wee bairn."

Fiona passed him his tea. He stood there, a huge man beside a tiny girl. Then he asked, "And she was washed up on the beach?"

"That's what it looked like," I confirmed. "She was below the tideline."

"What time was that?" Lyle was doing some calculations in his head.

"Around ten?" I guessed. "I didn't notice the time. I was on my way to bed."

Alf said, "The tide was turning, then. If she was thrown onto the beach by waves, it would have been hours earlier. She would have been dragged back out to sea in less than an hour, if you hadn't found her."

16

Lyle bent close to the girl, looking at her face. "What a tragedy!" he murmured, and reached for the quilt, covering the child properly.

We were all silent for a short while. The shutters rattled in the gale; a cacophony of storm noises screamed round the bothy.

"It's surprising you heard her from here, on a night like last night," commented Lyle.

"It is," I agreed. "And now I can't remember what it was that I heard. But something took me down to the beach."

"It was meant," suggested Fiona. "You were supposed to find the child."

"But it did no good!" I exclaimed. "If I had been able to save her, perhaps, but…" My comment trailed off. A wee dead girl lay under the blanket, a little life lost for ever.

With the body lying on the settle, there was nowhere for the men to sit. Alf went over to the desk where I kept the computer, and dragged the wooden bench across to the range. "So, what now?" he asked Lyle.

Lyle sat, stretching his long legs towards the warmth. Fiona, in the rocking chair opposite mine, held her hands round her mug as if to warm them.

"Well…" Lyle was thinking it through. "The lassie can't stay here. I could take her back up to the *fi'ilsted* and put her in their barn. It's cold there, but it's a bit of a junk hole. And the storm will be over in the next day or so, according to the Met Office. Then we can sort things out properly. I'll radio Sergeant Stensen as soon as we get reception."

"It's a rough night to be walking back to the village," Fiona pointed out. "And carrying the child too. Stop off at our place tonight and finish the journey tomorrow. We can keep the body of the poor mite in our old wood store." She looked at her husband. "That'll work, won't it?"

"It will," agreed Alf. "But we ought to set out at once."

Fiona turned to me. "Do you want to come with us?" she asked. "Stay a night or two? Get over the shock?"

She was kind, but "*Nei*, thanks," I answered. More than anything I just wanted to climb up onto my sleeping platform and shut out the world.

Lyle stood, patted me on the shoulder and said, "Then we'll leave you in peace. Can we take this blanket to wrap the wee one in?"

"Of course!"

I watched the three of them put on their coats and boots, wind their scarves round their necks and pull on their woollen hats and gloves. Finally, Lyle stepped over to the child, lifted her as if she were still alive, and wrapped her more securely, almost tenderly, in Duncan's blanket. He carried her the way a father would carry a sleeping child, her head resting on his shoulder, as if we had been having a pleasant evening together, eating and telling stories, and now they were just going home.

Fiona gave me a tight hug, rather clumsily because of all her outdoor clothing. Alf kissed me on the cheek. Then the door was open, a few stray flakes of snow whirled in while the sad little group left, and I was alone.

I made a sandwich of cold chicken and dandelion leaves, turned down the range and checked on the boiler. I changed into my warm winter pyjamas, climbed the ladder to the sleeping platform, and nestled under my duvet. The wind howled in my chimneys and rattled my shutters. I think I turned over once, finding just the right place on my mattress, and then I slept. I slept so deeply, I might as well have been dead myself.

The real name of the village, the one you will see if you look up En-Somi on a map or on the internet, is 'Gamla Husmannsplass'. It comes from the Norwegian and means something like 'the Old Homestead'. The oft-repeated joke of the locals back then was that there were more letters in the name of the village than there were inhabitants. What's more, in those days it was probably true. There were the two middle-aged men who ran the *fi'ilsted*, they were *un-fedii*, or outsiders like me, but like me they were, as far as I know, completely accepted. The schoolteacher was already widowed by the time of my story, I think, and her grown-up children were living right over on the other side of the island. The bothy where Lyle lived – and which still belongs to the *nasyonii*, the police force, to this day – was at the northern end of the settlement and there were two or three other habitations opposite Lyle, a little further down the hill. There is one main track running through the village, but a smaller path comes down from the fjell further inland and winds down to the coast south of me, forming a sort of crossroads. The village shop is right there, where the two tracks intersect. If you ever visit En-Somi, which is unlikely given the current travel restrictions, the first thing you'll notice about the shop is that it has a turf roof, still to this present day, just as it did back then. It was certainly the thing that made the biggest impression on me when Bjorn first showed me around. There was a goat grazing on the roof. It's a sight I'm used to now, but I think at the time it told me, more than anything else, how different life was going to be on the island. The three stone buildings east of the crossroad, further up on the moor towards the fjell, were derelict at the time I am telling you about now – very different from nowadays, when they are full of life.

Of course, we never call the village by its full name. Even when official letters come from the mainland, the name is abbreviated to 'Gamla Hus', and we generally just call it 'the village' or even just 'Hus'.

Patrick and Shona ran the village shop in those days. Like village shops everywhere, I suppose, it was our post office too, a bookshop (in a small sort of way) and the place where government leaflets were displayed and then ignored. Patrick was a thin, bearded man, prematurely grey but cheerful, and good with his hands. Shona was the talkative one, and a great singer. It was generally agreed that if they hadn't had so many children, the authorities wouldn't have allowed the village school to stay open. All their offspring had Shona's golden-red hair. My Duncan was the only dark-haired child in the school at one point.

When I woke up the morning after Lyle, Alf and Fiona had taken the child's body away, I knew at once, without having to think it through, that I would go into the village that morning. I could still hear the wind in my chimneys but the humming of the steel ropes anchoring my turbine had changed. It was late in the morning; late to be waking up, that is. I suppose it was about nine o'clock, but the shutters were still closed and so the bothy was dark. I clambered down the ladder into the main room, turned up the range, put the kettle on and then donned my jacket and boots.

We are, as you will realise, a very northerly island, but even so we don't often have snow that settles. It must be something to do with the ocean. Nowhere on En-Somi is more than a mile and a half from the sea, and even on the top of Fyrtarn Fjell, if you lick your lips, they will taste salty. Still, I wasn't surprised when I opened my heavy wooden door to see that the world had turned white. I took some feed round to the chickens and topped up their water, and then stood looking seaward. It was, I thought, beautiful. Out there, on the edge of nowhere, it was easy to forget the damage our species had done to the earth. Everything was wild. Everything was free. Down in the direction of my beach, a dozen or so gulls had found something to scavenge in the sea. They were wheeling and squawking and diving down into the grey waves.

I went back inside, made myself a proper breakfast, and sat over my coffee, thinking. Would the child still be in the Kullanders' wood store, or would Lyle have taken the body over to the village this morning? I wondered what Lyle's sergeant would say. Would they have to make all sorts of reports to the mainland? I would find out, anyhow, in Hus, and I needed to buy some bits and pieces and to see whether a letter from Duncan had arrived.

The wind was still blowing powerfully so that in places the stony path was clear and dry, and in other places there were sudden, unexpected snowdrifts. Even so it was easier walking than it had been the day before, on wet and slippery rock. My path to the village bypassed the Kullanders' place, taking me instead to the south side of the old stone wall, which still marked a boundary, although I didn't know whose. A lot of the land on our side of the island was owned by people in the east in those days, people who were not *bondii*, people we didn't know.

It took a good half hour, even in perfect conditions, to reach the village. On a distant slope of moorland, I could see a figure dressed in fluorescent orange, a man working his way along the line of yet another stone wall. It would be the crofter Jamie, checking that none of his sheep were buried alive. The air felt crisp and clean. It was good to be out.

I walked with my head up, I remember, the wind tugging at my jacket and woolly hat and smarting coldly against my cheeks. I saw the tracks of a blue hare in the snow and heard the baaing of sheep somewhere far away. The frozen air was hard on my lungs as I crested the hill, and then I was looking down into the valley where the village huddled.

Ancient civilisations lived on this tiny island; archaeologists have found artefacts going back 4,000 or so years before the

Common Era. There was a settlement even then, it seems, in this sheltered valley, and it was a well-chosen site. There's a deep inlet, a small loch really, below the village on the north side of the island, and a natural summer harbour where the men keep their fishing boats right up to the present day, dragging them up twenty feet or so away from the water's edge during the dangerous winter months, when huge waves roll up the loch and break with wrecking fury against the shore. It is debatable whether the north wind, coming from the Arctic, or the east wind, sweeping across from the frozen highlands of Norway, or the west wind, howling in from the wild North Atlantic, cause the most havoc on En-Somi, but Hus is sheltered from all three. You can't see the sea from the village. Norse Hill, which shelters the settlement, also blocks the view of the sea, but you can almost always hear it.

My path brought me from the ridge down to the school and the crossroads. Beyond me, the main part of the village (if you can call it that) was still in the shadow of Fyrtarn Fjell. I stomped the snow from my boots and opened the door of the shop.

The village shop was rather different in those days from the way it appears now. Even on these remote islands, the late twenty-first century is catching up with us. Of course, there are no drone deliveries here. A couple of the big online companies tried that a few years ago but too many packages went astray; the weather is just too wild and unpredictable. It was a decade or more, too, since any planes had landed on En-Somi. Even so, nowadays the shopper can sit at a computer and make an order of almost anything, and sooner or later it will arrive, over on the other side of the island where the ferries come in.

Back then there was no row of smart computers. Instead, where you can sit now to browse for the item of your choice, there were shelves from floor to ceiling, jammed full of all sorts of products people might suddenly need. You could buy gaffer tape and nails, printing paper and postcards, matches and candles, and tins of baked beans. The big wind-powered chest freezers filled up the whole of the centre of the store, and on the shelves to the right of the door were the books.

Patrick was with a customer. They had their backs to me, and Patrick was peering over the shoulder of the shorter man, a stranger to me, as they looked together at one of the volumes.

"It's the only history I know of," Patrick was saying, "that deals with anything on this side of the island beyond Hus. A couple of historians from Edinburgh wrote a short book about the Shetlands, En-Somi and the Faroes, but we hardly get a mention. There might be something in Oslo, if you read Norwegian? Or possibly in Iceland."

Shona came into the shop from the room behind the counter. "*Goddi morgoni*, Marie," she said, putting a plate of fresh-baked oat biscuits on the counter. "We heard about the child on your beach."

The two men turned to look at me. "*Morgoni*, Marie," said Patrick. "It must have been a shock. Where's the poor wee thing now?"

I took my gloves off and stuffed them into my pockets. "Lyle and Alf took her over to the Kullanders' place last night," I explained. "Lyle didn't think it was right to keep the body in the warm, at my place, and we couldn't contact the other side of the island."

"Still can't," said Patrick. He glanced up to the top shelf where a router similar to mine appeared as dead as mine.

The stranger was looking from one to another of us. "I had no idea," he said, "how cut off you all are over here."

"Oh, Marie," Patrick seemed suddenly to remember. "You don't know Malcolm, do you? He's just moved into old Cadha's place, up behind yours."

I was surprised. *Mori-mori* Cadha had died almost a year earlier, and before that she had lived with her daughter and son-in-law behind Fyrtarn Fjell for months after her fall. Her bothy had been empty all that time, and had been falling slowly into disrepair.

Usually, we all knew if there were any changes happening in our small community, but I had heard nothing of the cottage being sold.

"Is it even habitable?" I asked, then remembered my manners. "Welcome, anyhow!" I added.

He was a strange-looking man. He was not very tall, perhaps a couple of inches taller than me, but broad. He looked, somehow, like an outdoors man, with that shade of red hair which is not quite ginger, and a bushy beard. He was dressed just like one of us, not like an *un-fed*, with a thick, well-worn waterproof jacket and a red knitted hat that clashed with his hair.

"It was a sudden decision," said Malcolm. "I must admit, I've wondered about the wisdom of it, over the last couple of days. Such a storm!" Then he smiled, a wide, friendly grin. "And *nei*, the cottage is absolutely not habitable! I've got snow on the floor next to my bed!"

We all laughed. "How will you manage?" Shona wanted to know.

"I'm off down to the *fi'ilsted* when I'm done here," Malcolm replied, "to get a hot meal and to see if they can give me a bed for a week or two, while I patch the place up."

"They might at that," agreed Patrick.

"So, we're neighbours?" asked Malcolm, turning to me.

I laughed. "It depends what you mean!"

Shona explained, "It's a good twenty-minute climb from Marie's to yours, if you follow the burn. If you take the path round by Michaelmas Fjell, it's nearer thirty minutes. Still, I would say Marie's your closest neighbour."

"Or Jamie MacLoughlan," I suggested.

"Yes", agreed Shona. "He's closer as the crow flies, but you'd need a boat to cross Oden's Inlet."

Patrick asked, "Are you wondering what you've taken on, Malcolm?"

I must admit, I was thinking the same thing.

Malcolm didn't look at all perturbed. "I grew up on the east of the island," he explained, "but I've been away a long time. I came back a few months ago, but things've changed a lot over there. I think this is more like the En-Somi I remember."

Shona laughed. "You mean bleak and cold and isolated?"

Malcolm laughed too. "*Aja*, all of that, but friendly and – well, basic, I suppose."

At that point Sigrid, the schoolteacher, came in. She is long dead now, of course, but I had known her well while Duncan was in her care, and even before, and I was pleased to see her.

"Ah!" she exclaimed. "A gathering!" Then she asked, "So you've all survived the storm so far? A bit of a shock for you, Marie, finding that wee lass."

"What is this, about a child?" Malcolm asked.

Sigrid pulled a glove off and held her hand out to Malcolm. "You'll be Malcolm McDough, the man whose bought *Mori-mori* Cadha's place? Welcome!" She took off her other glove and eased her backpack onto the floor. "Petter told me just now. You found a little girl, dead, on your beach?" She was checking her facts with me, although Petter was usually right.

"She wasn't dead when I found her," I explained. "She died in the night. In my arms."

Shona put an arm round my shoulder. "You poor thing," she said, "and you alone in that bothy!"

"Who was she?" asked Malcolm. "Surely nobody round here would let their child go outside in a storm like this!"

Sigrid chipped in. "We don't know," she said. "You didn't recognise her, did you Marie? Nor did Alf or Fiona. Lyle and Alf tried to take the poor wee thing over to the town, but the pass is still closed. She's in the Kullanders' barn."

Malcolm had an expression of deep sadness. He said, "Some poor parents, somewhere!"

None of us said anything. I was thinking of Duncan. If anything happened to him… Who knows what the others had on their minds?

Sigrid broke the silence. "Well, she won't come to any harm in that freezing barn! And there's nothing to be done until this storm eases. And I need some flour, and treacle, if you have it!"

She had changed the mood by those few sentences.

Shona seemed suddenly to remember. "Oh, Marie, a letter came for you, three days ago!" She went back to the room behind the shop and returned with a green envelope. "Here," she said, passing it to me.

"It'll be that son of yours," said Sigrid. "Bright lad!"

"Cheeky!" I answered, smiling. Duncan had addressed the letter to *Mori-mori* Marie, which was a joke between us, because I was so far from being an old lady. I had been just twenty when he had arrived.

★ ★ ★

I had expected to go straight home once I had done my shopping. There was obviously no more news about the wee girl, and nothing to be achieved by staying in Gamla Hus until the long dusk started and the temperature dropped further. It was, therefore, a complete surprise when Malcolm said, "Well, I'm away to the *fi'ilsted* now, to talk about a bed and board, and to have a meal. Would any of you like to join me?"

Shona and Patrick declined. "I'm doing a roast this evening," explained Shona. "We finally killed that old hen."

Sigrid said, "Treacle pudding for me, tonight!"

I thought of my cosy little bothy, and the remains of a lamb stew already sitting in the fridge ready to be heated up, but then I thought of the warm hearth of the *fi'ilsted*, and of how pleasant it would be to drink coffee with some of Petter's good whisky in it, and I said, "I'll come!"

★ ★ ★

It's so long since I have even visited the mainland that I can no longer remember what pubs smell like. I visited a few, that year before I dropped out of university – sophisticated Edinburgh establishments with blackboards listing the specials for the day – but I was always with other people – at first, groups of fellow students, then Bjorn. I'm sure none of those institutions smelt like the *fi'ilsted*, of woodsmoke and peat, of coffee and fresh-baked piecrust, and of burning oil and wet waxed jackets hanging on the backs of chairs.

Petter was behind the bar, perched on a stool and doing a crossword puzzle from a dog-eared book of old *Times* crosswords from way back in the twentieth century. He had a pen in one hand and a pencil tucked behind one ear, for all the word like a character in an old film. The delicious smell of seafood stew was wafting in from somewhere behind the public room.

Malcolm looked around, his expression approving, at the low ceiling and the fish-oil lamps, and at the casks of whisky behind the bar.

"*Morgoni*, Petter," I greeted him.

Petter looked up from his crossword puzzle and raised an eyebrow. "Good morning," he said, formally, in English. He obviously hadn't met Malcolm.

I introduced them, and we took off our jackets and I removed my boots too and rested my feet on the brass rail fencing off the stone hearth. I listened as Petter and Malcolm sounded each other out, Petter assuring himself that Malcolm was, to all intents and purposes, a local and not any sort of *un-fed*, and Malcolm discovering that Petter was a friendly person, not inclined to judge a man for the foolhardiness of moving into a semi-derelict bothy at the beginning of a harsh winter.

Malcolm came and sat at the table by the fire opposite me, and Petter came out from behind the bar and asked, "Will you eat? Malchi has been cooking all morning, he's on fine form. I can heartily recommend his food!" He patted his round stomach and smiled happily.

27

So it was that we four, Petter and Malchi, Malcolm and I, sat by the fire and ate fish stew and dumplings and drank Irish coffee, and talked until it was dark. We talked about the village and the surrounding bothies, about the weather and the impossibility of getting round the island by boat during winter storms, about how good a *nasyoni* Lyle was turning out to be, despite his youth, and about the uselessness of our Wi-Fi connections. By mid-afternoon it was agreed that Malcolm could rent the back bedroom at the *fi'ilsted*, and Petter had volunteered to help with the installation of a ground-source heat pump and the erection of a turbine at Malcolm's.

"I can't cook," he said, touching Malchi's arm lightly, affectionately, "or build walls, but when it comes to carpentry or renewable energy…"

Then it was time to go. The wind had at last dropped. Calm nights are unusual on En-Somi, but that night, the sky was clear and the stars were bright and close. We stepped outside into the crisp cold, and Malcolm said, "I'll walk you home."

I laughed. "There's really no need!"

"I have to go and collect some of my stuff," said Malcolm. "And anyway, I'd like to know where my nearest neighbour lives."

We walked back, over the crest of the hill and away from the village, and down towards my bothy. We talked of this and that, but nothing significant. There was a sort of companionship about being out in the open, chatting inconsequentially about sheep surviving storms and about there being so few predators on En-Somi. Malcolm wouldn't come in when we reached my home, but I showed him the short way to his bothy, following the burn, and then went inside.

Even when I looked at the settle where she had lain, the death of the wee bairn and the two days following seemed somehow distant. I took an apple and a lump of cheese and munched them, standing beside my glowing range. Then I checked on the chickens, who were roosting contentedly, and went inside again. I felt deeply content. I hardly recall climbing the ladder and going to bed. It had been a good day.

The next couple of days passed quietly. The Wi-Fi came on at some point early the following morning. The radio had been on when the signal had gone down, so I was woken at twenty past five in the morning by the shipping forecast. I lay there listening as the calm, London-accented voice moved round the British Isles in a clockwork direction, "Humber, Thames, Dover... Lundy, Fastnet, Irish Sea... Rockall, Malin, Hebrides..." and finally, "Faroes and then South East Iceland," always the last two areas to be mentioned, and the only two to affect us.

I had quite a lot to do, I remember. I cleaned the bothy, let the chickens out into the relatively still air, picked some sprouts from my vegetable patch and put a pile of laundry into the machine. Although the storm was over, the air was still cold, and the snow wasn't melting. When I walked down to the old coal shed to collect a few potatoes I could see my breath in the air.

After lunch I put on my boots and jacket, pulled my hat down warmly over my ears, fished my gloves out of my pockets, and headed down to the beach. I needed to collect the driftwood I had seen on the night I found the child.

It was such a contrast to my last visit. A hazy, low sun gleamed dully through a slight mist. The sea was quiet; small waves lapped on the shore where just three nights ago they had crashed dangerously towards me. A small flock of black *muckle scarfs*, known to you perhaps as cormorants, was circling around the nearest of the stacks south of my beach, diving for fish, occasionally making their strange grunting call. I could hear sheep some distance away, behind me, and a dog barking.

I walked the length of my beach. It's more of a cove, really. I remember looking at the place where I had found the child, wondering again how she could possibly have got there, thinking gratefully of Duncan studying safely on Shetland, trying to decide whether to take Danish or Norwegian. There was nothing left to show that the little girl had been there, not even scuff marks amidst the gravel and pebbles.

I had brought Duncan's old sledge down with me. We had discovered years earlier, when he had still lived at home, that the best way of getting piles of driftwood up to the bothy, and later up to the *fi'ilsted*, was to drag it behind us.

It was just as well. At the north end of the beach there was a ragged pile of wood. Mostly it was broken branches, some quite large, but there were two planks, painted blue on one side. I wondered how far these offerings of the sea had come. From Norway? From Iceland? Or even from Greenland or the Canadian coast? There was no way of knowing. There were two torn plastic bags in amongst the debris too. Even then, so long after such things had been banned in every civilised society, we still saw them, and other plastic objects, washed up on our shores.

I piled the wood in a bundle onto the sledge and tied it securely, and then stood looking out to sea. The sun was about to set, but there were clouds just above the horizon, so that it looked as if there were mountains out there. I watched as the sky went from pale winter blue to streaks of gold and red, until the whole of the western horizon was glowing pink, and then the colours faded and the long winter dusk had started.

In those days I used to go quite a while without seeing anyone else. Of course, until he turned eleven, I had always had Duncan around, but once he went off to Shetland I was on my own during term-time. It never bothered me. The bothy, the chickens and my vegetable plot and kale circle kept me active and I had learnt the local knitting skills, unique to En-Somi, and could spend happy hours sitting by the range and (if the Wi-Fi was working) watching television programmes that left me feeling grateful that I lived where I did.

It was, therefore, a surprise when, the following morning, Lyle turned up.

I was sorting through the goods in the old coal shed. The storm of a few days earlier had reminded me that I ought to make sure I had everything I might need, if we were to have a winter as bad as two years earlier. The weather was totally unpredictable and all of us on the western side of the island had long since realised that we had to plan for the possibility of being stuck at home for almost any length of time once the winter had arrived. The wind had resumed its more normal, gusty mood by then, and I didn't hear Lyle's arrival. He had propped his bike up against my stone wall and was walking towards me when I heard his cheerful call.

"*Hei*, Marie!"

I turned and smiled. "Lyle! *Goddi morgoni!* Cup of tea?"

We went into the bothy, both of us taking our boots off at the door, and Lyle wriggled his toes inside his socks as he rested his feet on the fender.

"No storm damage here, then?" he enquired. "That stone wall along by the summer harbour has fallen. Forty-foot waves down there, I'm told."

"I'm fine," I said. "Just making sure I have everything I could need if the weather turns really bad."

Lyle gave a grunt of assent. Every bothy-dweller on the island would be doing the same thing.

"I came to give you an update," he explained as I passed him his tea. "About the wee lassie."

I sat opposite Lyle in the other rocking chair. "Who was she?" I asked.

Lyle frowned. "Well, that's the thing, Marie. The *nasyonii* over there know nothing about a missing bairn."

I was stunned. "She must belong somewhere!" I said, "I mean…"

"I know." Lyle looked sad. "Now that the internet's back, they've tried everywhere. Not just on En-Somi, but across the water too. There's no record of a missing child matching her description anywhere."

"So now what?" I wanted to know.

"So, they'll keep the DNA and the photographs, and the autopsy report when it's written, and bury the child on Aeloff's Hill. There's nothing else to be done."

"That's so sad," I exclaimed.

★ ★ ★

I walked out with Lyle when we had finished our mugs of tea, and so I saw Malcolm approaching, following the burn down towards me. The two men stopped and talked for a moment or two. Lyle had his back to me but I could see Malcolm's face, and his sudden smile at something the *nasyoni* had said. Then Lyle mounted his bike, turned and waved to me, and peddled off up the track towards the Kullanders'.

"There's tea in the pot," I greeted Malcolm.

"Excellent! Excellent!" he replied, following me inside, leaving his boots by the door, looking around at my snug dwelling. "Oh, this is lovely!" he said. "So, you decided to keep it as one room, like my place? Where's your bathroom? But you built a mezzanine floor!" He was looking up at my sleeping platform under the eaves.

I showed him the bathroom, on the opposite side of the north chimney to Duncan's sleeping nook.

"Very Scandinavian!" was Malcolm's comment.

I smiled. "Bjorn's brother – Bjorn was my partner – Bjorn's brother came over and did the work," I explained. "Nice, isn't it?"

Malcolm stood in the middle of the main room. The shutters were open; the view from the windows on the western side of the bothy was clear and stark.

"It's like the edge of the world!" exclaimed Malcolm, almost reverently.

"So, how's it going at the *fi'ilsted*?" I asked.

Malcolm grinned. "Amazing breakfasts!" he announced. "And good company. Petter wants to help with the bothy. I've fixed the roof for the time being, but it'll take time to finish the insulation."

"What about fuel?" I wanted to know. Back when Bjorn and I had been renovating our place it had taken forever to get all the necessary permissions, to say nothing of the parts, for the turbine and the ground-source heat pump installations.

"All in hand," said Malcolm, sounding confident. "*Mori-mori* Cadha's family had made all the applications. I bought the bothy knowing that."

We settled by the range. It was glowing cosily; there seemed no need for conversation. I was finding that Malcolm was a very easy person to be with.

After a while he said, looking at my kitchen cupboards in the south-west corner of the bothy, "I would say you did this place up about ten years ago, right?"

I chuckled. "Twelve," I told him. "How did you know?"

He was grinning that infectious grin again. "We had similar cupboards in our house in Edinburgh. They were very fashionable a decade or so ago."

"Are you saying I'm unfashionable?" I asked, in mock indignation.

He laughed again. "I'm not!" he said. Then he added, "I think Petter will build my furniture for me."

There was another peaceful silence. Malcolm was staring into the glass panel of the range, at the friendly glow, a slight frown on his face.

"How long did you live in Edinburgh?" I wanted to know.

Malcolm seemed to come out of a trance. "Most of my adult life," he said. "I was at university there, and then I got a job. And a wife. And a house. And then, over a few years, a son and two daughters."

34

I didn't know how to answer that. "Wow!" I said, rather lamely. "Will any of them be joining you here?"

He looked sad. He stood, poured himself more tea from the pot that was keeping warm on the range, and returned to his rocking chair. "Iona – my wife – succumbed to cancer when my youngest was only six," he said. "The bairns have all grown up now, with lives of their own. The youngest is at university in Glasgow. And I've retired. Well, given up, really. I sold the Edinburgh house, and I can live on very little here."

"I'm sorry." It sounded rather inconsequential, but what can you say?

There was another of those comfortable pauses. Then Malcolm added, "And to be honest, I was getting rather disillusioned with life in the city. I really needed to get back to En-Somi, to my roots." Then he flashed that bright smile at me again. "Although," he said, "if I spend all morning sitting at your snug hearth, I'll never have one of my own. I must get going."

He stood. Then he added, "Actually, I have to go over to Storhaven sometime soon, to pick up some stuff and sign the final registration papers at the town hall. I wondered if you'd like to come with me and grab some lunch. Petter says you don't get out much…"

I laughed. 'Getting out' was an Edinburgh concept. *Bondii* or common folk like us didn't 'get out', we just lived our lives, each day as it came along. Still, lunch at one of the two *fi'ilstedi* in Storhaven would make a good change before the worst of the winter set in, and I had a couple of *gensii* I had recently finished knitting, to drop off at the En-Somi craft shop down by the ferry port, where they would sell for a great deal more than they cost me to make.

"That would be fun," I agreed.

As I have already mentioned, back when travel was easier and En-Somi had more of a tourist trade, one of its attractions was the fact that the island council had decided against motorised transport. Later, when the environment was a big issue, people wanted to come and live here because of the clean air and what was often, rather patronisingly, called our 'simple lifestyle'. The reality, of course, is that things are not at all simple if you have no cars or buses. Our little horses, related to Shetland ponies but not pure bred, served us well back then, and still do, of course. We used them then, as now, for carrying anything around the island that can't be transported using human energy or boats, but only someone who has never had to manage with ponies instead of machines would call our lives simple!

Malcolm had borrowed two ponies from the village, along with a traditional hefty wooden cart, narrow but long, to meet the demands of our narrow tracks. I met him at the *fi'ilsted* in Hus, where he and Petter were standing talking while they waited for me to arrive.

"We can ride over," he said, "but I'm afraid we'll have to walk back. The cart'll be full."

"No problem," I reassured him. "I usually walk to Storhaven if there isn't a boat going round."

I remember that there was a strong easterly wind that day. While we were navigating the stony track out of the village it felt quite calm, but as we rounded the side of Fyrtarn Fjell, the wind hit us with full force. The ponies tossed their heads. They are sturdy creatures, accustomed to more or less anything the island climate can throw at them, but they are as entitled as the rest of us to object to air from the Norwegian tundra blowing directly into their eyes. Malcolm, who had been sitting next to me in the cart, jumped down and went to the animals' heads, making soothing noises and then walking alongside them.

Fyrtarn Fjell is the highest hill on En-Somi, and once we had followed the track round to the south of it, the rest of the island was spread out in front of us. It is a long, thin island, with no very defined shape. There are cliffs and coves and lochs, places where the moorland slopes gently down to inviting beaches and other places where great black rocks mark the stark boundary between wild land and wilder ocean. The track veers off to the north, linking several bothies and an old ruined chapel before following the slope of the land round to the south again, and down into Storhaven.

Malcolm stopped the ponies at the first sight of the little harbour town. He stood looking down at the roofs and quay, and at the fishing boats, rocking on their moorings.

"That's where I grew up," he said.

I climbed down from the cart and went to stand beside him. "Which was your place?" I asked.

He turned a little to the north and pointed. "You see that turbine? The one by the cairn? Our bothy is in the hollow down there. East facing. You can't see it from here."

"Who lives there now?" I wanted to know. It seemed odd that he would buy *Mori-mori* Cadha's derelict bothy if the family owned something close to the town.

"We sold it," he said. "Years ago. It belongs to *harkrav* now."

I winced. *Harkrav* is an island word, hard to translate. It means something like the English word 'elite' or 'the entitled people'. It carries a burden of implications, associated with wealthy outsiders buying up property and land which we *bondii* could never afford. It smacks of people with contacts in Edinburgh, London or Oslo, people who can get things done on the island which the rest of us could never achieve. It even has a bit of a feel to it of the medieval English word 'overlord'. No *bondi* would ever admit to wishing we were *harkrav,* but I'm sure that back then we all dreamt of what we would like to do if we were one of them.

We stood there for a moment in the cold wind. Storhaven is small; I suppose in those days there were about 5,000 inhabitants. Most of the older homes were down at the bottom of the hill, nestling between Frigg Moor and the harbour. Some, like our village store, still had turf roofs, but most had been built using the dark slates brought by boat from the Scottish slate islands. To the south, on a small ledge part way up Frigg Moor, was the building which housed the only twenty-first century industry on the island: a small electronics workshop of some sort. The larger houses of the *harkrav* were mostly built up on Floirean's Cnoc and were served by the only metalled road on the island. It was nicknamed 'The Road Less Travelled' because it led over the Cnoc and down towards St Matthew's Bay, where the airport used to be, and then stopped. The airport had only been operational for a few years. It was a part of the island I didn't know at all back then.

The ponies started tossing their heads again. Their instincts told them not to stand out on the exposed moors like that, and we set off, downhill, with Malcolm occasionally using the wooden brake like an expert.

Once in the town, our business took us in different directions. My visit to the craft shop was more successful than I had anticipated. Several of the *gensii* that I had knitted in the summer had sold, and I had two commissions on which down payments had been made. I was, of course, only one of a small team of home-knitters who supplied the market, but as the only person to knit the Fyrtarn Winter pattern, I was rarely short of work. About half the money I had earned from the items that had sold went on buying new wool, but the rest was mine, and I left the harbour area feeling unusually wealthy.

Malcolm and I met, as planned, at the Old Castle *fi'ilsted.* He was there before me and had taken a table by one of the small windows that looked out, down the cobbled street, to the harbour wall. We ordered Edinburgh Gin and chatted about nothing much while we looked at the menus.

"The chowder's good," remarked Malcolm. "Not like the America dish, but worth trying."

"Mm," I was wondering about conventional fish and chips.

"All the fish we eat here…" he said thoughtfully, "it's not surprising we're so healthy on the island. I could never convince my clients that fish was better for them than endless burgers."

"Your clients?" I asked. "What was your job?"

"Didn't you know?" Malcolm replied, looking amused. "I worked for a charity. The *Leith, Moredon and Craignure Social Outreach*. Our main concern was with deprived families, especially if there were children involved. Trying to work ourselves out of a job, and failing miserably."

I don't know what I had expected Malcolm to say, but as soon as I understood that he had been a sort of social worker, everything I had noticed about him seemed to fall into place. He had that mix of empathy and leadership you find so rarely, combined with the ability to see a funny side to things.

"A tough job, I should imagine," I remarked.

Malcolm looked thoughtful. "A young man's job, really. I think the worst of it was the contrast. Every evening I came home after a day of difficult conversations – you know, clients treating my suggestions with suspicion or downright hostility, and me scrabbling about for resources. I didn't blame them, but it was the hopelessness of the thing – and I'd walk into our house and Iona would be cooking the meal, the kids doing their homework or texting their friends, or practising their instruments… like a different world. Try as I might, I couldn't give to my clients what my family took for granted."

"*Nei*." I was thinking about raising Duncan on my own once Bjorn had left. Wherever I looked in Hus or the surrounding scattered bothies, I always had support. "You make me think how easy I've had it."

"I wouldn't say that." Our food arrived – two chowders with warm bread rolls and a second gin each.

"That child…" Malcolm started to say, after a mouthful or two of his meal. Then he said nothing further.

My mind was still on the children of the poorer parts of Edinburgh. "Which child?" I wanted to know.

"The wee lass – the girl you found on the beach."

"Oh." Of course, I had thought about her a lot – it was as if she were always there, just beyond the everyday matters that occupied me.

"You didn't know her." It was a statement rather than a question.

"*Nei.*"

"And neither did the *nasyoni* – the officer. Lyle, isn't it? Or Alf?"

"*Nei*, none of us recognised her," I agreed. "And they didn't know her over here, in Storhaven, either. Or on the mainland."

Malcolm paused in his eating and stared out of the window. The brightness of the day had already passed. The cobbles gleamed darkly in the pre-dusk gloom, and the sea was crested with white, spraying up over the harbour walls.

"She couldn't have come from the mainland," he said. "Not even Shetland, I would say. Not and still be alive on your beach. She could only have been in the sea for a short time."

"*Aja.*" The same thought had occurred to me.

"So, she came from En-Somi," Malcolm concluded.

"But Malcolm, nobody knew her!" It was frustrating because he had to be right, but how could he be? Everyone would know if an island child was missing.

We ate in silence until our bowls were empty and there were just a few crumbs on our side plates. Malcolm was playing with his paper place mat, curling up one corner and watching it slowly uncurl again. He was frowning.

"What do you know about the camp out by the airport?" he finally asked. I had a feeling that he had been wondering whether to broach the subject.

"Well – nothing," I said. "I mean… is it still there?"

Malcolm's eyes were still fixed on the place mat. "When I first got back," he said, "I stayed at the Frasers' place. Do you know Dougie Fraser? We were at school together, here in Storhaven and then in Lerwick. Anyhow, his wife, Ingrid, was talking about families still living out there. At the airport. You know – refugees."

"Well, but…" I was really taken aback. "Surely, there can't be! Didn't they close that camp years ago?"

Malcolm looked at me directly then. "So, you knew there had been a camp there?"

"Everyone did!" I thought for a minute or two. "Flights to En-Somi stopped completely two years after I arrived. They brought in the refugees the following summer, before Duncan started at the school in Hus. There was quite a fuss, over here, I think. Not on our side of the island, of course. We never even saw them."

Malcolm asked, "Climate refugees?"

"That's what we were told. From south of the border. I never knew much about them. The island council was up in arms about them."

"I can imagine."

I was remembering back to those days, discussing the matter with Bjorn. "I think people thought the authorities had just dumped them here. They didn't know anything about the highlands or islands – they didn't have any skills." I suddenly recalled something I had heard in the shop in the village back then. "One of them was a motor mechanic! In En-Somi, where we don't have motor vehicles! Can you imagine?"

"And then what?" Malcolm wanted to know.

"Well, I thought the authorities gave in," I said. "Didn't they take them all away again, by ferry, to… well, I'm not sure. To Shetland? Or back to Aberdeen? Somewhere where there would be work?"

Malcolm was taking out his card, settling the bill, and then standing. Outside it was nearly dark. "That's what I thought," he remarked, holding out my jacket for me to put on. "But according to Dougie's wife… Anyhow, I think we have a slow and cold walk home ahead of us. Let's go!"

★ ★ ★

The easterly wind hit us almost like a wall of cold when we emerged from the Old Castle, and we could hear the roar of the waves now that the tide was high, the ocean challenging our small rocky island for supremacy.

"The ponies are at Dougie's," Malcolm told me, his voice hardly carrying against the thunder of the sea.

We were standing just outside the *fi'ilsted,* still pulling on gloves and arranging our backpacks. Just at that moment, a group of three people came out of the Old Castle, talking and laughing. They weren't looking where they were going, and we shouldn't have been blocking the door, and they barged right into us, so that I staggered back, tripped and sat down, rather suddenly and inelegantly, on the ground.

"Hey, watch it!" exclaimed Malcolm.

It was a group of two men and a woman. It was the woman who replied. "Perhaps you should watch it yourselves!" she retorted. "Standing in everyone's way!"

I stood up. "Sorry!" I said, instinctively.

"I should think so!" said the woman.

One of the men remarked, "No harm done!" Then, addressing the woman he asked, "You're not hurt, are you?"

Malcolm looked indignant. "She's not the one who got knocked over!" he reminded the trio. Then he asked me, "Are *you* all right?"

"Of course she's all right!" said the woman angrily. "Why wouldn't she be? Perhaps it'll teach her a lesson!" Then, to one of her companions, "Come on, Dominic. We're expected at Loch House."

As they strolled away, we both clearly heard the woman say, "Honestly, they're such peasants round here. No manners at all!"

"*Harkrav,*" remarked Malcolm, and there didn't seem to be the need to say anything further.

★ ★ ★

We struggled up the hill away from the harbour and turned right into a narrow street where the houses on the east side sheltered us from the gale. Dougie's house was part of a terrace of single-storey homes with two windows facing the street and a door between, like a child's drawing. The stables which served all the houses were at the end of the row.

"We don't need to bother Dougie," said Malcolm. "He'll probably be over at his son's, anyhow."

The street was narrow and cobbled; the little houses looked inviting and warm, with lights shining from their windows, although it was barely three o'clock.

Halfway along the road Malcolm stopped and looked around him.

"What's up?" I asked.

"Well…" he answered, almost hesitantly. "What do you see?"

Right opposite us was the lighted window of someone's home. Inside, a child was sitting at a table, perhaps drawing. As we watched, a woman came over, looked at the child's work, and patted her on the shoulder. The little girl looked up and the two smiled.

"Just an ordinary family," I said.

"*Aja.*" Malcolm started to walk again. "You know, my clients in Edinburgh probably had more money coming in than these people, what with benefits and handouts. But on En-Somi – well, people just seem to get on with life."

I thought about it. "*Aja*," I agreed, "but it's different here, on the island, isn't it? I mean, I hardly ever need money except for groceries… You probably need to be spending money all the time on the mainland. And here we help each other out."

"We do," agreed Malcolm. "The *bondii*. But what about the others? What do the *harkrav* contribute?"

"Well," I considered. "I think they help each other out, too!"

When the Wi-Fi was working, Duncan and I spoke every Saturday. Back then he was living in a hostel in Lerwick, on the Shetland Islands, along with kids from various other islands or remote communities.

"So how long did it take you to get home?" Duncan wanted to know. I had been telling him of our trip to Storhaven.

"A good hour," I answered. "Malcolm had the cart piled high with stuff for his bothy, and the ponies were tired. But it was worth it. He and Petter are making really good progress, I'm told. The place is weatherproof and the heating engineers are supposed to be coming over on the next ferry. He reckons he'll be in by Solstice."

"Ah, Mam…" I could see the hesitancy on Duncan's face, despite the rather hazy picture on the screen.

"Uh ha?" He was going to ask me for something, I could tell.

My son looked away from the camera. He was in his study bedroom. I could see a row of books on a shelf and the corner of a poster. "The thing is…"

I wanted to make it easy for him. "The thing is," I suggested, "that you want to spend Solstice with a friend?"

Duncan laughed; a laugh that made me think of Bjorn. "Oh Mam!" he chuckled, "I never will get anything past you, will I? But it's not a friend – it's Paps."

"Your father?" I was surprised. Bjorn was living in Norway by then, in Tromso, remarried and with two small children and some sort of interior design business. He had always stayed in touch with Duncan, sent him cards and presents, but I didn't think they were close.

Duncan looked, I thought, a bit worried. He didn't want to upset me. "He's invited me over for Christmas."

45

"That's kind," I answered, trying to sound non-committal. If Duncan wanted to go to his father's, well and good, but it had to be his choice.

"So, Mam … would you mind?"

"Of course not!" It wasn't quite true, but I thought I sounded convincing.

Duncan gave me one of his huge smiles. "Mam, you're a hero!" he exclaimed. "I'll come to you for Solstice next year!"

I laughed. "Next year's a long way away!" I reminded him. "Say hello to your father from me."

★ ★ ★

If you have read the one guidebook still in print that includes En-Somi, you will already know that ours is not a particularly Christian community, in the traditional sense of the word. At the time that I am remembering now, there was certainly a Church of Scotland kirk in Storhaven, and children all across the island learnt some Bible stories at school. However, the old Methodist chapel on the track from Hus to the town was in ruins and there were no church buildings on our side of the island at all, populated or unpopulated. For a few years there had been a small group of Mormons, but they had failed to make any converts, and had gone somewhere else, where the harvest of souls might be more abundant.

Of course, all our festivals are influenced by the Christian calendar, but our traditions are older – the Christian elements are just a veneer. The two solstices were (and still are) focuses for our biggest celebrations, and of the two, the winter solstice is the one most beloved by islanders, especially the *bondii*. In fact, then as now, if you heard people talking about 'Solstice', you could be sure they were thinking of December 21st or 22nd. Long ago, the islanders had blended the 'real' Solstice with customs from the mainland and from things they had seen on television. We have no holly, ivy, mistletoe or fir trees on En-Somi, but it was not unusual for people to buy artificial trees and to decorate them. And, of course, to this present day we feast, but always on lamb, never on any sort of bird. I would be really surprised if any of the children, except among the *harkrav*, have ever tasted turkey.

The excitement and anticipation for Solstice builds up steadily right through the autumn. As soon as the children go back to school in the middle of August, they start collecting wood for the *solstice-brennii*, the big fires that are lit at the first moment light is seen in the sky on the shortest day of the year, and which are kept alight until well after nightfall. Great piles of driftwood appear beside bothies and in the hollow opposite the shop in the village, and more is taken up to the tops of fjells and down by the Hus summer harbour. Orders go in for fireworks, and in due course packages are brought over the track past Fyrtarn Fjell and dropped off at the shop for *bondii* to collect.

I wondered how I would spend Solstice with Duncan away, but I wasn't worried. Nobody ever spends it on their own; it's a community celebration. Often, like most of the people on our side of the island, Duncan and I had started off at the *brenni* of one household and moved, through the short day, to others, walking miles between bothies, eating and drinking more at every stage. Well, I decided, when the head of a pretty girl (one of Shona's daughters, I thought) appeared behind Duncan on his screen, and he told me he had to go, I would wait and see how things turned out.

Meanwhile, life continued, as far as I can remember, in an entirely normal fashion. The hens, all but my beautiful Wyandotte chicken, stopped laying, but with only me at home, one egg every couple of days was enough. Each day grew shorter and darker. I heard of floods in England and fires in Australia, and a small volcano erupted in Iceland and for several days we had stunningly beautiful sunsets. The children in the village school put on a concert of island music, the eerie, plaintive songs about elves and mermaids and mountain spirits, sung unaccompanied but with interludes played on the zither-like *langspil* by old man Olaf, who must have been of the same generation as *Mori-mori* Cadha. Everyone from our side of the island was there, and there was talk of *harkrav* visitors, the owners of the land bordering mine, but in the end they didn't appear. We gathered in the *fi'ilsted* afterwards and drank whisky while Olaf continued playing, and the children raced around outside in the darkness, playing with someone's luminous football.

It was a sociable evening, I recall. The Kullanders had come down from their place and one or two people from bothies on the other side of Fyrtarn Fjell were there too. Malcolm, who had been living in the *fi'ilsted* for several weeks by then, was helping Petter serve everyone, while Malchi came through from the kitchen every now and then with plates of *pylsa*, the lamb-based hot dogs that are so popular, covered in mustard and fried onions. Sigrid, Fiona and I were sitting at the little round table in the nook where the old sepia photographs of the village back in the nineteenth century are displayed. I seem to remember we were talking about knitting patterns, which were (and are) a matter of serious interest to every *bondi*, male or female, who was part of our cooperative.

I was beginning to think about going home when Malcolm came over.

"Ladies!" he said, with mock old-fashioned courtesy. Then he added, "I'm off into Storhaven sometime this week. Is there anything I can be fetching for you?"

"Oh, Malcolm," Sigrid was looking pleased. "Will you have the cart? There is a big box of books that came in off the ferry for the school. Could you pick them up for me?"

Fiona commented, "Alf and I went in last week. We won't go to town again this side of Solstice."

"You could drop off two *gensii* for me," I said, "but there's no urgency."

"I can do that," agreed Malcolm, "and *aja*, Sigrid, I'll have the cart. I'll be bringing the last of my stuff over for the bothy. I'm moving back in."

A huge burst of laughter came from the men by the door. Olaf had paused his playing and was telling them one of his fishing stories, which bore a much greater resemblance to myths than to history, and which were always funny. Sigrid and Fiona stood to go and join the men, and Malcolm sat where Sigrid had been seated.

"You could come over to Storhaven with me," he suggested.

I was rather surprised. "I don't really need…" I started to say, then I caught a look in Malcolm's eyes and stopped.

As if I hadn't spoken, he continued, still speaking quietly so that I had to lean forward to hear him above the laughter of the others. "I was thinking of taking a look at the old airport," he said. "Just to see for myself. I'm thinking that wee lassie might have come from there."

"Oh!" I had hardly thought about Malcolm's revelation that we still had climate refugees on En-Somi, until now. But of course, it was true – if that wee bairn had lived out there near the abandoned airport, then it was no wonder if none of us recognised her. "*Aja*, I'll come," I agreed.

Malcolm smiled, said a quiet "Thanks," and then stood. Rattling a fork against his whisky glass, he called for everyone's attention. Then, when the laughter had subsided enough for Malcolm to be heard, he announced, "I'm moving into my bothy this week, so come the Solstice, everyone is invited for fireworks and feasting at sunset!"

There was a general chorus of congratulations and of people accepting the invitation, and other people naming times when they hoped to see visitors: Lyle's to eat breakfast to start off the day, a stiff walk up Fyrtarn Fjell to see the sun rise, a visit to one of the bothies over on Hunger Moor, and so on. That's how it always worked. People fitted in with each other, and without any formal planning, the whole of Solstice was mapped out.

That second trip over to Storhaven was quite different from the first. We left a bit later because the days were even shorter, but we didn't have to contend with the bitter cold. A wind was blowing up from the south across the island, carrying drizzle in its gusts, leaving the rocks dark and slippery. We had different ponies, too; these came from a bothy down towards the Hus summer harbour. They were younger and stronger, probably a different mix of bloodlines, and game to carry us both right up and over the pass with barely a pause. Just beyond the ruined chapel we came across young Harris, stomping along the track wearing earpieces so that he could listen to his favourite music. Harris was a bit of a wild one back then, recently returned from the mainland and causing his parents some worry, I believe. That was before he got together with Elise, of course. Anyhow, we gave him a lift on the trap into Storhaven, and he entertained us with stories about his schooling on Shetland.

We dropped Harris off by the town hall, picked up Sigrid's books from the ferry office and took the ponies to Jamie's stable to rest while we did a few other jobs, staying together this time. By about twelve noon, we were ready. We harnessed the ponies to the cart again and turned north down by the harbour, towards the abandoned airport.

The plan had been, I believe, to attract tourists to En-Somi. The world had been mad for travelling when the idea was first mooted; people used to fly here and there all over the globe. The *harkrav* started buying up bothies and converting them into holiday cottages, and the Scottish Tourist Board persuaded the BBC to film one of their *Travel Show* series on the island. That was before I arrived here. The weather had already become unpredictable by then, but I don't suppose anyone realised how things would work out. In the end, so many planes were cancelled because of storms that the whole idea had become unworkable.

I knew that the track out to the airport was the only metalled road on the island, but I hadn't thought much about it. I should have realised that since so few people travelled that way, the surface would have been allowed to fall into disrepair. Actually, it was reasonably easy-going as far as the track up to Aeloff's Hill, because of the *harkrav* dwellings on Floirean's Cnoc looking out over the harbour and the rugged east coast. I suppose they used the road, but once we had got a little beyond the turn to the cemetery, the surface became terrible, full of potholes and with tufts of grass growing here and there. It wasn't easy for the ponies, but I remember that the views were lovely. There were clouds scudding across the sky, so that sometimes everything looked grey and dull in the low light, and sometimes it glowed with the weak winter sunshine. The road hugged the coastline and each time we turned another bend we saw a fresh sight: the Stacks of Seamus where James the Less is supposed to have been shipwrecked on his last missionary journey, the little cove where the schoolchildren from Storhaven have their summer barbecues – cliffs and moors and grey, heaving sea. It felt as remote as our side of the island, new but familiar.

Then the road turned away from the coast a little, following the contours of the land, and almost at once dipped down and south again towards St Matthew's Bay, and suddenly we could see the airport – or what was left of it.

Back in the days when I had been in Edinburgh, I had flown a few times, although it was already considered rather antisocial. My one trip to Greece had been by air, and I remember that Bjorn and I once went by plane down to London for a big charity rock concert. On another occasion I flew with Bjorn to visit his parents in Bergen, although we came back by ferry. Maybe more to the point, I had seen lots of airports on films and television series dating back to the old days.

Perhaps, then, I shouldn't have been surprised. Compared to almost any other building on the island, it was ugly – and the buildings on En-Somi could never be called pretty! Why would somebody decide to build in concrete when there was so much good stone about? And why have a corrugated iron roof? To the north of the depressing, weather-stained building was the runway, a broken line of greening asphalt with sheep grazing at the far end. To the east of the larger building was a smaller hut-like edifice with a taller construction, which I assumed to be some sort of control tower.

Malcolm drew on the reins to stop the ponies and we sat there, looking down at the shambles below us. One end of the long, low main building had obviously suffered some sort of storm damage. There were rocks piled onto the roof, as if to hold the corrugated iron in place, and further along, someone had attempted to create a turf roof. There were no windows that we could see from there, but there were black marks streaking upwards on the stained concrete, as if there had been a fire.

And there were signs of life.

At the near end of the runway, some sort of contraption had been built. For a moment I thought it was a makeshift football goal with rags hanging from it, until I realised that I was looking at a washing line. We were quite sheltered, with the moors beyond Aeloff's Hill blocking the worst of the wind, but when there was a sudden gust from the east to disturb the air, I realised that there was smoke issuing from one of the holes in the roof. Then, as we sat there, the ponies staring ahead passively as if they had seen it all before, I heard the unmistakable shout of a child, and two small figures appeared from behind the rocks down towards St Matthew's Bay and ran, calling to each other, across the open space. They vanished again behind the building. They had obviously gone inside.

Malcolm drew in his breath. "So!" he exclaimed. "It's true. There are still people living out here."

For a moment I didn't say anything. To be honest, I hadn't really thought we would find anyone. "So, what now?" I asked.

Malcolm took off his hat and wiped his forehead with his hand, as if he were hot, which he couldn't have been. Then, "Would you mind if we went down there and spoke to them?" he wanted to know. "Or would you rather not? I can come back another time."

"Oh," I answered at once, "we've come all this way! Let's go down there."

Malcolm twitched the reins and the ponies obediently set off again, clip-clopping down the track.

Since one of En-Somi's attractions was the lack of motor transport, there had obviously never been a car park. Instead, there was a row of metal stands where ponies could be tethered while their owners waited for new arrivals. Malcolm drew the cart up to the space closest to the main building, jumped down to tie up the ponies, then looked up at me and asked, "Do you want to stay here, or go in?"

"Oh, I'll come with you," I answered, although I'll admit I felt a little nervous.

★ ★ ★

The wall we could see, the western wall, had no windows, as I have already mentioned, so we walked round to the other side of the building. There were no windows there either, but there had obviously once been three huge, wide entrances. Two of these were boarded up, but the third opening, the one closest to us, had a sort of makeshift door created out of rusty corrugated iron, set into whatever material had been used to board the whole place up.

We walked towards it, looking around us. Someone had used one of those metal litter bins in which to light a fire. You could still see some of the writing on the side, *Property of Storhaven.*

Please recycle. There was a single shoe lodged against some sort of large, metal basket on wheels, which once, I supposed, had been used to move luggage around. A notice on the wall reminded people in English and Norwegian that there were no motorised vehicles on the island and gave a phone number in case the reader wanted to call for a pony and trap. The yellow stains below the notice suggested that the wall had been used as a urinal.

Malcolm pulled open the corrugated iron door and we stepped inside.

For a few moments, while our eyes adjusted, it was difficult to see anything. The atmosphere was smoky and a few degrees warmer than outside. Light from flames made strange, distorted patterns dance on the breeze-block walls. We were in a huge open space, and further along, people were sitting around a fire, made on the floor approximately below a jagged hole in the roof. They had all stopped talking as we came in.

A woman stood and came towards us. She was oddly clothed, in a long coat that looked like a man's overcoat, and with her hair up in a turban made of checked material, like a tablecloth. Her face was thin and grey, in a way that suggested dirt rather than old age.

"Can I 'elp you?" she asked, in a tone that suggested anything other than a desire to be of assistance.

Malcolm smiled at the woman. "Hello," he answered. "I'm Malcolm, and this is my friend Marie."

"Huh!" said the woman. "What does you want? We got nofing for you 'ere."

Malcolm was very calm, as if he hadn't noticed the hostility. "I didn't know anyone was living out here," he explained, "until a couple of weeks ago."

"Those who needs to know, know," muttered the woman obliquely. She obviously didn't intend to tell us anything. Nor did I see any reason why she should.

Just then a small girl separated herself from the group round

54

the fire and came up to us. I thought she must be about five or six. She clutched at the woman's coat, and said, "Nan?"

The woman didn't look down. Instead, she just said, "Go back to the fire, Shirley, and stay with your uncle Eric."

"Not an ideal place to bring up a child," Malcolm suggested, his eyes on the wee lass, who hadn't moved.

"That's our business," remarked the woman.

"How do you survive?" I asked.

"We survive," the woman responded flatly.

"But…" I felt terrible. There were people here, camping out in the derelict arrival hall! How could that be? But a hand grasped mine – Malcolm, signalling me to stay quiet.

A second person joined the woman and child. He was about the same height as the woman, with sticky-looking fair hair and a long, dark-green coat that almost reached his ankles. A dirty blue and white scarf hung loosely round his neck, a dingy yellow lion depicted on one end of it. He was barefoot.

"'Ave we got a problem?" he asked the woman. "Anyfing I can 'elp with?" His voice was quiet, but definitely threatening.

"I can 'andle it, Jarvis," the woman replied, not taking her eyes off us. "You go on back to the others. These people is just going. Ain't you?"

"I'm sorry we intruded," Malcolm said. "We mean you no harm. Is there anything we can do to help?"

"You could go away," the woman said, "and leave us alone."

Malcolm was pulling his phone out of his pocket. "If you wanted to contact me…" he was saying.

The woman snorted. "We could send you a pigeon!" she retorted. "We don't 'ave no phones 'ere!"

Malcolm seemed unperturbed. "Maybe I'll come back another time," he said. "Just to see if you need anything."

"Good of you," responded the woman sarcastically. Then, as we opened that makeshift door to let ourselves out, she added, "We could do with some privacy."

The sun had set behind the mass of the island when we emerged into the open air, and the temperature was dropping fast. I felt shaken. I suppose that all the time I had lived on the island I had been sheltered from poverty, the sort of poverty where people lived in squats and their faces took on that gaunt look of the woman we had just met. Malcolm was still holding my hand, and I was glad of the reassurance.

He let go, of course, when he untied the ponies, backed the cart up and turned it around, and we climbed back up and started our journey home. We said nothing to each other until after the first bend, when, if we had looked behind us, the airport would already have been out of sight.

Then Malcolm said, sounding thoughtful, "It must be a decade since those refugees were dumped here."

"*Aja*," I agreed.

"But where did they house them? I mean, surely they didn't start out living in the departure hall?"

I remembered the rumours I had heard back then. "I think they put up tents."

Malcolm sounded indignant. "But it's sub-arctic here!"

"*Aja*." Then I recalled something Shona had told me when I had taken Duncan, still a toddler, to play with her youngest. "They thought the refugees would get work here, integrate. Assimilate. There's that electrical business, whatever it is, just outside Storhaven. I suppose they thought we might get more light industry."

"Huh!" Malcolm was clearly unimpressed, as indeed we had all been at the time. "That shows how little they knew about En-Somi!"

The wind was veering round to the east, and it was cold in the long, drawn-out winter dusk. The journey back to Storhaven seemed to take longer than it had going out to the airport, and my spirits were low. We still had to load the cart up and travel the length of En-Somi to get home again, and we hadn't eaten all day. I shivered.

"I wonder why they didn't leave?" Malcolm remarked, apparently thinking aloud. "Didn't they take the rest of them away when it was obvious it wasn't working out? Why would anyone stay?"

I wasn't sure Malcolm wanted an answer, but it was a good question.

"Perhaps where they had come from was worse even than this?" I suggested.

"Maybe."

We rounded another bend and came, at last, to the better road surface. Up on the moors to our right we could see scattered lights from the larger homes of the *harkrav*. After another rise, we were looking down at Storhaven. I had never seen the town from this vantage point before, and the thought came unbidden to my mind: '*How small it is!*'

As we started the deep descent into the town, Malcolm said, "When I worked in Edinburgh, I came across the same thing."

"What thing?" I wanted to know.

"This reluctance to change. You know, I think people can put up with so many initiatives from others, changes that are supposed to improve their lot, so many new projects, so many schemes, and then they think, '*That's enough!* They don't see the point any more of going on this training course or enrolling their children on that programme. They know from experience that nothing's really going to change anything for the better. They just want to be left alone. I saw it all the time."

"So, what did you do then?" I wondered. "I mean, when the people you were trying to help had given up?"

"Well…" Malcolm was navigating the last, steep bend into the town. "I bought them trainers. Or gave them food vouchers. Depending on their age. I just helped them to cope that day."

★ ★ ★

We didn't talk about it again until we had called in at Dougie
Fraser's, drunk some tea with his wife Ingrid, accepted two
enormous sandwiches to eat on the walk home, loaded up the
cart with the last of Malcolm's things, and set off again for Hus.
It was pitch dark by then, and the stars were startlingly bright in
the clear, cold night sky. Malcolm was leading the ponies and I
was walking alongside him. The track up to Fyrtarn Fjell pass
is gentler on the Storhaven side, and the travelling was easy. We
kept a companionable silence. I was wondering how long it was
since I had spent this much time with another human being
– other than Duncan, of course. To the best of my memory, I
decided, it was almost two months ago, when Shona and I had
agreed to help each other with our potato harvests.

"I think that's the tack I will maybe take now," Malcolm
suddenly said.

"Pardon?" I had no idea what he was talking about.

"I'll just take them stuff they need," he explained. "The
refugees. Food and clothes. Not try and make them change. Just
help."

"Why?" I asked.

Malcolm sounded surprised. "Because they need help!" he
exclaimed. Then he laughed and added, "Because that's what
I've always done! If you can't stop the blows from falling, you
can at least soften them."

The first day of December is *Huldufolk* Day on En-Somi, and it marks the beginning of the big lead-up to Solstice. A strict member of the Catholic Church in Edinburgh once told me that December 1st is not really the first day of the Christian Advent, but advent calendars always seem to start then, and our island children kept that custom too. That year – the year of the dead child, the year Malcolm arrived among us – *Huldufolk* Day fell on a Friday, and a general agreement had been made that we would celebrate it in the village as we always did, beginning in the school and working our way down to the summer harbour via the Kullanders' place and the Sinclairs' bothy over on Hunger Moor.

You probably know that the *huldufolk* are the little people – a bit like elves. They live on these northern Atlantic islands, keeping themselves very much to themselves most of the time, but interacting with humans at special times. It is the *huldufolk* who plant flowers in people's gardens where those flowers hadn't grown the year before. It is they who tell the bees where there are new sources of nectar, and who tell ladybirds where the aphids are. They are often busy at night, and when, in a spring dawn, the birds sing especially beautifully, it is to the *huldufolk* that they are singing.

The *huldufolk*, like humans, are generally benign. They look after each other, provide for those in need and have been known to take in other small, lost creatures to care for, in an emergency. It is said that the *huldufolk* will rescue the chicks of small birds if the black-backed gulls are after them, and that they once guided a child who was lost at the foot of Fyrtarn Fjell back to her bothy, in the time of *Mori-mori* Cadha's youth. It is possible, though, to get on the wrong side of the *huldufolk*, just as one can fall out with a neighbour. One of our island stories tells of a family of crofters (over on the east side of the island, of course) who needed to build a new stone wall to stop their sheep from straying onto someone else's land. They had a good supply of loose rocks, ideal for the purpose, down by their beach, but it was going to be hard work carrying them up to the site of the new wall. So, instead, those lazy crofters dug out the stones they needed from a nearby bank – and in so doing, destroyed the homes of three *huldufolk* families. Needless to say, the wall mysteriously fell down the very night after it was completed, the sheep escaped onto the neighbour's property, the neighbour refused to return them, and the crofters starved to death. The *huldufolk* should always be treated with respect.

A rather wind-blown group of *bondii* met at the *fi'ilsted* just after midday. Some of the villagers had obviously had a drink or two, to warm themselves up in preparation for the afternoon, but Jamie MacLoughlan, Lyle, Patrick and Shona from the shop and several other folk from surrounding bothies had spent the morning in the school, where the children had needed adult help to make the final touches to the wee houses. When the little crowd from the school emerged, children and adults alike dressed in warm waterproof jackets and boots, they were carrying six or seven of these little, brightly painted wooden 'houses' which would be our offering to the *huldufolk*.

We formed a ragged procession, the children at the front with Sigrid, then their parents and helpers, followed by the rest of us. The children were, as always, equipped with makeshift drums – old saucepans with wooden spoons, a wooden box which one of the twins was beating with a small mallet, and one proper drum that looked rather the worse for wear. The parents were carrying the wee houses.

Just as we set off, not following the track that led directly to the harbour but clambering up the steep side of the moor towards the Kullanders' place, Malcolm arrived.

He fell into step beside me. "It certainly brings back memories, doesn't it?" he remarked cheerfully.

I laughed. "The first time we did this with Duncan," I recalled, "Bjorn had to carry him the whole time, and he didn't stop crying. It was the noise. But he was only three."

"I brought the children over here once, to Storhaven," Malcolm said. He seemed less breathless than me on the steep climb, which surprised me; I thought I was pretty fit. "It was after Iona had died. I wanted them to see it for themselves. They didn't like it, though. They thought it was childish – the whole idea of the *huldufolk*. And, of course, that was the year that it rained non-stop all day."

I laughed again, although it seemed sad to me that Malcolm was a true *En-Som-in-Fedi*, islander, and his children hadn't learnt our customs.

"But when I was a boy," Malcolm continued, "well, those celebrations were wonderful!"

We were still climbing steeply; the children were drumming only intermittently because they needed their hands to grasp the rocks, and there was a certain amount of panting and grunting from the adults.

"There have always been more children on the east of the island," I prompted, hoping to hear more of Malcolm's memories.

"Oh yes, at least two classes, sometimes three!" he agreed. "And, of course, the school is only a couple of hundred metres from the harbour, but it was really not so different. We made our wee houses in the morning, and then processed to a couple of bothies in the afternoon, before returning to Storhaven. The biggest difference, when I look back on it now, is that the *harkrav* used to join in."

I was amazed. I actually stopped and stared at Malcolm, who was just behind me on the last, steep part of the ascent.

Malcolm chuckled again, that infectious laugh of his. "Well, you know how they are…" I made one last effort up the slope, and at last I was on the flatter land in front of the Kullanders' place. "Their bairns didn't go to the village school, but one or two of them would make wee houses at home and join in the festivities. And their parents would take photographs."

"At least they were learning our customs," I said, but I think Malcolm didn't hear me, because just at that moment the children started beating on their drums with increased energy, and calling out, "Food for the *huldufolk*! Food for the *huldufolk*!"

Then Fiona and Alf were bringing out toasted cheese sandwiches which, I may say, were certainly not devoured by the little people!

★ ★ ★

The Kullanders' place is on the other side of Hus valley from Hunger Moor, which was our next destination. Once we had devoured the food for the *huldufolk* and the adults had warmed themselves up with Alf's home-brew whisky, we set off downhill. Alf, Fiona and their youngest son Andy, who was being home-schooled that year, joined us, bringing their own wee house.

It took a couple of minutes to assemble the procession in the right order, not least because just as we were about to leave, half the children and several adults needed to visit the bathroom. Malcolm had been talking to Jamie MacLoughlan about the moorland beyond their boundaries, which was owned by a member of the *harkrav* whom Malcolm had yet to meet.

"He'll do his share of the walling," Jamie was saying, "but he won't repair the stiles. Says he's worried about *un-fedii*, outsiders, walking their dogs on his land and worrying his sheep."

"We get a lot of *un-fedii* round here?" Malcolm wanted to know.

Jamie laughed. "None at all!" he said.

When the procession finally reassembled – children at the front making a renewed clamour now that they had been fed, then the parents and Sigrid carrying the wee houses, and lastly the remaining adults – Malcolm joined me again.

The path we followed down into the valley again was more northerly than the track that would take Malcolm or me back to our lands, but the views were just as stunning. There is something about the sort of light we see on winter afternoons when the sun is low; it has always seemed to me that there's a sort of magic in the clear air and the long shadows. At one point, where two stone walls meet and there's a stile, we could see down to the summer harbour, but then we were back in the shelter of Norse Hill, crossing the burn, and climbing again, up onto Hunger Moor.

The Sinclairs were a young couple back at the time I am telling you about; I seem to remember that their first child might have been on the way. I recall very distinctly, though, that those steps from the track up to their bothy had already been built, because Malcolm commented on them. "Has the National Trust been working here?" he joked.

It was a crazy remark, and I'm sure he knew it, but it made me laugh. "Old man Sinclair did all this," I told him. "It was a wedding present for his son – not Yanni who lives here now, but the other one, the one who works on the ferries."

Just at that point the children, who had reached the bothy first, set up the traditional cry of "Food for the *huldufolk*!" again, and thumped their makeshift drums with great enthusiasm. Malcolm laughed, and as soon as the Sinclairs appeared at their door with plates of scones, he joined in the general clapping and cheering.

From the Sinclairs it is only a matter of a twenty-minute scramble, avoiding a dark, rocky outcrop and circling behind the marshy area, and suddenly there it is – the summer harbour, and beyond it, the loch, and somewhere not so far away, the Arctic Circle.

By then, I remember, the sun had gone behind the moorland to the west, and it was cold. Even though we had been on the move for most of the day, the rising wind, blowing up the loch from the ocean, seemed to have a bite to it. Still, spirits were high enough, and people set to at once, building the fire and balancing all the wee houses on it, like bothies on a hill.

Malcolm was looking around him with interest. "I haven't been down here before," he remarked.

"Well, *nei*." I was not surprised. "It's only a summer harbour."

"I suppose…" he started to say. "Of course, Storhaven has a proper harbour, they use it all the year round."

"*Aja*," I agreed. "But you should see this place when it's stormy." I pointed to the rocky ledge where the rowing boats were tied down against the winter weather. "The waves can get up as far as that."

"It must be an amazing sight," Malcolm said, almost reverently.

A cheer went up as the fire caught, the flames dancing orange in the dusk, already licking at the wood or cardboard walls of the wee houses. When the highest house took light there was a sudden silence. All the children held their hands out to the glow and made their wishes. The *huldufolk* would hear them, and look after them, because they had shown their respect.

We were almost back at Norse Hill, walking in the dark on the familiar track back to the village, when Patrick spoke, using an ancient traditional formula. "Look, *En-Som-in-Fedii*, fellow islanders and *bondii*, the Little People are blessing us!" He was pointing behind him, back towards the loch.

We all turned and looked. It was the northern lights, glowing pink and green, weaving their colours over the black ocean.

There were murmurs of pleasure and approval. Did any of us really believe that by our strange and ancient customs we had brought blessings on our community? Yet I know it felt as if we had.

"How magical," said Malcolm, and held my hand in the dark, all the way back to Hus.

"Have you met the minister?" Malcolm asked me, sitting companionably in the rocking chair opposite mine. He was holding his mug of tea and balancing a plate containing several oat biscuits on one knee.

"The minister?" For a moment I couldn't imagine what he was talking about. My mind had gone immediately to politics.

Malcolm laughed. "The church minister. The woman who serves St Andrew's Kirk in Storhaven."

"Oh!" I have probably mentioned before that we on En-Somi are not a particularly religious bunch – maybe less so in those days than now, some would say. Perhaps I had known, if I had thought about it, that there must be a minister at St Andrew's. After all, a few people took their babies over there to be christened, and there were marriages and funerals. I suppose, though, that I thought of the kirk as the domain of the *harkrav*, as alien to me as their frequent comings and goings to Oslo or Edinburgh.

"I met her on Saturday," continued Malcolm. "She's an interesting person."

Malcolm had come over that morning to ask me a favour. He was, he maintained, nicely settled in his bothy, and Petter had almost finished the cupboards he was building, so most things had been put away. "I just wondered, though…" Malcolm had been hesitant. "Would you knit me a *gensi*? A really traditional one? I'll pay, of course!"

I was delighted. I had learnt to knit as a child, but never much liked it. Only when I arrived on En-Somi did I become interested in taking it up again, and that was partly through Sigrid's influence. It was Sigrid who founded the cooperative and it was she who had encouraged me to learn the Fyrtarn Winter

65

design. It had taken us ages, all one winter, working together from old photographs and an incomplete pattern, to discover how to create it, using four needles and five colours. I had made careful notes, so that it wouldn't be forgotten again, but at that time I was the only person actually knitting it.

So, I had measured Malcolm up, discussed colours, and refused the offer of payment, and now we were sitting drinking our tea.

"You've been back into Storhaven, then?" I wanted to know.

"Yesterday. I walked over," he told me. "I had to sign some more papers at the town hall, the final documents for my wind turbine. So that spare electricity can go into the grid."

This was pretty routine on the island. It meant that if one of us had problems with our turbines, we would still have power.

"Anyhow," continued Malcolm, "I met her at the Frasers'. It seems Ingrid goes to St Andrew's. Dougie doesn't."

"What's she like, this minister?" I asked.

"Well… quite interesting, actually," said Malcolm. "I have mixed feelings about the clergy. We used to meet them, a few of them, in Edinburgh. Some of them really understood what our clients were up against but some of them – well, let's just say that they really didn't!"

"And this woman?" I wondered. "I'm guessing she's the understanding kind?"

"Mm." Malcolm sipped his tea and ate one of his biscuits in two mouthfuls, looking contented. "She knew there were people out by the airport."

"*In* the airport, really," I corrected.

Malcolm chuckled. "*Aja*, you're right." He looked thoughtful. "She's been out there, once or twice, this minister."

I stood up to fetch the teapot from the top of the range where it was keeping warm, and to pour us both second cups. "What sort of a welcome did she get?" I asked, thinking of the way we had been received.

66

"Much the same as us, I gather," answered Malcolm. "But she doesn't want to give up. I was wondering whether we should enlist her help."

I noticed the 'we' in Malcolm's last comment. I hadn't thought I had committed myself to anything, but it felt right.

"I'd like to meet her," I said.

Malcolm gave me a huge, almost conspiratorial grin. "That's what I thought," he said. "I've invited her to my place for Saturday lunch. Can you come?"

★ ★ ★

This was to be my first visit to Malcolm's home. The last time I had visited the bothy was back when *Mori-mori* Cadha had lived there, and I used to take her firewood. The weather was dry enough that Saturday for me to climb up to his place by following the burn, and I arrived just before midday.

He had made a lot of changes. There had obviously been significant work done outside, no doubt to put in the ground-source heat system, and the wind turbine was one of the newer ones, erected on the hill above the cottage. The appearance of the bothy itself, as I approached it from the north, hadn't changed much – the windows and doors were still in the same places – but somehow Malcolm had got hold of some slate, and had made a sort of covered patio at the front. I could imagine that, in the summer, especially the late summer when the midges had gone, it would be the perfect place to sit and watch the sunset. He had built a stone bench, too, so that a person could sit down to put on, or take off, muddy boots.

I knocked on the door rather than just opening it and calling out a greeting, the way we usually did, because it felt a little formal, visiting for the first time.

Just as I did that, Malcolm came round the corner – he must have been doing something in one of his sheds – and made me jump.

"*Hei*, Marie!" he said just behind me.

I laughed. "Goodness, Malcolm! You nearly gave me a heart attack!"

"Let yourself in," he said, chuckling. "I haven't even put a lock on the door yet!"

If the outside hadn't changed on my approach from the north-west, the inside was entirely different. I was really surprised. He had taken away a lot of stone from the southern wall, which I couldn't see from the direction I had approached the dwelling, and created a line of five long, narrow glass windows, through which you see the corner of Jamie MacLoughlan's land, the sea and the *muckle scarf* stacks that I can see from my beach, but not from my bothy. Instead of a range, he and Petter had installed something that looked like an open fire. Of course, like my range, it wasn't the real thing. Both were powered by electricity from our turbines, but it looked completely convincing. He had arranged two sofas so that anyone sitting on them could see the fire and the view. The kitchen area was in the south-west corner, just as it had been in *Mori-mori* Cadha's time, just as, traditionally, cooking areas always are in our island homes, but now it was separated from the sitting area with a countertop.

Close to the door there was a spiral staircase.

"You've made a mezzanine floor, like mine!" I exclaimed.

"Well, not quite like yours," Malcolm corrected. "Go up and look."

My sleeping platform was – and still is – at the northern end of my room. Malcolm's ran north to south and was half the width of the cottage, and when I had climbed the stairs, I saw that it was divided into two sections. "I don't plan to sleep up there," explained Malcolm, standing at the foot of the staircase. "It's just because I hope the bairns will come and visit sometime. To make space for them."

I came down the steep stairs backwards. "It's really lovely,"

I exclaimed. "And the whole of this end of this room is your sleeping area!"

Malcolm had built a low wall, about waist high, to separate the bedroom space from the rest of the bothy. There were books on top of it, the full length of the wall. Beyond it, the room looked much more like a conventional bedroom, with a large bed and cupboards either side. There were doors either side of the old, north-facing chimney. "Just like yours!" said Malcolm. "A cupboard one side, a bathroom the other."

"Goodness!" I said, rather lamely. It made me feel that my home was rather basic, by comparison.

Malcolm was filling an electric kettle, switching it on and taking mugs out of a cupboard. There was something simmering on the hob, and the smell of lamb stew wafted towards me. "It all looks rather shiny and new," he remarked, "but it'll mature, and then it'll look more homely, like your place."

Just then, the door opened and a bundle of outdoor clothes appeared, with a smiling face visible underneath a woolly hat. "Anyone home?" asked the visitor.

"Verity, come on in!" welcomed Malcolm, walking across to the door. "Just leave your jacket there, I haven't put up enough hooks yet! And let me introduce you to Marie."

She was so different from my concept of a church minister that it was hard to believe that she really was one. She looked young, probably in reality not much younger than me, but I had lost that youthful appearance years ago. I found out later that she was in her late twenties. She was slim, with blonde hair cut short, and she was wearing jeans and a round-necked *gensi* with a white band at the neckline that gave the impression of being a clerical collar, but wasn't.

"Marie, hello!" she said, holding out her hand to shake mine. Her accent was almost English.

"Hi!" I replied in English. "It's good to meet you."

Verity was looking around the room. "What a beautiful

cottage," she said. "Sorry – I mean bothy. I ought to know by now!"

"That's okay," I reassured her. "The two words are pretty much interchangeable."

"I've been in a few of these little homes," she said, "since I arrived on the island. There're several not far from Storhaven, but none as attractive as this." She went over to the windows at the south end of the room. "What a view!" she exclaimed. "Most of the folk who live in bothies over on the east of En-Somi don't seem to be kirk people."

Malcolm chuckled again. He had lined up three mugs on the counter. "Help yourselves," he suggested, indicating the teapot, sugar and milk. "The Church of Scotland is an import," he explained. "We *En-Som-in-Fedii*, islanders, don't have much to do with it."

"I'm beginning to realise that," agreed Verity, pouring milk into her tea. "My Sunday congregation seems to be small and wealthy. Where do the rest of the population worship?"

By then it had dawned on me that Verity must have been a very new appointment. "How long have you been here?" I asked.

"Oh dear!" exclaimed the minister. "Is that not a question I should have asked? You're right, I don't know anything about the islanders really. I've been here for a month. Have I put my foot in it, asking where other people worship?"

"*Nei*, not at all," I reassured her.

Malcolm sat on the sofa next to me, and Verity curled up on the corner of the other sofa, looking comfortably at home. "I read everything I could find about En-Somi before I came, but honestly, it wasn't much. There seemed to be a lot more about Shetland and the Faroe Islands. I thought they might all be similar, but it seems not."

Malcolm looked thoughtful. "These island communities…" he started to say. Then he changed tack. "You know how, on remote islands and over hundreds of years, species develop differently? Well, culturally that's what we're like. We're so remote, each island community has its own way of doing things."

"More than that, even," I explained. "Our own stories and legends, our own dialects and accents, our own songs and poems…"

Verity drank some of her tea, taking in what we had said.

Malcolm changed the subject. "So, how are you settling in?" he enquired.

Verity smiled. "Oh, okay, I suppose. The moderator warned me I'd find it tough. She wanted me to be on a team in one of the big parishes on the mainland to get more experience. But En-Somi appealed to me – the remoteness, and the challenge of making something of the parish after it had gone so long without a permanent minister. But the church people seem very conservative, after Aberdeen. And then there's the poverty."

I was so surprised by her last statement that I nearly choked on my tea. "Poverty?" I asked. "What poverty?"

Malcolm laughed. Of course, he had talked to Verity before at the Frasers' place. "Not us," he said, "not *En-Som-in-Fedii*. Remember, I told you, Verity went out to the old airport."

"Oh, *aja!*"

Verity seemed not to notice my surprise. She went on, "Of course I've seen news broadcasts about climate refugees. Who hasn't? And while I was at Highland College, we visited several of the camps on the Borders and around Oban, but they all seemed to be quite well run, with proper facilities. I had no idea we had people living like those people live."

"It's not an official camp," I explained.

Malcolm said thoughtfully, "We ought to be able to do something to help."

"*Aja*," I agreed. Now that I knew that they were there, it didn't seem possible to go on living my comfortable life and doing nothing.

Verity said, "Good. So where do we start?"

71

We hatched out our plan, such as it was, over lamb stew with mashed potatoes. Verity was keen to involve some of the people from her parish. "It'll do them good," she insisted. "They're a bit insular." She had made a few enquiries and discovered that none of the refugee children attended the school in Storhaven. In fact, the refugees seemed never to visit the town at all. "It's a mystery to me how they get hold of the things they need," she said.

Malcolm was quite quiet. I had the feeling that he didn't think Verity's plan would work. I had my doubts, too. St Andrew's congregation were mostly *harkrav*. Nothing in my experience of the island suggested that they had much interest in anyone outside their own group. Still, Verity was their minister, and presumably she knew what she was doing.

By the time we had drunk some more tea, and it was three in the afternoon and already dusk, we had agreed that Verity would raise the issue with the elders of the kirk. "I'd like you two to come, too," she said. "You could stay over at my place."

"Oh, that would be grand," agreed Malcolm. "What do you think, Marie?"

I was still feeling unsure, but I had no particular reasons for holding back, so, "All right," I agreed.

Verity looked pleased. "You'll be my first overnight guests!" she exclaimed. Then a look of uncertainty passed over her face. "The only thing is…" She seemed almost shy. "I don't know if you two are an item. I mean, will you share a room?"

"*Nei!*" I said, possibly a little too fervently.

"Not yet," said Malcolm, rather more quietly, so that I wasn't sure if Verity had heard.

★ ★ ★

If the visit over to Storhaven had been planned for the next day or two, I think I would have felt quite awkward with Malcolm. To be honest, my experience with men was limited – a few boyfriends in Melrose where I grew up, a romantic but rather unrealistic summer with Xander in Greece, and then Bjorn at university, and since Bjorn had left, nobody. It was pretty naive of me, but I had thought of Malcolm only as a friend. As I sat by my range that evening, I considered the situation, how he had held my hand when things were difficult out at the old airport, and again as we walked home on *Huldufolk* Day, how he had chosen to walk with me all that day, and how he had twice invited me to go over to Storhaven with him.

He was a good man; of that, I was sure. A bit older than me, but not too much – maybe ten years, perhaps fifteen? And I felt very comfortable in his company. But a woman didn't become 'an item' with someone, as Verity had put it, just because she liked someone and felt comfortable with him! It was a bit unsettling.

By the following morning, though, I was already beginning to feel less bothered. Perhaps Malcolm had just been teasing; he had a funny sense of humour. And didn't we all say things that were a little inappropriate now and again? Probably he regretted saying "Not yet" by now. The best thing would be for me just to forget the whole thing. As the grandmother who brought me up might have said, I shouldn't make a mountain out of a molehill.

We met in the late morning at the top end of the village, where our two rather vaguely defined footpaths met, and called into the shop to buy chocolates for Verity before setting off for Storhaven. The sky was clear and blue, the breeze icy cold but not very strong, so that initially the walking was easy. Most of the tracks on En-Somi are narrow, just wide enough for two ponies, but that's also a good width for two people walking companionably along. Malcolm seemed to be in a particularly

73

good mood. His Wi-Fi was connected at last, and he had been talking to his children the evening before. His youngest daughter, Beth, was loving university, where she was studying medicine and had also started to play in a chamber orchestra. "They're all so sophisticated, compared with the way Iona and I were at that age!" he said. Then he added as an afterthought, "Or now. Iona would have been so proud of them."

Then we talked about Bjorn, how I had been much too young to settle down when I had met him, but how I had clung to the first relationship that came along after my grandmother had died. "En-Somi was the saving of me," I told him. "I found myself plonked down in the middle of a well-established community. Sigrid took me under her wing and Patrick and Shona helped me with Duncan when I didn't have a clue about baby stuff. I sort of found my feet here. So, when Bjorn got restless and left, I found that I was fine."

We climbed up over the high point of the Fyrtarn Fjell pass at that point, and then I continued. "I didn't really miss him at all – Bjorn – when he left. Duncan did, of course, and I was sad for Duncan's sake, but not on my own behalf."

We were quiet for a while, enjoying the bright, cold morning, the clear air and the peaceful sounds of the island. Somewhere out of sight someone was whistling signals to a sheepdog; closer to the track, a squabble of black-backed gulls was fighting over some carrion close to the chapel ruins. It occurred to me for a moment that I wouldn't mind if Malcolm held my hand again, but he showed no sign of doing so.

"The weather's on the change," remarked Malcolm after half a mile or so.

It was true. To the north the sky had turned a dark grey-blue, and the breeze had become stronger.

"But we've got fifteen minutes, I would say," he added.

We could see Storhaven by now. The low sun reflected off the squat, stubby tower of the kirk, but most of the little town was in shadow. Our days are so short in the winter. Then it seemed like no time at all before we had passed the turn that led to the bothy where Malcolm had grown up, and we were walking on cobbles, instead of freezing mud or rock, and following Verity's directions to the manse.

★ ★ ★

I had been south of the border a few times in my life and had watched all sorts of films and series on television, and I knew that many villages in England, as in a lot of Europe, are really pretty. In Norway, their buildings are also distinctive and attractive, deep red in the countryside but brightly painted in some of the towns. I don't know what it is about the Scots, that so many of our buildings look so heavy and dark, when the people themselves are so generous and kind. Verity's accommodation was typical. It was not a manse at all, but a flat above a bakery just down from the Castle *fi'ilsted*. Verity had pinned a note on the door next to the shop, saying '*Just come up*' so I pushed open the heavy blue door and we climbed the stairs.

From the outside, the building looked austere, made of cut stone with tall, unfriendly windows. Inside, it was warm and smelt of scented candles. Verity was wearing black, dressed, I guessed, ready for the meeting of elders that evening, but she had on a bright green apron with the motto, '*Save water, drink whisky*', which I thought was quite funny to see around the waist of a Church of Scotland minister.

Over our meal she explained to us what would happen. "The court of elders is pretty informal," she told us. "Actually, they don't call it a court here – it's a *domstol* – I think that's a Nordic word. We have an agenda that covers several items which are really just to do with the church. I've put those after the matter of the folk out at the airport. You'll need to listen quietly to the discussion, and not speak until it comes to questions. There'll be another visitor too, a member of the church."

By the time we set out for the church, the bad weather which Malcolm had spotted on its approach had arrived. The wind was blowing up from the harbour, from the east, and the moisture it was carrying was sleet rather than rain. Down by the harbour there was white foam spraying up above the walls, and we could hear the steady roar and crash as the waves broke.

It was only a dash across the cobbled lane and down a few hundred feet before we reached the kirk. Verity pushed open the door and we entered the plain old building.

Suddenly it seemed very quiet. Malcolm stood stock still in the aisle, a look of surprise on his face. "But you can't hear anything in here!" he exclaimed.

Verity, who was ahead of us, turned and smiled. "It's amazing, isn't it?" she agreed. "When the Church of Scotland resolved to try to make all their buildings carbon neutral, it seems St Andrew's got a grant from some green agency or other, and they put in triple glazing at the same time as they did all the insulation. I can hear the sea almost all the time in my flat, but I never hear it here!"

We walked down one aisle of the dimly lit sanctuary and through a door by the steps up to the pulpit, and found ourselves in some sort of church meeting room. A group of eight people, mostly men but including Ingrid Fraser, were standing around holding mugs and chatting. There was an old wooden table with chairs round it, ready for a formal meeting, but nobody was sitting down.

We were greeted with various cheerful welcomes. "Here she is!" and "Is this weather to your liking, minister?" and "Coffee, Verity? And for our visitors?" I saw that some people had papers with them, and a couple of the men had devices. Most had the look about them of *harkrav*; it was something to do with the way their hair was cut, or the clothes they were wearing, or even their posture. *'These are good people, Kirk folk'* I reminded myself, and wondered why I felt at a disadvantage when they were being so friendly.

The meeting settled down quickly. Malcolm and I were shown to chairs to the side of the room, where an elderly woman was also sitting. We were right by a radiator, and it was extremely comfortable. After a walk over from the west of the island, a big meal at Verity's, and now a warm, quiet seat… I feared I might go to sleep.

There were, of course, prayers to start with, and then general introductions. Each of the elders gave his or her name, and Verity introduced Malcolm and me. "They've been over to the old airport too," she explained. "They've seen first-hand what conditions are like out there. I thought you might like someone else's take on it, as well as mine."

Then she moved on to the woman next to us. "And if anyone can be considered an expert," she announced, "it must be Jean. As some of you know, Jean came to En-Somi as a climate refugee in the first group, but most of us know her now as the owner and excellent manager of the Copper Kettle tea house next to the school."

Now that, I thought, was interesting. So, some people had settled and assimilated? Well, one person at any rate!

Verity spoke well to her elders. I could see why the church had allowed her to take a parish on her own, young as she was. She was calm and unemotional as she told the *domstol* about what she had found at the old airport, but her descriptions were, nonetheless, quite graphic. She spoke of people who were deeply suspicious of all outside interference, who wouldn't talk about how they managed to feed themselves, or of what they did when they needed medical help. She spoke of plumbing that hadn't been repaired, of a departure lounge that had been ransacked so that beds could be made of the old seating, of hovels erected inside that barn of a building, like a shanty town in some developing country. She spoke of people dressed in rags, with dirty hair and dirty faces. Then she spoke of the response she thought would be expected of any Christian anywhere. She quoted verses from

77

the Bible about 'do unto others' and 'what you do to the least of these my brethren.'

On one side of me, Malcolm was nodding in agreement, but there was a strange tension in the way the woman, Jean, to my right, was sitting and breathing.

When Verity had finished, there were several seconds of absolute silence. At last, one elderly gentleman announced, in a strong island accent, "And I can see nothing but truth in what yon wee minister tells us!"

One or two others sitting round the table nodded, but several of them had frowns on their faces, and didn't look at Verity, but down at their notes or devices. One younger man, who stood out in the group because he was wearing a tie, said, "It's strange we've known so little about these people until now."

"Well," admitted another man, rubbing at his weather-beaten face, "I knew they were there, I just didn't…"

"Whose land are they on?" asked someone else.

Everyone looked around the table at each other. Land ownership on En-Somi is a strange business because, over many years, parcels of moorland and little patches of hillside have changed hands as people married, or died without heirs, or moved away and left one family rearing sheep on another person's property, until the whole island has become a sort of patchwork. Back then I knew, for example, that there was land belonging to Malcolm's bothy that was wedged between Michaelmas Fjell and Jamie MacLoughlan's high grazing ground, but that it was always used by Sigrid for the few sheep she kept. Mind you, there were always people who knew who owned what, if you asked around enough, at least on our side of the island.

Verity chipped in at that point. "They're on airport land. So, who owns the airport?"

The man with the tie was sifting through his papers. "I checked it out," he said. "The island council owned the land when the airport was built. It was sold when the venture failed."

"To?" asked Ingrid.

The man with the tie looked down at his papers again. "Someone called *North Atlantic and Nordic Holdings*" he read out. "Sounds like some sort of company, or maybe a trust."

"Whoever it is," remarked another elder, "they obviously don't mind that the refugees are still there."

"Or they don't know," suggested someone else.

I felt Malcolm tentatively raise his hand beside me. When Verity nodded to him, he asked, "But isn't there some sort of law that only *En-Som-in-Fedii*, islanders, can buy land here? I had to prove I was native born before I could buy *Mori-mori* Cadha's place."

There were nods of agreement and a few grunts of assent round the table.

Jean raised her hand. "Yes," she explained, "but you can apply for island status, after ten years, if you've lived on En-Somi all that time."

There was some more silence while we all thought about that. Then Verity brought us back to the real issue. "Well, it would be interesting to know who owns the land, but it doesn't really affect us, does it? I mean, there are people in need out there – great need – and we should be doing something to help them."

Ingrid Fraser spoke again. "I agree, Verity," she said. "I didn't even know they were there until a few weeks ago, and I think that's a scandal. If there are people in need not six miles from our town, surely we should be doing something?"

An older man with a shiny bald head half raised his hand to show that he had something to contribute. When Verity said, "Dominic?" he took a moment before contributing.

"I think," he said, speaking slowly as if he were thinking aloud, "I think that we should be very careful here." He looked around the table, but didn't include the woman Jean, or Malcolm and me, in his glance. Something about the way he acted made me think he was used to addressing board meetings. "These people – these refugees – what do we really know about them?" He left a dramatic silence so that we could take in his point. I could tell he didn't want an answer. "We know that they are squatting on someone else's land. We know, from what our youthful minister has told us, that they are living in squalor. It seems as if they have been there for years and done nothing at all to improve their lot. Are we really sure we want to get the kirk involved with people like that?"

Jean raised her hand to speak again, and when Verity nodded to her, she stood. She was clasping her hands tightly together in front of her, and her voice sounded nervous as she started to speak. "It's like the minister said," she nodded, "I know more about them refugees than you, because I was one. And I can tell you, they live out there like that because they choose to. I don't know why, but they're lazy. If they had wanted to, they could 'ave done what I done, they could 'ave made a life for themselves 'ere or they could've gone off with the others to somewhere where they could've got work. But they like being refugees. They like other people bringing them food and clothes and being sorry for them because they been flooded out of their 'omes. I don't see why we should 'elp people what don't choose to 'elp themselves! I think it's wrong!" Then she sat down, rather abruptly.

The man with the tie added, "Of course, we don't want to be hard-hearted. A lot of those climate refugees have had a very bad time. But we have to consider – do they really want to change?"

Jean didn't stand this time or wait for Verity to bring her into the conversation. "I'd only been on the island for three or four days," she declared, "when I started to look for work. And you know, it's a long walk from there into the town, and I 'ad the wrong shoes an' all, but I did it. And I went from shop to shop, and I asked for work. And if those people out there 'ad any intention of making new lives for themselves, they would've done the same."

"Hear, hear!" applauded the bald man.

Ingrid was looking rather unhappy. "I wonder if that's really the point?" she asked. "Are we supposed to weigh up the merits of anyone before we decide to help them?"

The bald man was looking triumphant by then. "Well, hen," he said patronisingly to Ingrid, and patted her hand, "I would say that's exactly what we ought to do!" He looked around the table again. "No point in spending time and effort on people who won't spend any time or effort on themselves!"

I was impressed by how calm Verity was. I was feeling furious, and Malcolm was jiggling one foot up and down rhythmically. Verity, on the other hand, seemed almost casual as she asked, "And is that the general consensus?"

The elderly man with the strong island accent coughed, almost apologetically. "Well," he said, "I'm not so sure about that. It seems to me that the Gospels are quite clear."

The man with the tie seemed a little impatient. He looked across the table to answer. "But, Holti!" he remonstrated, "Think about it! How long has your family lived on En-Somi?"

"Well – maybe always," answered Holti.

"Quite!" agreed the man with the tie. "And in all that time, have you ever accepted charity?"

Holti looked, I thought, a little intimidated. "We help each other out, me and mine," he said, slightly defensively.

"Of course you do!" answered the man with the tie, sitting back in his chair as if he had just proved a point. "You look after your family, and they look after you, and that's the way it's supposed to be!" For the first time he looked across at Malcolm and me. "And over on the west of the island, do you receive charity? I mean, it's hard living over there, isn't it?"

When neither of us answered, he spoke for us. "Of course you don't!" he exclaimed. "You wouldn't dream of it! You scrimp and save and you work all hours, and you keep your independence, and you keep your self-respect!"

The bald man, Dominic, chipped in at that point. "The thing is," he explained, patronising us as well, "if we start giving assistance to those people, we'll just make them even more dependent than they are already. They'll start to think that they have a right to the help we have given them. They'll just want more and more from us, and they'll never give back. They've got to stand on their own two feet. That's life!"

Verity said quietly, "You do know there're children out there?"

Dominic said, "Yes, well – that's a pity, but we won't help anyone if we start giving them handouts!"

★ ★ ★

As we stood to leave the meeting, Verity came over to us.

"The flat's not locked," she said. "You can go back there if you want. Or I could meet you at the Castle for a nightcap when we've finished?"

Then she turned to Jean, who was still looking angry, and in a way, withdrawn. "Thanks, Jeanie," Verity was speaking quietly, "that must have taken some courage." And she touched the woman's shoulder gently, almost reassuringly.

We left the elders to their meeting. Jean came out with us and went off up the cobbled street to her home. Malcolm and I stood in the howling gale and looked at each other.

"Let's go down to the harbour!" Malcolm shouted above the roar of the wind and the waves.

I nodded, and he grabbed my hand as we battled against the strong easterly wind, down towards the harbour wall.

The tide must have been right in. Even though Storhaven harbour is relatively well protected by a natural outcrop of rock and some well-maintained walls, the waves were rolling in that night, driven by forces no man-made defences could control. Huge spumes of spray reached up into the night sky as the ocean crashed against the harbour wall. Small boats rocked and swayed precariously on their moorings; the windows of the houses down at the bottom of the town streamed with sea water. We felt the spray a good twenty feet before we made it to the quay.

It was wonderful. Both sea and air seemed to tear at us, pummelling us, pushing and pulling at us, demonstrating its mastery over all things, showing us how small we were. It was probably silly to be so close to such wild water, but it was exhilarating, exciting, challenging. A great sheet of spray arced over us as we stood there, and fell on us like a heavy rainstorm, and instinctively, so it seemed, Malcolm put his arm round my shoulders and held me tight, secure. We laughed and whooped, and another wave crashed over the harbour wall and somewhere there was the sound of breaking wood. Then we turned and struggled back up the cobbled street to the Castle, to have a drink and to wait for Verity to finish her meeting.

"Well, I admit I'm disappointed," reflected Verity as she fried black pudding and eggs in two separate pans, her back to us. "They're really such nice people. I thought they'd jump at the chance of helping the refugees."

Malcolm was sipping his tea while we waited for our breakfast. I thought he looked a little stern, and it occurred to me that this might be his professional face, the way he must have looked when he was worrying about his clients.

"You've a lot to learn about *En-Som-in-Fedii*," he remarked. He put his mug down and spooned in some sugar. "Everyone is a bit clannish out here."

"Yes, but..." Verity turned round to look at us, holding a spatula up in the air like a sort of flag. "They've been so lovely to me from the moment I arrived. I was a bit worried, you know, in case they thought I was too young and inexperienced, but not a bit of it. And they've been so generous."

She turned around to serve the food onto the three plates she was keeping warm under the grill, and then sat with us at the kitchen table. It was nine o'clock, but still dark outside. There was a splatter of rain against the window.

"You couldn't ask for kinder people," agreed Malcolm as he tucked into his food, "but that's when we're with our own." He chewed thoughtfully. "It's as if there are three tribes living side by side on this tiny island. There's the *harkrav*, for a start. They're mostly descended from incomers, but not recently – sometimes centuries ago. As a general rule, they have money."

"And connections elsewhere," I interrupted. "They come and go from the island."

"*Aja*," Malcolm agreed. "And then there's the *bondii*. We're the ordinary folk."

"Descended from the Vikings," I put in.

Malcolm grinned. "Well, maybe. That's what my mam told me. And the *bondii* are divided into two groups, depending on whether we live to the east or the west of Fyrtarn Fjell."

I thought that needed a bit more clarification. "Really, all the *bondii* are one group," I insisted. "There're families with members on both sides of the Fjell. Like Jamie MacLoughlan – his brother lives away to the south of Storhaven up on the moor there, where the lighthouse used to be."

"*Aja*," agreed Malcolm. "Culturally we're all the same, pretty much – the *bondii* – but the westerners are more traditional. And we mix less."

Verity was stirring her tea thoughtfully. "So why did you say, Malcolm, that the *bondii* are divided into two groups? You sound quite united."

"*Aja*," affirmed Malcolm again. "Culturally united, I would say. So, for example – did you go to the *huldufolk* celebrations?"

"Yes, I did," answered Verity. "Although I wondered whether I should, it being pagan…"

"Well," said Malcolm. "I grew up on the east of the island and I took part in *Huldufolk* Day every year until I went off to secondary school. But somehow this year's, over on the west of the island, was different. More like the original, I suppose. More traditional."

That interested me. I had never been to any celebrations east of Fyrtarn Fjell in all my time on the island. "Different how?" I wanted to know.

Malcolm buttered another piece of toast before he answered. Then, "Well, for a start, everyone there took part. Over here, on the east, there were always some people who just watched. You know, they were there when we set off from the school, and there again when the *huldufolk* fire was built by the harbour at the end of the day and the wee houses were burnt, but they didn't walk with us to whichever bothies were selected that year. In the west, it's still an occasion for everyone."

I was feeling glad, as I listened to Malcolm, that Bjorn's family had come from the west.

"And another thing," added Malcolm. "There aren't any *harkrav* actually living west of the Fjell. It's the *harkrav* who bring new ideas onto the island, so everyone living in the east seems to be more connected to the outside world. I've really noticed the difference, growing up on the east of En-Somi and now living in the west. It's things like not having reliable Wi-Fi and being cut off when the Fyrtarn Fjell pass is closed. The western *En-Som-in-Fedii* have to be much more self-reliant."

I had finished my breakfast and was feeling content and full. I sat back in my chair and corrected Malcolm. "I wouldn't say we're self-reliant," I suggested. "We rely a lot on each other."

"*Aja! Aja*, that's right!" agreed Malcolm.

Just at that moment there was a fresh spattering of rain against the window. It was still dark.

Verity asked, "Will you go home today? In this weather? I think I made a wasted journey for you. I'm really sorry, I was sure that the elders would want to do something."

Malcolm had finished his meal too. He tipped his chair on the back two legs and grinned at Verity. "I didn't think they'd be interested!" he announced.

"But why not?"

Malcolm said, "Remember, I grew up here. Those kirk folk, they're good to their own kind, but they don't see beyond their own concerns. It's not so much that they don't care, they just don't know. They can't imagine."

"And I thought Jean would want to help," continued Verity, as if Malcolm hadn't spoken. "She came here as a refugee. She must know what it's like out there, at the old airport. And Holti told me that some of the kirk people have really helped her – invested in her business. Fox-Drummin, who was there last night – Holti told me he put money into the tea house. So I thought he might want to get involved too…"

Malcolm looked sad. "In my experience," he commented, "people run out of compassion very quickly. And sometimes it's the folk who have made it who are the least sympathetic to those who haven't."

Verity sighed. "I suppose you're right," she agreed. "But you'd hope it wouldn't be like that, wouldn't you? Especially in a kirk!"

We realised then that we needed to plan our day. Over the stacking of the dishwasher, we listened to the radio. The forecast promised a break in the rain by noon, so we decided that if we set off during the dryer weather, we should make it over the pass and home before it was really dark again.

"In that case," suggested Malcolm as we stacked the dishwasher, "why don't we visit the Copper Kettle, and talk to Jean?"

★ ★ ★

The Copper Kettle was quite a steep climb up a cobbled footpath between the rears of two rows of those small, single-storey houses so typical of Storhaven, their heavy slate roofs shiny with rain, their windows small, from the days before triple glazing, when everything had to be done to keep out our winter storms. We came out into the main street opposite the tea house, just down from the school. Rainwater was pouring down the guttering in the centre of the road, down towards the harbour. Not too far away, the waves were still crashing and foaming, and the wind was whistling through a mast in the school playground where, at times, I supposed, a flag was flown.

I had to admit, the tea house looked inviting. The rain-darkened stone was brightened by the red-painted window frames and door, and inside we could see red-checked tablecloths.

"Can you make room for more coffee?" Malcolm asked me. It was less than an hour since breakfast, after all!

"I should think so," I answered, as Malcolm held open the door and we went inside.

Jean was behind a wooden counter where interesting confectionery was displayed. In the far-left corner of the room there was an artificial Christmas tree, decorated with coloured lights and silver baubles. Instead of a star at the top, someone had placed a wee house. At the table next to it, a young woman was seated, nursing a baby. Her toddler sat beside her, his face smeared with chocolate, a look of intense concentration on his face as he tackled a large éclair. There was nobody else in the room.

We took a table by the window, putting our rain-soaked jackets on the backs of our chairs, and looking around us in appreciation.

Jean came over almost at once. "*Goddi Morgoni*," she said, the words sounding not quite right in her English accent.

"*Morgoni*," we both responded. Then Malcolm went on, "You've really done well with this place. It used to be a tool shop, I think, when I was a boy. Old Calum owned it, if I remember rightly."

I thought Jean was looking at us rather suspiciously. "You were at the elders' *domstol* last night," she said, and it sounded like an accusation.

"We were!" agreed Malcolm cheerfully. "We didn't really have time to talk then. I'd love to hear your story. It sounds as if you've managed to make a life for yourself. We'd love to know how you did it."

He knows how to defuse aggression, I thought, and felt glad I was with Malcolm.

Jean looked slightly mollified. "Well, yes," she responded. "I likes it 'ere."

Malcolm suggested, "If you're not too busy, why don't you tell us about it? Marie here is really an *un-fed*, an outsider – or at least, she was when she first came here. And I'd really like a glass of Irish coffee," he added. "Marie? And why not have one yourself? And come and join us while you can."

Over in the corner by the Christmas tree the young mother had finished feeding her baby and was winding him. The toddler was still engrossed in his éclair. Jean went behind the counter, prepared three Irish coffees, and joined us.

"It's so nice in here," I commented. "Had you run a tea room before? I mean, before you came to En-Somi?"

Jean was relaxing. She stirred her coffee before answering. Then, "Years ago," she said. "I didn't really run it, but I was employed there for a while, and saw 'ow it worked – the ordering and the bookkeeping, and attracting customers, all that. I loved it."

"So, what brought you up here?" Malcolm wanted to know, although I think we could both guess.

"Erosion," answered Jean, looking sad. "The sea levels was rising, the storms was getting worse, and they said there was no way of defending our coastlines. In the space of just two years, or maybe three, my whole village was washed away." She glanced across at her other customers, but they didn't need anything. "The 'ouse we lived in went. When I was little, there was a whole row of bungalows between our 'ome and the dunes. It was all just washed away, just like that. In only two or three years!"

"How awful!" I had heard of such things, but I couldn't really imagine it. En-Somi is all rock, like a fortress. The sea and the storms batter against it in vain.

"There was so many climate refugees," Jean continued. "At first, they said they'd re'ouse us in our own area, but that really weren't possible. And no one wanted us. Well, you can't blame 'em. So we was sent up 'ere, to En-Somi."

"You were in Norfolk?" asked Malcolm. "I was living in Edinburgh the year of those huge storms – Hurricane Xavier, wasn't it?"

"Yes, *aja*," responded Jean. "Xavier was one of them. Vincent, Wendy and then Xavier, one after the other – and the town had gone." She didn't sound bitter, more resigned.

"And some loss of life, I seem to remember?" prompted Malcolm gently.

Tears welled up in Jean's eyes. For a moment she didn't answer. Then, "My 'usband and our two kids was in the 'ouse the night of Xavier," she told us. "I went to work that evening and never saw 'em again."

Malcolm put his hand over Jean's. "I'm so sorry," he said, and I knew he was. I was too; this was a terrible story.

The little family were putting their coats on, ready to go. The baby was sleeping, the toddler's mouth had been wiped, but there was still a smear of chocolate.

"Thanks, Jeanie!" said the young mother.

"You're welcome, love!" answered Jean. "Now you be a good boy, young Alexander, if you wants Father Christmas to bring you any toys!"

We had all finished our coffee. Without us asking, Jean poured us more, topping it up generously with whisky. Then she sat again.

"But they kept the survivors together?" Malcolm wanted to know. "You weren't brought up here with a crowd of strangers?"

"Well, I was really," she explained. "Lots of people 'ad family they could go to. I 'ad a sister in Felixstowe, but I didn't want to live close to the sea no more. It didn't feel safe. And any'ow, we never really get on. So I registered to be re'omed." She paused and sipped her coffee. "Yeah," she said. "Re'omed. That's what they called it. Like a dog."

It was a pretty appalling story. We all sat quietly for a few minutes. Outside, the rain had eased off and the sky to the north was brighter.

Jean didn't need any prompting to go on. "I was in no fit state to make no decisions," she told us. "I 'ad lost my whole family. It was like being in a nightmare. A waking nightmare.

90

For weeks, I just went where the authorities told me to go and did what they told me to do. I was at some sort of military camp somewhere – I don't even know where. Then we was living in an abandoned ware'ouse. That might've been in Birmingham. By then there was nobody left what I knew, we was just a bunch of people who'd given up. It was obvious that they didn't know what to do with us, either. And then they brought us 'ere."

"I heard that they expected you to live in tents," I said.

"Yes. *Aja*," agreed Jean. "We arrived on the ferry. 'Alf the people was sick. Then they put us in carts pulled by 'orses. And we was taken out to the airport. And when we got there, there was these big old green tents. And that's when I sort of woke up. It was as if I'd been in a trance, you know? And then the 'orse-drawn carts, and the tents… I thought, *This place is primitive.* I thought that if I didn't pull my finger out, I would just die. Just not make it through the winter. Just end it all, on this lump of rock I 'ad never 'eard of."

"What were they thinking of?" Malcolm was angry that anyone could have been treated like that.

Jean looked at him but went straight on with her story. "I thought, *I 'ave to get work! Nobody's going to 'elp me. I'm on my own.* So, after about two days, maybe three, once I 'ad got over the ferry trip, I walked into Stor'aven." She looked reflective. "It seemed to take ages," she told us. "I'd never been anywhere like this before – the 'ills and the moors, you know. And no trees. It was all so alien. And I thought I'd find a proper town, you know, with a High Street and shops and offices, like in England. But there were just three shops. But one of them was Calum's tool shop."

"He was an old man when I was a wee boy," remarked Malcolm.

"Even older when I met 'im!" said Jean. "But so kind! 'E wanted someone to take over 'is business. 'E said I was an answer to 'is prayers. 'E didn't mind what I did with the place, as long as I didn't convert it into an 'oliday let!"

Malcolm laughed out loud at that. "Just like old Calum!" he exclaimed.

"So I turned it into this tea house," Jean finished.

"That must have cost a bob or two," remarked Malcolm, encouraging Jean to keep talking.

"I managed!" retorted the woman, a little stiffly.

I looked around me. The tables were simple metal constructions, obviously imported, and the chairs all matched. The counter had probably been built into place by a local carpenter, but the covered containers for displaying cakes and biscuits looked as if they had come from a specialist supplier. How could someone who arrived with nothing manage to set up a business such as this? I hadn't known old Calum, but it occurred to me that perhaps he had provided the capital. I felt a surge of warmth for the kindly people of En-Somi.

Malcolm changed the subject. "Where's Calum now?"

"Oh, 'e died a couple of years ago," answered Jean sadly. "'E used to live next door. I made 'im 'is breakfast every day. Every single day of the year."

Just as were leaving, Jean paused in the clearing of our table and called out to us, "When I got back to the airport, you know, they 'ad stolen all my stuff. Everything. Even my photos. The lot. They're scum, them people out there. Scum."

★ ★ ★

Sure enough, the rain stopped at about noon. We set off for Gamla Hus with the east wind behind us, our stomachs full, but our moods sombre.

"The things some people have to go through!" said Malcolm after a while.

I kicked a loose stone off the track. "I thought she was just some bitter *un-fed* last night," I told Malcolm. "She was so mean about the refugees. But now…"

"*Aja.*"

We were both quiet for a while. Then Malcolm said, "I suppose everyone always has a story, if only we'd listen."

It was nearly three in the afternoon when we arrived in the village, and the sun was low in the sky. The Hus valley is sheltered by the moorland which lies behind my bothy; it looked shadowy, and the lights from the houses and the shop seemed warm and kindly.

Malcolm wanted to check whether his favourite brand of coffee had been delivered the previous day when the weekly deliveries were brought over the pass, so we went into the shop and Shona teased him about his sophisticated Edinburgh tastes – they didn't usually sell much coffee except to the *fi'ilsted*. We stayed to chat about the *huldufolk* celebrations and about the fact that several people had spotted a pod of orcas in Odin's Inlet in the last few days. This was not so unusual, but always a matter of interest. As we left the shop, school finished, and a little ragtag group of children emerged, heading off to the houses opposite Lyle's cottage, or up one or other of the steep footpaths to the bothies.

We saw young Andy Kullander emerge, talking in an animated fashion with a smaller boy. When they saw us, they rushed up the slope to greet us.

"*Hei*, Marie," called out Andy.

"*Hei*, Andy!" I answered. "So, are you back in the wee school now?"

Andy chuckled. "*Nei*, Marie! I'm helping Sigrid with the reading for the little ones!"

Malcolm was standing back a bit. Obviously, he was known by now, at least by name. I said, "Andy, you know Malcolm, do you, from *Mori-mori* Cadha's bothy?"

"*Aja!*" Andy grinned at Malcolm.

The other lad was young Christian from the village – the son of a second cousin of Bjorn's, although I didn't know his parents as well as some people.

Andy said, "It's dead lucky you being here, Marie. I wanted to ask you something."

"*Aja?*"

Andy shuffled his feet a bit, as if he were a little uncertain. "Me and Christian – we wondered if we could collect some wood off your beach, for our big Solstice *brenni*?" he finally blurted out.

Christian said slightly sheepishly, "Mam said we shouldn't ask, because you have a deal with the *fi'ilsted*, wood for fish, but the thing is…"

"Your beach has the best driftwood round here!" finished Andy.

I laughed. Actually, it was true – it still is. There's something about the direction of the currents and the prevailing winds which means that I have an almost regular supply of driftwood.

"We've probably got enough daylight left for you to collect one load right now!" I suggested.

★ ★ ★

Malcolm headed off home at that point and the two boys joined me. They chatted cheerfully to each other and to me, unselfconscious in the way of the western *bondii*, who generally don't learn shyness until they go off to secondary school. We dropped off my backpack, picked up some biscuits (I know about the appetites of children when they've just come from school), grabbed Duncan's old sledge, and we headed down to my beach.

By then the sun was setting. There were streaks of gold and red on the horizon, so bright that even the stones seemed pink.

Andy stood with his hands on his hips at the edge of the water. "It's bonnie," he commented.

Christian looked around. He walked over to the rocks at the south end of the little bay. "Is this where you found the dead lassie?" he wanted to know, and I thought his voice sounded slightly strained.

"*Aja.*" I walked across and stood next to him, looking down at the place where the child had lain. "Poor thing."

Andy came and joined us. "My mam says that if anything happened to one of us, she'd never smile again," he remarked.

"We won't die," asserted Christian confidently, "because people love us. She was a wee bairn out on her own in a storm, who nobody cared for... an *un-fed.*" He stared at the patch of beach where I had found the lass. "It *couldn't* happen to us!" I thought there was an air of desperation in his voice. The idea of a bairn lost in the dark waters was frightening. Then he looked right, to the other end of the little beach where the driftwood usually collected, and his face brightened. "Hey, Andy," he added, "there's loads of wood!"

And that sums it up, I thought. *The dead child was un-fed, an outsider, as easy to forget as a passing gull.*

★ ★ ★

The boys headed off back to the village, dragging the sledge and chatting excitedly about Solstice. Everyone west of Fyrtarn Fjell was going to be at Malcolm's for the last big event of the day, all of Andy's siblings would be home, and Alf was going to slaughter a sheep. There was a lot to look forward to.

I stayed on the beach a little longer, to watch the last of the setting sun. With the wind still blowing from the east, my west-facing bay was unusually quiet. Little waves lapped against the rocks and pebbles. I thought I could see movement further out, towards the *muckle scarf* stacks, and wondered for a moment if it was a sighting of the orcas, but then the sea calmed again without anything exciting appearing. I watched the last of the sun dip below the horizon and at once it felt colder.

I turned to leave.

And that was when I saw it. It was just a glint of brightness, a flash of pink-gold in the last light of the day, right at the point where the turf gives way to the pebbles.

I bent to pick it up.

It was a small silver cross on a chain, black in places from the peaty earth. I breathed on it and polished it on my glove. The front was smooth, reflecting back the last of the sunset. The back seemed scratched. Had it been damaged in the sea? Had someone tried to mark it?

Two thoughts came into my mind, almost simultaneously: *None of the bondii ever wear crosses*, and, *It must have belonged to the little girl*.

I walked back up to my bothy, suddenly overwhelmed with a sense of grief. Since that first night, I had hardly cried for the poor wee thing, but I wept then – wept all the while that I checked on the chickens, all the while that I sorted out my laundry and turned up the heating, all the while that I showered and made a meal. Then, as I sat to eat, I resolved to visit the child's grave and to bury the cross with her. Somehow it gave the poor lassie an identity.

That night I dreamt about her again, about finding her on the beach, about her dying in my arms.

★ ★ ★

I phoned Malcolm in the morning and told him about the cross, and what I wanted to do. He was quiet for a moment, but at last he said, "I think you ought to talk to Lyle first."

"*Aja*," I agreed.

Perhaps my tone sounded flat. On the other end of the line, Malcolm said, "I'll go over with you, if you want, to bury the cross, if Lyle thinks that's okay?"

Life was much easier with the phones working. Lyle had to be over at Storhaven the following day, and anyhow, he couldn't see any urgency in the matter of the cross. He suggested lunch in the *fi'ilsted* later in the week, and we agreed on the day following. It made life easier for me. I had fewer chores to do around the bothy in the winter, but I felt the need to do some thorough cleaning, especially the windows, which so easily fog up with salt from the westerly winds. One of the other chickens had started laying again, which was strange given the time of year, and I used the extra eggs to make a cake. In the evening Duncan and I had a long video call, full of laughter. He was excited to be going to his father's. Bjorn had bought him a ticket on the ferry to Bergen. It was an eleven-hour journey and his papa had booked a cabin for Duncan.

"I've never slept on a ferry before!" he claimed.

"You might not this time either!" I laughed, thinking of the probability of heavy seas. "A ferry crossing from Lerwick to Bergen, in December!"

★ ★ ★

I woke to the sound of waves crashing on the beach. The wind had changed direction again, and the tide was high. When I first came to En-Somi I had found these massive winter gales threatening. It didn't seem possible that the island would not be pummelled to death and washed away. Gradually, though, through that first winter, my feelings had changed. There was something about watching the spray and foam around the stacks, the birds wheeling and diving into the thunderous seas, the clouds scudding urgently across the sky, that started to speak to me of permanence. I remember standing with Bjorn at the place where our path slopes steeply down to the beach, the hill and the bothy behind us, the wind in our faces, and thinking, *It has been like this for thousands of years!* By the time I am telling you about now, the year that Malcolm came home to the island, the sight and sound of monster waves inspired in me only awe – awe and gratitude.

Malcolm called for me, which meant that he had taken a very long way round to get to the *fì'ilsted*. He had brought me a small three-legged stool which he said he didn't need, so that I could reach the top of my kitchen cupboards. We walked together, up the track to the village, the wind behind us pushing us forward, whipping our words out of our mouths so that it was impossible to have a conversation.

Lyle was already sitting at the table by the fire, a glass of whisky in front of him, and Petter and Malchi were standing behind the bar, talking. Malchi was regaling the other two with the story of some catastrophe that had taken place in the kitchen that morning and which, he said, explained the smell of burning.

"*Morgoni,*" greeted Petter. He served us Irish coffee, then said, "We'll leave you to your important police business!" Those last two words, 'police business', he pronounced in a mock-English accent, imitating a popular TV series from south of the border.

Lyle and Malcolm made quite a contrast, the one large and sturdy, looking younger than his years, the other squat and bearded and somehow always dishevelled. I felt a great sense of fondness for them both.

I took the little box in which I was keeping the cross and chain out of my backpack. We all three leaned over the table, looking at it.

"My boss isn't really interested in it," Lyle told us. "He thinks it could've come from anywhere. Don't you get driftwood that's come all the way from Newfoundland on your beach?"

I laughed. "We did once," I answered.

Malcolm said, "But isn't that a bit of a stretch? I mean, wouldn't metal sink?"

Lyle picked the cross out of the box. It looked so dainty in his huge hand. "Hard to believe this was washed in by the sea," he agreed.

"I was thinking to bury it in the wee child's grave," I explained.

"*Aja.*" Lyle was thoughtful. "That would be a kindness. They gave her a Christian burial, you know. The new minister did."

Malcolm reached over and took the cross from Lyle. "If the *nasyonii* had had this, they could have asked around, whether anyone recognised it," he pointed out.

"They won't do that now," Lyle warned us. "The case is closed. She was just some *En-Som-fly-Kninger*," he explained, using an uncomplimentary dialect word for 'refugee'.

We were all quiet. I was thinking of Christian, how easily he had designated the unknown child as *un-fed*, an outsider. "She was just a wee bairn," I said.

Malcolm placed his hand comfortably over mine. "We'll do what we can for her," he suggested. Then, of Lyle he asked, "Would the *nasyonii* mind if we showed the cross to the people over in the airport?"

Lyle looked thoughtful for a moment. Then, "I'm not sure they'd ever know," he pointed out. "And it's a free country!"

It seemed to me that we three had made an important decision, sitting there in front of the fire, a sort of pact. To seal it, we ordered mutton pie (which was not, despite Malchi's warnings, at all burnt!) and made room for Olaf, who came in soon after for his midday meal.

Over the next couple of days, it seemed as if Malcolm and I were on the phone together every few hours. We were planning to go out to the airport again at least once before Solstice, and we thought we should take things which the people out there would find useful. I looked through Duncan's old clothes, and also chose a couple of items of my own clothing that I had brought over from Edinburgh, and now never wore. We thought that it might be good to take some food, too. I made piles of oat biscuits and Malcolm said he had tins of food he didn't want. Almost at the last minute I put in an old colouring book that Duncan had turned his nose up at when he was about four (*Mam, it's for girls!*) and some colouring pencils.

Dragging my offerings up to the village on the sledge before it was even light was hard work, but I knew Malcolm would be laden down with his own contributions. He was there before me, talking to the owner of the ponies and cart, and laughing about something. He greeted me with that great smile of his and loaded my stuff onto the cart while I took the sledge round to the back of the *fi'ilsted*. It was about eleven in the morning by the time we left, and the sun was just rising behind Fyrtarn Fjell.

The cart had a sort of bench seat at the front, and beneath it, Malcolm had wedged a box. "There's a flask of coffee in there," he pointed out, once we were over the bumpy part of the track where the little stream that flows into Oden's Inlet crosses the path. He had laced it with a touch of whisky, as is the custom, and it felt good, riding the cart next to Malcolm as the track climbed towards the pass.

"We'll have to come home in the dark," he remarked after a while.

"*Aja.*" I had already thought of that. By mid-December we are down to only about four hours of daylight out of every twenty-four. "Those poor refugees, they must have wondered where on the earth their government had sent them."

★ ★ ★

We didn't stop in Storhaven but we had to drive through it; there are no tracks round the edge. The town seemed quite busy. A ferry had come in, and there was a lot of bustle around the quay. Depending on the North Atlantic weather, it could have been the last ferry before Solstice, so people had come down from the outlying bothies to collect packages ordered from elsewhere. There were several *harkrav* families visible too. Some of the private schools would have finished for Christmas and the children would join their parents on the island for the holidays.

It was one of those fresh, cold days. The air seemed startlingly clear, the sky an icy pale blue, the moorland green and grey. I had my scarf wound round my face for warmth, Malcolm was humming under his breath as we followed the road round the coast.

The journey seemed quicker this time. It was about one in the afternoon when we arrived, tying up the ponies exactly where we had done before. We covered them with blankets, unloaded our bundles, and headed round to the entrance.

There seemed to be more activity around the place on that second visit. Two children were kicking a ball near the end of what had been the runway. Someone had lit a fire on a patch of concrete, and several people were standing around it, drinking out of a mixture of tumblers and what looked like jam jars. As soon as they saw us, they all stopped talking, and watched us warily as we approached. I recognised the woman who had been less than pleased to see us last time.

Malcolm shifted the old sports bag he was carrying more securely over one shoulder to free up a hand, and gave a sort of wave, as if he were greeting friends. Once again, I realised how his professional experience stood him in good stead.

"You again!" said the woman grumpily. "I fought I told you we like our privacy?"

Malcolm smiled and put his bag down at the feet of the woman. "And I told you we'd be back," he said. "We've brought some stuff we thought you might like."

For a few moments nobody said anything. The woman didn't look down at the bundle but continued to stare at Malcolm. The fire crackled in the stillness, and the children on the runway called to each other.

"No 'arm in seeing what's in there," suggested a grubby-looking man in a baseball cap.

"Might be some use," agreed another.

The man called Jarvis disagreed. "We don't need nofing from them geezers," he grumbled, his face angry.

The woman still didn't look down, but obviously she had heard what her friends had said. She nudged the sports bag towards the fire with one foot.

At once, the others, all but Jarvis, dived towards it in a sort of mad scrabble. They pulled out the tins of food and then some saucepans. One man grabbed a coat and put it on at once, another was holding up a pair of jeans, checking the size.

The woman watched them for a few minutes, a look of scorn on her face. Then she turned back to us and said, "Huh! No cloves for the women and children, then?"

I passed my bag across. Disdainfully, as if she were clean and tidy and I was some suspect street person, she took the bundle and opened it.

Her expression changed a little as she examined what I had included. She opened the biscuit tin and sniffed the contents, and for the first time I saw the glimmer of a smile on her face.

She pulled out one of Duncan's old jackets and held it up. Over her shoulder she said to the crowd by the fire, "This'll fit Shawn, won't it?"

The man in the baseball cap stepped over to us and looked at the jacket. "Fink it will," he agreed. Then he held his hand out to Malcolm. "Name's Charlie," he said. "Grateful for this lot." He waved his hand vaguely over the two bags, the contents of which were now scattered on the ground around the fire.

"No problem," answered Malcolm in a casual tone. "Anything you'd particularly like us to bring, if we came again?"

The man called Jarvis spat on the ground at that. Muttering something under his breath, he turned and slouched away.

Another person joined us. I thought for a moment that it was another man, perhaps younger, although the ages of these people were hard to guess. Then, when she spoke, I realised it was a woman. "Somefing for the girls to wear would be good," she said. "You've only brought cloves for the boys."

"Right!" Malcolm seemed entirely accepting of the fact that nobody but Charlie had introduced themselves, or thanked us. "We'll be off, then," he added, and put a hand on my shoulder as if to guide me back to the trap.

At once, the older woman jumped between us and our ponies. "Wait a mo!" she commanded.

We stopped. The woman looked us up and down – like a person deciding whether to slaughter a sheep, I thought.

Then, "'Ave a drink wiv us before you go!" she instructed.

Malcolm gave her his warmest grin. "I thought you'd never ask!" he replied, and we joined the circle.

It was some sort of rough spirit they had in those glasses and jam jars, not recognisably whisky, or anything else really, but definitely alcoholic.

"'Ome brew!" announced Charlie. "Cheers!"

"So, can you speak too?" asked the woman, addressing me.

"*Aja!*" I said, then changed to the English, "Yes. I'm happy to meet you."

"Ha!" responded the woman. "'Appy, are you? Well, there's no accounting for tastes!" She scrutinised me again, then added, "We might be 'appy to meet you, being as you've brought us some bounty, but why would you want to meet us? You know what they call us round here? *Sommy klingers.* It means 'rubbish'. That's what we is. Rubbish. And they calls this place 'the pit'." She paused for a moment. "Which it is!" she added.

Of course, I knew what she was referring to. Somewhere she had come across the dialect phrase, *En-Som-fly-Kninger.* I wondered where she might have heard it. "It means 'refugee'," I told her. "Whoever used those words was saying you are refugees."

She was not easily convinced. The woman gave me that calculating look again. "Don't sound like they're saying 'refugees'," she told me. "Sounds like they're swearing at us. Sounds like 'darkie' or 'Pikey' in our language."

"I'm sorry," I responded, although my reply seemed inadequate. And she was right, in a way. The phrase carried negative undertones. Any welcome newcomer would be called an *un-fed*, an outsider, not *En-Som-fly-Kninger.*

"And anyhow," butted in Charlie. "'ow long do you 'ave to live on a piece of rock before you stop being a refugee? We got children what was born 'ere!"

"How many children are here?" Malcolm wanted to know.

Immediately, the faces of the crowd took on that wary look again.

"Why would you want to know?" the woman demanded.

"Oh, sorry!" was Malcolm's instant response. "I didn't mean to pry. It's not our business."

The woman looked slightly mollified. "No," she agreed. "It ain't! Still, no 'arm in asking." I noticed, though, that nobody answered.

"We'll be away, then," said Malcolm, putting his empty jam jar down on the ground. "It's a long way home and it'll be dark soon."

"It's always dark in this godforsaken land," said one of the men.

"Or always light," said another.

Malcolm smiled his cheerful smile again. "So it is!" he agreed, and taking my hand, he led me away from the fire.

★ ★ ★

"Well, it seems that they have contact with someone on the island," mused Malcolm as the ponies climbed the slope away from the airport. "Someone who speaks dialect – or a corruption of it, at any rate."

"*Aja*," I agreed. "Someone they don't like."

"I've heard that before, you know," he said. "The phrase that woman used, *sommy klingers*. I was called that once, when I was a lad."

"You were?" That made no sense. Malcolm is island stock, going back countless generations.

"Mm," he agreed. "But I don't think the person using it knew the dialect. It was just an insult."

"Who was it?" I wanted to know. "Who called you that?" I was feeling quite indignant.

Malcolm shrugged. "Just some *harkrav* lad. Down by the harbour in Storhaven. I can't remember why, now."

We were both quiet for a while. The ponies were trotting along, apparently content. A light shone from a dwelling up on the moors, bright in the winter dusk.

"I'll tell you what," remarked Malcolm after a while. "If I drank much of that hootch it'd be an early grave for me!"

I 've heard it said that back in the old days it was the job of the owners of the *fi'ilsted* to decide on the exact day of Solstice each year. It makes sense – there's quite a lot of drinking involved in the celebrations, and as well as that, back then, only the men tended to congregate there, bringing their knowledge of times and seasons. By the time of my story, the date was calculated far more scientifically, and easily discovered on the internet well in advance. I think it was probably on 22nd December that year, the closest Solstice ever gets to Christmas.

As is the way among the *bondii* west of the fjell, plans for the day had somehow clarified through discussions at the shop or over drinks and meals. The first big gathering, to see the rising sun, would happen on top of the fjell, for those able to climb it. Already, wood and various flammable cast-offs had been carried up there and a *brenni*, or fire, had been built. At the same time, breakfast would be served at the school for those villagers unable to climb the hill, because there's a good view of Fyrtarn Fjell from there.

Sunrise isn't until well after eleven in the morning that late in the year; there's never any need to make an early start on Solstice. Nevertheless, the climb to the top is steep and demanding, and people need to eat before attempting it. Generally, then as now, neighbours met with friends and made the ascent together.

Lyle had invited several people to his place, myself included. I suppose it was about eight in the morning when I arrived. It was a bitterly cold day, with icy rain in the wind, but I remember being happy with that. The weirdest Solstice I had experienced before then had been accompanied by a southerly breeze, and the mild air all day had made us uncomfortably aware of how the climate was changing.

Sigrid the schoolteacher, Malchi, Petter and Malcolm were already there, and Sigrid's youngest daughter, over from Storhaven for the holidays and obviously pregnant. There was the delicious smell of frying food coming from the kitchen area of Lyle's bothy.

"*Hei!*" Lyle greeted me; the others turned round from the various places where they were sitting or standing, and there was a chorus of "Happy Solstice!" Lyle had coloured lights draped around the room, his nod to the forthcoming Christmas festival, and the place was warm and cheerful. Lyle didn't really have a table large enough for us all to sit together, and I remember balancing my plate on my lap and laughing at some story Sigrid was telling about one of the children in the school.

It was still pitch dark when we set off. As I knew he would, Malcolm fell into step beside me while the track was still wide enough for two. We didn't talk much – it is hard work climbing the fjell, although Lyle was quite talkative, I seem to remember. Sigrid and her daughter had stayed down in the village to supervise the big breakfast in the school.

The first time I had ever climbed Fyrtarn Fjell had been a few days after my arrival on En-Somi. Bjorn had taken me up there so that I could get an idea of the geography of the whole island. We had taken a picnic, and Bjorn had insisted on carrying everything we needed, because I was pregnant. Then it had been a bright autumn day. After that, I hadn't climbed the fjell again until Duncan was about six, and desperate not to be left behind at the school with the old people and the babies. Since then, I think I had climbed it every Solstice except one, and every time, I had been surprised at the way that one minute you are scrambling around on the steep and apparently endless slopes, and then suddenly you are there, at the top.

So it was that morning. Malcolm was ahead of me, I remember. He gasped, "Made it!" and reached down to haul me up the last rocky three feet or so, and we were standing there, side by side, able to see into the darkness in every direction.

Lyle was inspecting the *brenni* with his torch, adding a little oil so that it would light easily, kicking sheep dung off a large, flat rock so that people could sit down. We heard voices and saw the flashing lights as another group climbed up on the eastern side of the fjell – Olaf and his crowd, who started off in the lower, northern part of the valley towards the harbour. Other people arrived too, Jamie MacLoughlan and all his family, even their little one in a sling, and the Kullanders, who were responsible for the fireworks that year.

Some years the weather had been so bad up on top of Fyrtarn Fjell that it had been nearly impossible to stand upright, and once, the sleet had actually put the fire out, but everything was just as it ought to have been, the year I am describing here. We knew that the sun was supposed to rise at about eleven twenty, so we all stood looking east towards Storhaven, and saw the horizon gradually lighten. Lyle was ready with his matches and Alf had the first rocket in position, so that when Olaf announced, "Sun-up!" the *brenni* was lit and simultaneously, the first rocket shot up into the air, exploding in sparks of green and blue.

We all cheered, the baby cried, and Petter handed round spiced dandelion tea, the traditional drink with which to welcome the rising sun. For a few minutes, ours was the only bonfire lit, and the only fireworks. We were higher than anyone else, and the first to greet the sun. Then, bit by bit, as if an invisible hand were moving down the slopes, more *brennii* were lit and more fireworks set off, until last of all, the two bonfires at our summer harbour and on Storhaven quay were burning, and all across the island were the flickers of fire, the explosions of fireworks and, occasionally, carried by the wind, the cheering of islanders.

It was a good day. From Fyrtarn Fjell we walked south and a little to the east, and were at the Stewarts' place by lunchtime. Theirs was an unusual home. Some *harkrav* family had bought the cottage once and renovated it to let as a holiday cottage, but when the tourist industry came to nothing, they had sold it back to the Stewarts. As a result, it was divided up inside into different rooms, and it is the only bothy I have ever been in that doesn't have the cooking area in the south-western corner.

For those who were so inclined, the serious drinking started at the Stewarts'. The feasting, too. And, of course, after all that walking and climbing, our appetites were enormous. Some of the younger families had come up from the school, and there seemed to be children everywhere. The Stewarts had a huge *brenni* on a rocky area just down from their home, and there were potatoes baking in the fire, as well as kebabs on long metal skewers to hold into the flames, for those who could stand the heat. When he had eaten his fill and tasted each of the three different whiskies provided by the Stewarts, Olaf produced his *langspil* and played us a mixture of traditional island songs and Christmas carols.

I was sitting on a wooden bench, talking to one of the Stewart girls, when Malcolm came over to me.

"They're coming to me next," he reminded me. "I need to go ahead and get ready. Do you want to come, or will you stay here?"

"Oh, I'll come!" I answered at once.

Young Andy Kullander overheard. He wanted to know, "Where're you going? Can I come?"

I saw Alf and Fiona look at each other, and Alf said, "You stay here with us, my lad!"

"*Nei, nei!*" argued Malcolm. "He can come with us. There's lots to do!" Then, looking at Andy, he asked, "Are you good with fires?"

"*Aja!*" said Andy with great emphasis.

"Well then, we need you!" said Malcolm. "I haven't lit my *brenni* yet!"

★ ★ ★

The day ended as well as it had started. By the time the crowds arrived, half an hour or so before sunset, the fire was lit, the lamb, which had been slow-roasting inside all day, was carved, every cup, mug or beaker was arranged on the breakfast bar and five bottles of whisky were lined up ready for people to help themselves.

We arranged ourselves on the new slate porch overlooking the sea and watched the sun sink slowly down. There were cheers and more fireworks, and a lot of singing, and some storytelling, and gradually, as it got colder and colder, and children became tired, the crowd thinned out until finally, there was only Malcolm and me. We sat on the bench which Petter had made, wrapped in a huge blanket that Malcolm had brought out, and listened to the fading voices of the last of the people to leave.

That was the first time Malcolm kissed me.

It was a perfect Solstice.

It was early in the afternoon, and from the row of long, narrow windows in Malcolm's bothy, we could see the darkening sea and the dusk-blue sky, lighter still in the west. We were almost too full to move. Malcolm had offered to make Christmas lunch and had used some of the mutton left over from Solstice to make a delicious pie, and I had provided some Kentish wine which I had bought years earlier and had never felt like opening. There was ice cream in the fridge, but neither of us was ready to eat anything more.

Christmas isn't a big deal on the island, except perhaps for some families with children and maybe the *harkrav*, but it's rarely ignored altogether, and both of us had been in the habit of celebrating it when we had lived on the mainland.

"We ought to go for a walk," groaned Malcolm contentedly. "Burn off some of that lunch!"

"*Aja*," I agreed, not moving. I was stretched out on one sofa, Malcolm on the other.

"It looks cold out there," he commented.

"*Aja*."

He groaned again, then swivelled his legs around so that he was sitting upright. He stood, came over to the sofa that I was on, grabbed my hand, and said, "Come on, lazy bones! Time for some fresh air!"

I let him pull me to my feet. "You're a slave driver!" I complained.

It was indeed cold outside. The wind was coming from the north-west, bringing a few icy flakes that were neither rain nor snow. We huddled into our jackets and set off, up the track behind the bothy, past the wind turbine, and on up to the ridge where an old track goes north–south across the island. From there we could see clear down to Oden's Inlet and across to Jamie MacLoughlan's bothy.

We stood together looking out at the wild landscape.

"I didn't know how much I'd missed this," Malcolm commented, "until I came back."

"I can't imagine living anywhere else, now," I agreed. I thought of the winters of my childhood. "I wonder what Granny would have made of all this?" I added. "You know, she never visited any of the islands in all her seventy years!"

"Have you still got that cross?" asked Malcolm thoughtfully, after a few minutes.

"*Aja.*" I had put it in the drawer alongside my wedding ring from the days when I had been married to Bjorn. "We never did show it to the people out at the airport."

"There's still time," he mused.

"I had wondered about Hogmanay," I said. "But they're English, aren't they? Do the English celebrate Hogmanay?"

"Marie!" exclaimed Malcolm, as if I had put forward a brilliant idea. "Of course! *Aja*, the English do celebrate, but not as much as us. But we could take stuff over to them – food and fireworks! Let's celebrate Hogmanay with them!"

★ ★ ★

That gave us a week to prepare. I phoned Verity and told her what we were planning, and she asked us to call in on her on our way; she had collected some clothes and toys from the few elders who had shown any sympathy for the refugees. Malcolm, meanwhile, was engaged in business of his own. Having borrowed ponies and a trap from villagers several times, he had decided to buy his own, and while the internet was working, he was spending time on his computer and on the phone, negotiating for two ponies from Shetland which were partly of Faroe Island stock, and a cart made by an artisan carpenter on the Cowal Peninsula on the west coast of the mainland. These purchases would have to be brought to En-Somi by ferry, however, and in the meantime we were going to borrow from Robert in the village again.

We didn't see each other during that week. Solstice and Christmas had been lovely, but on the following morning, Boxing Day, I suddenly started to have doubts again. I think it was talking to Duncan that set me off. He had Skyped soon after breakfast, wishing me a happy Solstice and Christmas, and excited about the overland skiing trip that was planned for the following day.

"And you are having a good time?" I had asked, although I suppose I'd known he was. He would have phoned or messaged me sooner if there had been any problems.

"*Aja*," answered my son. "I thought it might be a bit strange – you know, being with Paps and Gudrun, and having two little half-sisters. But they're sweet, Mam, and Paps seems so happy with Gudrun. They seem to be really close. It's nice."

When the call was finished, I remember that I had felt rather hollow. Of course, I didn't want Bjorn to be unhappy or to spend the rest of his life alone, and I had no illusions about our marriage. We had been far too young, and I had been far too needy, to make the sort of commitment that we needed to make. I don't suppose we would have stayed together for as long as we had if it hadn't been for Duncan. But still… the thought of Bjorn being deeply in love, still, after two children had come along… it made me feel like a bit of a failure.

So, then I started thinking about my relationship with Malcolm. I had really only known him for six weeks. It was true that we had slipped easily into a very good friendship, and I believed that Malcolm was becoming fond of me. But did I love him? Did I even know what being in love was really all about?

And somewhere, behind those thoughts about my present situation, and my friendship with Malcolm especially, lay the deeper questions which, I suppose, had always been with me. Somehow, you embark on life thinking certain things will happen, and events take over, one thing after another. Now, here I was in my early thirties, my son away at school – and what was it all about? What was the point of it all? I had last asked myself these sorts of questions, as far as I could remember, when I had lived with Granny, and perhaps in the first few weeks of university, before I met Bjorn. Now it seemed I had never answered them, just pushed them aside. I realised that I didn't know what I wanted in life. To grow old on my own, on En-Somi? To grow old with Malcolm? With someone else? To wait until Duncan had struck out on his own, then to go back and finish my degree? How had I managed to spend more than a decade so contentedly on the island, without considering these things?

In the evenings, to occupy myself, I worked hard on Malcolm's *gensi*. It was going well. I was using En-Somi wool, natural beige and blacks (almost certainly from Jamie's brother's flock), and the other colours dyed using traditional island potions. I had developed several small variations on the Fyrtarn Winter pattern, which made the business of knitting just engrossing enough to occupy my mind, but even so, I was aware that I didn't feel completely at peace with myself.

The one thing I did feel confident about, though, was the rightness of going over to the old airport again. Whenever I thought about those people, I felt a sort of tug towards them. It wasn't any longer just about the wee dead girl. It was all those living people, the bleakness of their environment, the seeming emptiness of their existence. Perhaps I related a little to them, now that all those questions had arisen in my mind. I was asking myself what the purpose of my life might be, but I was wondering about the purpose of theirs, too.

★ ★ ★

It was deathly quiet when I woke up on the last day of the year. I could hear no sea, no sheep, no rain or wind. I knew at once what that meant. I climbed down from the sleeping platform, pulled a coat on over my pyjamas and opened the door.

As I had known would be the case, I could hardly see the old coal shed, so dense was the fog. Of course, it was still dark too. I wondered briefly whether this would make us alter our plans, and I felt a small pang of disappointment at the thought. But *nei*, I knew that we would go over to the airport if it was at all possible. Fog might slow us down, but it wouldn't stop us. My backpack was ready by the door. At the last minute, I remembered the little cross. I took it from its resting place beside my old wedding ring, thinking to put it in an inside pocket of my bag, but at the last minute, I paused. Then, not feeling quite sure why, I put it round my own neck under my warm winter clothes. It seemed right, somehow, that it should be against living flesh.

As we had done before, we met outside the *fi'ilsted*. Petter and Malchi were there, but not the owner of the ponies. Malcolm had already loaded some bits and pieces onto the cart, and I had very few offerings this time, so we were away quite quickly.

It was bitterly cold. We both wore our scarves over our mouths and wore the fur-lined hoods of our jackets up, so there was no conversation possible. We knew enough about En-Somi in a winter fog to be wearing layers of clothes, so we looked like two shapeless bundles, with steam issuing forth each time we breathed out.

Crossing the pass was tricky. The track was easily wide enough for the cart and the ponies knew the way, but at one point there's a steep drop on the right – the south side of the path. Malcolm jumped off the bench seat at that point and went to the ponies' heads, just to be safe, although they were sure-footed enough. Then we were negotiating our way down the gentler eastern side of the fjell and making good progress to Storhaven.

"I wasn't sure you'd come," smiled Verity, when we had knocked on her door and called up the stairs to the flat. "Do you want to come up?"

"*Nei*, thanks," answered Malcolm, then checked with me, "unless you want to?"

"*Nei*, let's just keep going," was my verdict, "if that's all right with you, Verity?"

She was coming down the stairs, laden with several bags of different sizes and shapes. "These are from Ingrid Fraser," she said, piling the bundles onto the back of the cart. "And good old Holti collected all these from some of the people up on Frigg Moor. And hold on a moment…" She ran back up the stairs, returning with one of those colourful paper carrier bags you get when you buy Christmas presents in the more expensive Edinburgh stores, "There's some treats for the children in there, from me."

We climbed back up onto the bench seat. "I wish I was coming with you, really," she said. "Oh well… Have a good day."

She stood in the street and watched us as we left, the sound of the ponies' hooves muted in the fog.

★ ★ ★

Although it was light by the time we reached the old airport, the fog had barely thinned at all. There were no signs of life this time. We settled the ponies, covering them with blankets as before, and headed round to the corrugated iron doorway.

My first impression, as we stepped into the old concourse, was that it was almost as foggy inside as out, but almost at once I realised that it was woodsmoke thickening the air. During such weather, smoke hardly rises at all; it was drifting around the whole building from two fires lit where once passengers would have sat, waiting to be called to departure gates. We made our way, loaded down with all our bags and bundles, to the closer of the two fires.

117

The reception we received this time was completely different.

It was one of the children who noticed us first. She tugged at the arm of the older woman, the one who seemed to be in charge, and whispered something. The woman looked towards us, then got to her feet and walked towards us. She wasn't smiling, but she didn't have that suspicious look any more.

"Good as your word, then!" she said.

"Happy Solstice," I said. "And happy Christmas, and happy new year!"

"Hmm. And the same to you," she said, looking at our baggage.

Malcolm said, "We celebrate Hogmanay on the island, like they do on the mainland. We wondered if we could see in the new year with you?"

For the first time, something we'd said or done seemed really to surprise the woman. "What, 'ere?" she asked. "In this dump?"

"Why not?" asked Malcolm, as we put our bags and bundles down by the fire.

At once, several grimy hands reached out, but, "'Old it! 'Old it!" demanded the woman. Then she called across to the people at the other fire. "Charlie, come over 'ere!"

The man with the baseball cap shouted back, "What?"

"Come over 'ere," repeated the woman, "got something for you!"

He stood to his feet and came across the dirty floor, followed by most of the others who had been sitting or lying around the second fire.

"What's up?" demanded Charlie. Then he saw us. "Oh, it's you again!" he said.

"Hello!" I answered. Following Malcolm's example, I had decided to treat the people with courtesy, however rude they seemed.

The man gave me a look, disdain and surprise written on his face.

When almost the whole crowd had gathered, the woman spoke to them.

118

"These people 'ave come to see in the new year wiv us," she said. "So, let's make 'em welcome, shall we?"

"What've you brought?" demanded a boy, who seemed maybe a little older than our Andy Kullander.

"See for yourself," suggested Malcolm.

Again, hands reached out for offerings, and again the woman stopped them. "No!" she said. "First things first!" Then, turning to us, she said, "I'm Frances – Frances Atkins. They calls me Frankie."

"Charlie."

"Mandy."

"Joe."

"Si, and this is Marigold, my oldest. And Thistle, the baby."

"Thistle?" I was intrigued.

"Not many flowers grow on this lump of rock," said Si, "but lots of thistles. Seemed better than calling 'er Lily or Rosemary!"

"I still think Jasmine would 'ave been prettier," said a woman. "I'm 'er mum. I'm Rose."

"'Ave a drink?" invited Frankie when the introductions were done and the whole crowd – or almost everyone – had seated themselves round the fire.

Someone passed a dirty-looking piece of cloth over for us to sit on.

I could see Malcolm hesitate. Frankie must have noticed too. "We're on tea," she said. "Not booze!"

After that, it became easier. Our packages were opened, and clothes and toys were passed round for general examination. The food was kept aside by Frankie, who was obviously the boss, but we were offered some sort of sweet biscuits from the tin I had brought over before. They tasted smoky – cooked over the fire, I guessed – but were perfectly edible. The 'tea' was strange, made from dandelion leaves, I guessed, and drunk black, but it was warm at least.

There was some idle chat around the fire. Frankie checked the bag donated by Verity and decided, "For this evening."

Malcolm pointed out that he had brought some good whisky, but that it, too, was for the new year celebrations.

"You're really going to stay 'ere with us, then? Overnight?" queried Frankie.

"It's a bit far for us to go home," joked Malcolm, "if we don't leave here till after midnight!"

Charlie was smoking some sort of cigarette. "We'd better bring them ponies of yours in," he remarked. "The poor fings'll die of exposure out there."

"I'll 'elp!" volunteered the child called Marigold, who jumped to her feet.

Outside, the fog had finally started to clear, and it was actually daylight, but the wind which had sprung up was cold. Malcolm and I pulled our hoods up again to protect our ears, but Charlie and Marigold seemed unperturbed by the weather. Just as I turned to say something to the child, I saw a figure moving away, round the corner of the building.

"Who was that?" I asked, feeling, for some reason, alarmed.

"Oh," Marigold answered. "That weren't nobody. Just Jarvis. 'E don't like no visitors. 'E'll go off on 'is own until you is gone. 'E ain't too friendly, Jarvis ain't."

"That's a pity," Malcolm remarked casually.

"I don't like 'im," volunteered Marigold. 'E frightens me."

"Where can we put them, the ponies?" I asked, changing the subject. Jarvis made me feel uncomfortable too.

"Inside, with us," answered Marigold, skipping a little. "I likes ponies."

I decided she wasn't as old as I had originally thought. She was only, I realised, about nine or ten. She must, surely, have been born here, on En-Somi?

We untied the ponies and walked them round to the entrance of the building. We encountered some difficulty there. The makeshift corrugated iron doorway was too narrow for the animals and they tossed their heads with reluctance when Charlie tried to coax them forward. In the end, Si came to help, and the whole doorway contraption was taken down, to let the ponies in, then reassembled. They were tied up in a dark corner away from the fires, and given water and oats, which we had brought with us. Marigold shyly patted their noses and stayed watching them eat when the rest of us went back to the fire.

I t was a strange day. To begin with, most of the adults sat around the fire, a few of us on odd pieces of old fabric, but several others on parts of plastic chairs, presumably torn from the places where they had originally been anchored when the building had still been an arrivals and departure lounge. At one point I needed the *cludgie*, and Frankie directed me the full length of the hall to the facilities still marked 'Ladies' and 'Gentlemen', and I saw how the whole place had been vandalised, dismantled so that the refugees could use the original furnishings in ways that best suited them. The facilities looked worn and shabby, but there was cold water in the taps and the toilet, in the one cubicle that had a door, flushed. On the way back, I noticed that there were two figures asleep by the far fire, wrapped in sleeping bags and wearing woolly hats. "Quincy and Mo," said Frankie. "They've both been ill for ages."

"Bunking off," remarked Charlie scornfully.

"Bunking off from what?" I wanted to know. This was our third visit and so far, we had seen no signs of anyone working.

For a second or two, nobody said anything. Then, "Just bunking off," said Frankie. "From life."

At one point there was a sudden surge of activity. It was odd, I didn't hear anyone say, "It's lunchtime" or "I'm hungry", but one moment nobody seemed inclined to do anything but shuffle up as close to the fire as they could and make the odd, desultory remark, and then the next moment there was activity. Someone produced a large saucepan from a pile which seemed to have been stored in the dilapidated ruins of a shop of some sort on the concourse (I recognised one of the pans Malcolm had brought over on our previous trip), and someone else was emptying tins of soup into it, with, as far as I could tell, no concern about the different flavours that were being mixed. The woman called Rose fetched a plastic bowl which she had filled with water, and started peeling potatoes, and the boy Shawn went off in search of bowls and spoons.

It took a while for the meal to be prepared. Heating things up over a fire isn't an easy business, but everyone seemed patient enough. Several loaves of bread appeared from the stores, and I could see at once that this was not home made. It was bakery bread, the sort of food you might buy in Storhaven. More 'tea' was made, our mugs and repurposed jam jars were refilled, a strange variety of crockery and cutlery was distributed, and at last, lunch was served.

"Tuck in," invited Charlie and, with happy slurps and sips, we did as we were told. The concoction which was ladled out was thick and tasty, a cross between soup and stew, although what exactly it tasted of was difficult to say.

By that point in the day, most people seemed quite comfortable with us. Malcolm and I were still sitting next to each other, but Malcolm was talking to Shawn, and Marigold had plonked herself down on the other side of me. I was finding the accents of most people strange, after hearing En-Somi accents for so many years. It added to a general feeling that I was on a film set, or visiting a foreign country.

"Is them your ponies?" Marigold wanted to know.

"We borrowed them," I explained.

"Nicked them?" She obviously wanted clarification.

"*Nei*," I laughed. "Borrowed – we'll return them tomorrow, to our neighbour, Robert. Or Malcolm will."

"Is 'e your bloke, then, Malcolm?" was the next question.

"He's my friend," I answered, and wondered again what there was between the two of us.

"You talks funny," remarked the child. "Not like a boss. Like…" she was obviously struggling to think of a way of explaining my strange speech. "Like a boat man!" she finally decided.

"A boat man?" I couldn't imagine what she meant.

"Yeah, you know, a bloke what…" She stopped very suddenly. Si, who was sitting on the other side of her, had slapped her face.

At once, even before I could do anything, I felt Malcolm's hand rest on my knee. *Don't react*, he was warning me. I swallowed the objection that I had been about to utter, and gulped.

"Is there any more tea?" asked Malcolm, as if he hadn't noticed Si's surprising behaviour, and Frankie stood to retrieve the huge kettle from beside the fire. The moment had passed.

★ ★ ★

A couple of the younger bairns had run outside as soon as they had eaten their soup. Now they reappeared. "Sun's out!" they announced. "Can we go and collect wood?"

"Let's all go," suggested Frankie.

Charlie turned to us. "You can see our beach. It's lovely."

Actually, it was a bit of an exaggeration to say that the sun was out. The fog had certainly cleared completely, but there were grey, ominous clouds racing across the sky allowing occasional glints of brightness. Nevertheless, it was good to be out of that smoky atmosphere.

From the airport you can't see St Matthew's Bay, although I've heard that in the days when the airport was actually an airport, the views as the planes came in to land were lovely. The children ran ahead, past the old control tower and up, over a rocky outcrop, and out of sight. The rest of our motley bunch followed, leaving behind only the two sleeping members of the community and Rose, who was feeding baby Thistle. Marigold skipped along beside her father, apparently not in the least upset by having been slapped, and Malcolm fell into step besides me.

"There's a mystery or two here, wouldn't you say?" he asked.

"*Aja*," I agreed. "Bosses who speak differently from me,

124

boat men, and bread that was baked in a proper bread oven somewhere…"

"And two people who bunk off – from what?" added Malcolm.

Just then Marigold rushed over to me. "Come on! Come on!" she demanded. "If we collects the most wood, we gets an extra potato!"

"We do?" I exclaimed, pretending to be excited. "Come on then, Marigold! I'll beat you to the beach!"

★ ★ ★

Even with a biting easterly wind blowing in from the sea, whipping up the foam from the crashing waves and making our cheeks smart, it was glorious to be on the beach. It's the sort of bay that you see on calendars, almost half-moon shaped, with steep, rocky cliffs on either side. I had wondered how, on an island with no trees, the people at the airport found wood for their fires, but I realised at once that St Matthew's Bay, like my beach, must catch just the right currents and tides to bring in a steady supply of driftwood.

The children were obviously used to this sort of beachcombing – the adults too. Once we were over the rocks and down on the sand, everyone separated and started hunting along the shoreline. I realised almost immediately that wood was not the only thing they were looking for. Everything and anything man-made was brought to Frankie for inspection and most of it was kept. Before long, as well as an impressive pile of wood, there was a stretch of plastic netting, some orange rope, a very tattered looking flip-flop and, weirdly, an English car number plate.

"I found a purse, once," confided Marigold, "but there weren't nofing in it."

In a surprisingly short space of time, there was quite a respectable heap of wood, and the sun, such as it was, had gone down behind the moors west of the airport.

"Best get back," remarked Frankie, and we all did as instructed. There was no doubt who was in charge.

★ ★ ★

"I'm going to walk the ponies," said Malcolm as we entered the huge building again.

"I'll join you," I volunteered.

"Did you say you've brought fireworks?" Frankie wanted to know. "Because if so, we ought to build a fire outside and cook them spuds in the embers. Like Guy Fawkes' night when we was kids."

"Yeah," agreed Charlie, "let's!"

Malcolm and I each took one pony by the reins and Charlie helped us manoeuvre them through that makeshift doorway again. Outside, it was already getting dark, with a sharp easterly wind but no more clouds. Some of the children followed us out and, with Si, they started building the bonfire. We led the ponies towards the beach again.

Once we were out of earshot, Malcolm wanted to know, "So, what do you make of this set-up?"

"Well…" To be honest, I had begun to feel the way you do if you are reading a novel and accidentally turn over two pages at once. "I can't work it out, to tell you the truth."

"*Nei*," Malcolm agreed. "Verity said they never go into Storhaven. It's possible that they grow their own potatoes out here, but that bread… and some of the tins of soup looked like the stuff we brought over last time, but some definitely wasn't. The labels were in Norwegian."

I hadn't noticed that. "So, someone else is supplying them with food? Do you think it's Verity?"

"*Nei*, I don't think so." We had reached the rocky incline that sheltered the airport buildings from the sea, and we turned around and started heading back. "She would've told us, I'm sure."

By the time we had rubbed the ponies down a bit, checked on their feed and water and mucked out their area of the building, the bonfire was built. Rose had passed baby Thistle to Marigold, who had wandered over to us, holding the infant against her shoulder expertly, jogging her gently. It was obvious she'd taken her turn in caring for her little sister any number of times. I was reminded of those pictures you see on the news of refugees in other parts of the world, where babies seem often to be cared for by children who aren't so much older than them.

"Them ponies is good," she commented.

"I'm going to get two of my own soon," remarked Malcolm.

"Where from?" Marigold looked around the smoky space, as if they were somewhere close by.

"They'll be brought in on the ferry, when the weather's good enough," I explained.

"Ferry?" Marigold seemed not to know what I was talking about.

"*Aja* – yes," I said, "haven't you seen it? The big boat that comes into Storhaven harbour."

"Ain't never been to Stor'aven," the child answered, jogging the baby gently. "They says it's dangerous. Safer to stay 'ere."

By now, we had wandered over to the indoor fire, which had burnt down quite low because nobody was tending it. I added a chunk of wood, which sizzled and hissed on the embers. It hadn't dried out from its immersion in the sea.

"I've been to Storhaven lots of times," commented Malcolm casually. "Why is it dangerous?"

The girl looked at him with big eyes; for a moment she stopped jiggling the baby. Then, "It just is," she said. "If you don't know, I ain't gonna to tell you."

I thought it best to change the subject. "You're very good with the baby," I remarked. "When I was your age, I wouldn't have had a clue. I had to learn it all when I had my son."

"What's 'is name? Your boy?" Marigold wanted to know.

"Duncan," I told her.

"That's a boss name," was her response.

"Is it?" I tried to keep my tone neutral, almost disinterested. "My husband and I liked it. It was the name of his grandfather."

"So where is 'e now, your 'usband? If it ain't 'im?" She nodded her head towards Malcolm.

"We're divorced," I explained.

"Done a bunk," decided the girl, sounding entirely satisfied. Obviously, it made sense to her.

Baby Thistle started to grumble in her sleep. Marigold patted her soothingly on her back and rocked a little from side to side. "I likes babies," she commented.

"Me too," I agreed.

"We always used to fight, me and Lavender, about 'o would look after 'er."

"Who's Lavender?" Malcolm asked gently, poking the fire with a stick as if he wasn't really paying much attention.

Marigold made a sort of squeak. I looked at her, surprised. There was a look of alarm on her face.

"Marigold," I prompted her, "who's Lavender?"

For a moment, a look of utter panic crossed the child's face. She looked from one of us to the other, and then almost wildly round the room. "Ain't nobody 'ere called Lavender!" she exclaimed, getting to her feet almost clumsily because of the baby in her arms. "Ain't never 'eard of no Lavender! I's going to see me dad!"

She almost ran towards the corrugated iron door, and was gone.

Malcolm and I were left looking at each other in the gloom. "Marie," he asked, and his face looked sad. "Do you suppose that the wee lassie you found on the beach was Lavender?"

★ ★ ★

128

To be honest, the evening dragged a bit. The general consensus was that the fireworks should be lit at midnight, so everyone, even the children, stayed up. There was some discussion about how we would know when the time had come. It turned out that nobody among the refugees had a watch that worked. "We all used our phones till the electric was cut," explained Charlie. "Now we just guess."

"Last year we saw fireworks over there," Rose reminded people, pointing to the moors that loomed darkly to the south-west.

"Floirean's Cnoc," I said.

"What?" Several of the people who were gathered round the bonfire looked at me as if I'd spoken a foreign language.

"Oh, sorry!" I was coming to realise that these people knew almost nothing about En-Somi beyond their own small patch of territory. "There's an area over there, towards the town, where the *harkrav* – the rich people – live, called Floirean's Cnoc. They probably let fireworks off at midnight. It's Hogmanay for them."

"We saw fireworks a few days ago," commented someone else.

"Solstice," said Malcolm. "The shortest day of the year. We light bonfires and set off fireworks at sunrise and sunset."

"I'm figuring '*arkrav* is bosses, then?" asked Frankie. "Does you work for 'em?"

"No!" Malcolm and I spoke forcefully, in unison, and then laughed. "We work for ourselves," clarified Malcolm.

"We don't have much to do with the *harkrav*," I added. "They don't live on our side of the island."

"Fortunate!" uttered Frankie under her breath, and I was left wondering whether this was her earlier sarcasm emerging again, or whether she had personal reasons to believe that it was best to keep away from the richer islanders.

Towards the end of the evening, Si and Rose produced what looked like a catering-sized can of cooking oil. It turned out to be more of the home-brew we had been offered on our last visit.

"Ah!" exclaimed Malcolm. "We can do better than that!" and he retrieved the whisky we had brought with us.

It was at about that time that the two refugees, the people they had called Quincy and Mo and who had been sleeping beside the far fire, emerged.

They were relatively young, not teenagers or children, but perhaps in their early twenties. Quincy had a bushy beard and long, scraggly hair. I'd noticed that none of the refugee men were clean-shaven. Mo gave the impression of being skinny, although it was hard to tell because they were both wearing blankets like shawls, wrapped round their shoulders. In the flickering light of the bonfire their faces looked worn and haggard. I thought that they actually did look ill, not the way you would expect a person to look if he or she was just malingering.

Everyone made room for the late arrivals round the fire. The children were mostly sitting down, dangerously close to the embers, I thought, and some of the adults had dragged bits and pieces to sit on: a broken wooden bench, an old crate, even a couple of breeze blocks. Malcolm had enlisted the help of Charlie and Harry to arrange some rocks away from the buildings, so that the fireworks could be lit safely. Frankie organised the removal of the potatoes from the fire, and they were served, liberally sprinkled with salt, on the same strange assortment of crockery that had made its appearance at lunchtime. Si came round with Malcolm's whisky, and people started making toasts.

"To the new year!"

"To proper drink!"

"To our visitors!"

Mo was standing next to me. She was hunched up under her blanket, holding it together at the neck with one hand, and she had taken a jam jar of whisky in her other.

"So, what's this all about?" she asked me. "And who're you?"

"It's new year," I answered. "We call it Hogmanay up here. I'm Marie. We've just come over to celebrate with you."

She glanced at me, almost furtively, as if she didn't want me to know that she had looked at me. "Nobody comes 'ere to celebrate," she announced.

"Well, we did!" I told her.

There was a pause, then, "Why?" she demanded. "What's in it for you?"

Her question took me aback for a moment. Why had we come over? "To be neighbourly," I finally answered.

"Huh!" remarked Mo. "A good time to start being neighbourly, ten years after we got 'ere!"

She had a point, and I felt embarrassed. "I know," I said. "I'm sorry!"

This time, Mo looked at me more steadily. "So what?" she persisted. "Are you new on this island, then? That vicar came over 'ere a couple of times when she was new. Never came back, though."

"I've lived here for years," I said, "but I live over on the other coast. I didn't even know you were here until a few weeks ago."

"Did you *choose* to live 'ere?" Mo sounded utterly incredulous.

"*Aja*," I answered. "I came here with my boyfriend… well, my husband… well, my ex-husband, and I've been here ever since."

"They say you can get away," reflected Mo, "if you 'ave any dosh. Me and Quincy, we don't 'ave no dosh."

"Don't you like it, then?" I asked. "I mean, didn't they offer you all places somewhere else if you didn't like it here? That's what I heard. Why did you stay?"

"Yeah, well…" Mo took another swig of her whisky. She was getting through it at quite a pace. "We was kids then, me and Quincy. We didn't want to go back and live in them old barracks again and be made to go to school. And the boss said if we stayed 'ere we'd be free. Free! Huh!"

"The boss?" I queried. Frankie had talked about 'the bosses' as well. It was not an idea that belonged on the island.

Mo glanced around the circle of people. Nobody seemed to be paying us any attention. She lowered her voice, so that I could hardly hear what she was saying. "The bosses are the blokes what we works for. They *owns* us. They says 'jump', and we jumps. They says 'work', and we works. They says 'shut yer mouth', and we sure as 'ell shuts our mouths."

Just at that moment, Malcolm called out, "All right, everyone. It's nearly midnight! Who can count down from a hundred?"

Most of us, it seemed, could. When we reached about thirty, there was a show of sparks from the direction of Floirean's Cnoc – the *harkrav* had started their fireworks, but Charlie held his nerve and it was only when we chanted "… eight, seven, six, five, four, three, two, ONE!" that he lit the touch paper and the first rocket went shooting up into the sky, exploding in a shower of crackling, golden sparks.

Baby Thistle cried, one or two of the children rushed to their parents, others rushed towards Charlie, and there were lots of "Oohs!" and "Ahs!"

Mo laughed. "They ain't never seen fireworks before!" she explained to me. "The kids what was born 'ere. I seen 'em once, when I was a kid. Pretty."

"*Aja.*" I rather liked Mo, and the things she had been saying intrigued me. It was hard to talk, though, now that the fireworks were banging and crackling around us.

Young Marigold came up to me then. "Ain't they brilliant?" she exclaimed, her eyes shining in the firelight. "This is the best night ever!"

★ ★ ★

I woke feeling cold and dirty. Frankie was poking the fire and resting the kettle on some metal contraption that had been rigged up. She saw that I was awake.

"Cup of tea?" she offered. "It'll be brewed soon."

I crawled out of the tangle of my blankets and pulled my boots on. Like everyone else, I had slept in my clothes. I joined Frankie by the fire.

"Thanks," I answered.

"Never really thought you'd stay," commented Frankie. "Our first proper visitors."

"You have it hard, out here," I said.

"Yeah. Yeah, it's 'ard."

We were both quiet for a moment. Malcolm was snoring slightly, a gentle, soothing sound. Then, "We was taken in, you know," offered Frankie. "We should've left wiv the others, but we was conned. And now look at us."

We both looked around the semi-derelict, barn-like building, at the smoke stains on the walls, the filthy floor, and the piles and heaps of blankets, by the two smouldering fires, that were people sleeping.

"Is it too late?" I asked. "I mean, Mo said last night that you are owned by a boss, but that can't be right. Not on En-Somi!"

"Mo, huh!" Frankie was clearly unimpressed. "She don't understand. 'Er and that Quincy just fink they can go! Just leave this island and go somewhere, make a fresh start! 'O do they fink 'as brought 'em food all these years? 'O 'elped us move out of them tents and into this building? 'O brings some doctor woman 'ere when babies is born? We owe them bosses. Mo and Quincy, they say we don't owe 'em nothing, but we does! And we can't never pay 'em back. So, we just 'ave to make the best of it! And not bunk off!"

I was finding it hard to take in what Frankie was saying. "But Frankie," I said, "I don't think it's legal, getting people into debt like that, so that they're not free! Who are they, these bosses? Maybe if Malcolm and I went to the *nasyonii*, the police…"

Frankie put down the stick with which she had been poking the fire. She placed one hand over mine. "Now look, girl," she warned, her voice low and serious, "don't you go stirring fings up. 'They's hard men, them bosses, and there's no knowing what they might do. You come over 'ere, evenings and 'olidays, if you want. You bring us stuff, too – that's kind. But you keep well away when we's working, when it's just an ordinary day, and you don't say nofing to nobody about no bosses. Otherwise – well, it'll be us what pays, not you."

I could hear the warning in her voice, and the fear. "Can I just tell Malcolm?" I asked. "If he promises not to do anything that'll hurt you?"

Frankie looked across at Malcolm, still sleeping by the fire. She smiled. "Yeah, you can tell that bloke o' yours. I wouldn't expect nofing else!"

★ ★ ★

"So, what do you suppose they do?" I asked Malcolm. We were in the trap again, heading back to Storhaven. To our left, the waves were crashing onto the rocks. Even when we couldn't see the sea, we could hear it, and sometimes we saw great fountains of spray reaching high into the freezing air. I had repeated everything that Mo and Frankie had told me, and Malcolm had listened, nodding a little now and again, frowning into the cold wind over the ponies' heads.

"Well…" For a few moments he was quiet. Then, "I think it must be something illicit, don't you? Something someone would need slaves for."

"Slaves!" Pictures of sugar plantations came unbidden into my mind.

"*Aja.*" Again, Malcolm was quiet while he thought. "We came across it once in Edinburgh," he continued. "Immigrants from

Eastern Europe, working on a building site, so badly in debt that they were completely trapped. Or thought they were."

"But it can't be legal!" The thought of those people out at the airport living like that, believing they couldn't do anything about it, made me angry. "If we just reported it, surely the *nasyonii* would do something about it?"

"We can't do that," Malcolm pointed out. "Didn't you give Frankie your word that you wouldn't? And anyhow, do you realise that we don't have any proof? Just the words of people who are scorned by everyone. Remember how the *domstol*, the meeting of the elders, talked?"

After that we were quiet for a while. I was having a job taking it all in.

As we rounded the bend that gave us our first view of Storhaven, all grey slate roofs and stone walls, nestled down by the harbour, Malcolm suggested, "Let's see if Verity's home, shall we?"

★ ★ ★

"She'll be over in the church!" We had tried knocking on the door of Verity's building to no avail, when an elderly man addressed us. "There's a place for tying up ponies over there too," he added. "By the bike racks."

We found the rails the man must have been talking about, tethered the ponies and opened the door into that large, silent building.

One light was on, the light over the central pulpit. Beneath it, sitting in the front pew with her head bowed, was Verity. Of course, she heard us coming in, and turned.

"Oh, hello!" she greeted us, and her solemn expression turned a little more cheerful. "How did it go?"

"*Hei*!" we both answered. We walked down the aisle and settled ourselves next to the minister.

"Interesting," said Malcolm.

"Worrying," was my comment.

We were sitting in a straight line, all looking forward, facing the heavy wooden carvings round the base of the pulpit.

"I didn't expect it," said Verity, almost to herself. "When I came here, to En-Somi, I thought I would find… well, something different. I expected that people would be simple, straightforward. You know, in touch with the land and themselves. Good people."

Malcolm sounded sympathetic. "We probably are good people," he suggested. "Well, as good as anyone anywhere. But you know, Verity, people are just people wherever they live."

Verity sighed. "Yes, of course," she agreed, but it was obvious that she was dealing with real disappointment. "But wouldn't you think that here, where people have to cope with the elements all the time, that they would become more sympathetic towards their neighbours if their neighbours weren't coping? I can't get over the way the elders reacted when I raised the question of the refugees!"

"Not all of them," I pointed out. "Not Ingrid Fraser or Holti."

"No, okay," agreed Verity. "But they're not typical, are they?"

The absolute stillness of the church was strange. On En-Somi, we live with wild noises, wind and sea and birds and sheep, all the while. We three sat there for a while longer, saying nothing.

"How do you suppose they survive?" I asked Verity.

Verity sighed. "Oh, I'm afraid they're being used," she said. "That's what I'm finding so hard. It isn't just that nobody's helping them, it's that someone's taking advantage of them. When I went over there, one of the children mentioned a workshop. He said his dad had hurt his hand in the workshop. I didn't see a workshop. Did you?"

"We heard mention of bosses," I said.

Malcolm sounded thoughtful. "There's only one workshop I know of on the island, and it's on the steep side of Frigg Moor. They couldn't get there without going right through the town."

"I was told that building isn't used," Verity told us. "One of the elders told me when they showed me round the town."

We were all quiet again. The old kirk creaked a little and there was a subdued ticking sound of a heater warming up.

Finally, Verity broke the silence. "I was trying to pray," she said.

"That's something I haven't done since I was a wee lad," commented Malcolm.

"I prayed a lot, when Granny was ill," I said. "I wasn't quite sure what I was doing. Anyway, it didn't work. She died. I gave up on praying after that."

Again, we were all quiet. Verity changed her position, stretching out her legs. "The Quakers call it *'holding in the Light'*," she added. "They do it all the time. Just lift up people or problems to the Light, like children showing a teacher their paintings. Just showing God the problem so that he can sort it out."

"When I prayed for Granny, I just pleaded with him – or her. Whoever God is. Just pleaded and pleaded for Granny to get better, so that I wouldn't be alone."

On one side of me, Malcolm put out his hand and rested it over mine. Verity replied, "Yes, that's what people do. We tell God what we want. *'Give us this!'*, *'I need that!'*, *'Help us!'* But you know what Jesus is supposed to have taught, *'Thy kingdom come, thy will be done, on earth as it is in heaven.'* God's will, not ours."

"All very well," commented Malcolm, letting go of my hand. "But how do you know what God's will is?"

"Perhaps you don't have to know," I suggested. "Perhaps you just accept whatever happens is God's will?"

"That can't be right," argued Malcolm.

"No," agreed Verity. "The Quakers say that you listen to the things that come into your heart – ideas that are loving and truthful," she said. "I suppose if you think something is neither loving nor truthful, then it can't be God's will."

Again, we were quiet. Then, "I think the offer of a cup of coffee might be loving," suggested Malcolm, and we all three laughed, and went back to Verity's flat.

L ater the same day we were sitting in the *fi'ilsted* by the fire. Old Olaf was regaling Petter with yet another of his fishing stories, and Malchi was in the kitchen preparing our lunch. We had returned the ponies and cart and were fortifying ourselves for the last legs of our journeys home.

"I think," meditated Malcolm, looking thoughtfully at his whisky glass, "that the next thing we need to do is to find out exactly what's going on over there. I don't see how we can do anything before we get some more details."

"How'll we do that?" I wondered.

"Spy on them," answered Malcolm, in a matter-of-fact tone of voice.

"Honestly?" I was surprised. "Do you think we should?"

"Actually…" he was thinking it over. "It could be risky," he pondered. "We could do with some more help."

"But I promised…" I pointed out.

"I didn't," Malcolm reminded me.

"We're in for a storm," commented Malchi, coming out from the kitchen with two plates of mutton curry and a basket of warm bread, balanced carefully along his arm. "Just heard it on the radio. Have you got everything you need for the next week or so? Or you could stay here. We've got the space."

"*Nei*," I answered, picking up my fork. Goodness, the food smelt great! "I've got chickens to think of."

"I want to get back, too," agreed Malcolm. "Is this a new recipe, Malchi? It looks grand!"

"I'll buy some more milk before we leave the village," I told Malcolm. "It's the one thing I hate to run out of!"

"Ah!" Malcolm was making speedy inroads into Malchi's

offering. "As long as I've got the condensed stuff in cans, I'm all right!"

And so it was that the biggest storm of that winter became the focus of our attention, and the refugees, and all thoughts of spying on them, suddenly disappeared from our minds. If you live on En-Somi you don't ever take storms lightly!

★ ★ ★

A storm like that one, a century earlier, would have gone down in history, but by the winter I'm recalling here, the world had seen such terrible weather that it was difficult to keep track. I remember parting from Malcolm as we left Hus and agreeing to keep in touch for as long as we had communications. I wasn't at all worried. Before Wi-Fi and mobile phones, the people of the island had always had to be prepared to be isolated for long periods during the winter. We had never lost the skills.

Back in my bothy I showered and put on fresh clothes, throwing a pile of laundry into the machine. I checked on the chickens and collected four eggs, and brought tins of food up from the old coal shed in case it felt too wild to be going out at all in the next few days. I checked the dials for the ground-source heat pump, and the tension regulator for the turbine, and all the while I listened to the radio.

The storm was sweeping across the North Atlantic. Greenland had been entirely cut off from the rest of the world when their communications went down, although that had happened before, and the people had come to no harm. Iceland and the Faroes were bracing themselves for a rough week, but they, too, were well prepared. There was talk of flying in extra supplies to Shetland from Norway, and En-Somi even got a passing mention, when we were told that the ferries were cancelled.

At about six in the evening, Duncan Skyped me. He looked happy, with rosy cheeks from his skiing trip. He was excited by the possibility of really bad weather. "Paps says I can stay here," he told me enthusiastically. "Just till the storm has passed. It's going to be our job, Paps and me, to dig us out every morning. He says he never saw snow on the island like they get here. Once, the house was nearly buried!"

"Sounds fun!" I said. I realised that I had hardly missed him for the last few days, so taken up was I with the refugees – and, to be honest, with Malcolm. "I'm all set, here. I don't expect we'll be able to stay in touch for a few days. Be good, won't you?"

"Mam!" exclaimed Duncan indignantly. "I'm always good! I'm so good, I'm boring!"

I laughed to myself as I settled down in my rocking chair to work on the *gensi* for Malcolm. If this was a really bad storm, I thought, I might finish it. There is nothing like being grounded by the weather to encourage me to finish a project!

★ ★ ★

There's something really wonderful about big storms observed from a safe place. I woke once in the night to hear the waves crashing onto my beach and the cables that anchored my turbine humming in the gale. I had closed the shutters before retreating to my sleeping platform, so there was no sound of rain on the windows. I knew that Duncan was safe with Bjorn, that Malcolm had found that all was well when he got back to his bothy a few minutes after me, and that all my friends in and around Hus would hunker down and see the storm out, as we had all done many times before. I wondered about the refugees, but even they had a secure building of sorts, and as they were on the east coast, they would be sheltered from the worst of the storm by the moorland to their west. I dreamt about Granny, a recurring dream in which she is putting me to bed, stroking my hair, singing to me. It's a dream that has come to me many times through my life, a dream of comfort and security.

I remember waking quite suddenly, feeling snug and warm but ready for my day. I was hungry and was out of bed and down the ladder to the main room almost at once. While the kettle was heating up and the oil in the frying pan was warming on the hob, I started to walk round the room to open the shutters.

Like everything Bjorn had done to the bothy, the shutters were cleverly designed, with a mechanism to enable a person to open and close them from the inside without having to open the windows. I went first to the kitchen window but, unusually, it was stuck. I tried the small window next to the door, but it was firmly closed too. That was probably when I realised. I went to the door and opened it.

There was a solid wall of snow about waist high, frozen into place so that I could see the imprint of the door on the white wall. For a moment I was surprised, but then, I remember, I started to chuckle. Duncan had been so excited about experiencing really heavy snow at his father's, and here I was on En-Somi, and the arctic weather had come to me!

I closed the door and turned on the radio. At that point it was still working, although the signal was breaking up a bit. The announcer, a woman with a Shetland accent, was describing the movement of the storm and repeating the warnings that we should all stay at home. *As if I have any choice!* I thought to myself, and I chuckled again as I fried my bacon and eggs.

Malcolm phoned around nine in the morning. He sounded cheerful. He had already been out to clear the snowdrifts from his west-facing windows and was planning to use his time studying until he could get out again. "And I'm thinking I'll buy some goats in the spring, and obviously, two ponies and a trap," he told me. "So, I need to brush up on everything I used to know about goat keeping!"

As soon as I had cleared up the kitchen, I donned my warmest outdoor clothes, broke my way through the wall of snow against the bothy entrance, and ventured into the swirling white outdoors.

At once, I felt the force of the wind. Later, I learnt that it was blowing at eighty miles an hour, and the front of my bothy has no shelter. Everything – the ground, the air, the sky – was white. I couldn't see as far as my old coal shed. The gale had heaped the snow up in strange and unrecognisable shapes, and just reaching my west-facing windows to clear them so that the shutters could open was hard work. I shovelled a path round as far as the chicken coop, gave the birds some fresh water and checked on their feed, and decided that I had done enough outside for the day.

That was the first of five days of storm. Each morning, I cleared the snow from my doorway and the west-facing windows. I have always enjoyed being able to see out, although very little light came in during that wild week. The Wi-Fi didn't go down until the second day, but after that, all I heard was the whining and creaking of the turbine cables, the howling of the wind, and the waves breaking on the shore. I kept myself busy. I took some lamb mince out of the freezer and batch-cooked shepherd's pie and bolognaise sauce. I reread McIntosh's *The Mystery of Liten Stein*, about the lost civilisation of that remote, but once inhabited, rock, and in the evenings, I sat by the range and worked on the *gensi* I was knitting for Malcolm. It was, to be honest, a time of peace. By the end of the fifth day, I felt rested and calm, as if my life had somehow been ironed out. Every night I slept deeply and long, and every morning I woke feeling happy.

Then, on the sixth day, the storm was over. I lay in bed in the dark, and everything seemed quiet – no wind, no waves, no shutters rattling. I rolled over and checked my watch. It was seven-thirty; nearly two hours until sunrise.

I clambered down to the main room and was walking across to the bathroom when I heard a new sound: a soft, high-pitched scream, seeming to come from the unused chimney by Duncan's bed-cupboard.

I stopped still to listen. For a few minutes, I heard nothing, then, there it was again.

I held my breath. The cry came again, the call of a bird which rarely visited us on En-Somi. I had never been fortunate enough actually to see one in all the time I had lived here.

I threw my jacket on quickly and pulled on my boots. I opened the door carefully, slowly; I didn't want to frighten it. Outside, the air was still and bitterly cold. The skyscape was wonderful, thousands of bright stars sparkled like frost, and the snow crunched under my boots. I had to stand far enough back from the bothy to be able to see the chimney at the northern end.

And there she was, as I had hoped. Sitting on the closed-off chimney, preening herself, was a beautiful snowy owl. Even as I stood still and watched, she raised her head and gave that cry again, not a hoot but a screech. I felt a wave of thankfulness surge within me. She was the most beautiful creature I had ever seen, I thought, excluding Duncan when he was new-born.

I must have stood out there in the bitter cold for almost half an hour. I think she knew I was there. I felt as if she were looking at me. Once, when she gave that high-pitched call, it seemed to me as if she were warning me to stay away. Then, at last, she took to the wing, flying almost lazily right over my head and towards Oden's Inlet, until I lost sight of her behind the snow-covered moors.

The Wi-Fi was still down that morning, but the day felt entirely different. When the sun came up over the moors, there were long golden shadows across the snow. The air smelt different – not salty, but clear and fresh, the smell of frost. For the first time since the storm had started, I clambered through the snow drifts, past the chicken coop, to clear the snow from the small windows on the east side of the building. By eleven, when the sun had topped the slope behind the cottage, light streamed in, the icicles hanging in the window making patterns on the settle where once I had lain that wee child.

I took my mid-morning tea outside. It was desperately cold and very bright; I had to root around in the kitchen drawer to find my sunglasses. The view was stunning, the sea a bright, deep blue, the sky even bluer. *Muckle scarfs* were sweeping through the air and diving into the sea, and black-backed gulls were gliding on the thermals. I saw movement way out to sea, and wondered if it was the orcas, but whatever it was, it was too far away to tell. I felt like the only person alive in a recreated world.

Just as I was about to go back inside, though, I heard a much more human noise: the 'swish, swish' of overland skis, and then the unmistakable sound of voices.

"Now, careful on the slope," came the sound of Lyle's calm instruction. "Remember what I told you! Yes, Andy, that's right! Gently does it, Elin. Great, Christian!"

Then, appearing above the slope of the moors, wearing woolly hats and huge smiles, appeared the little group. Andy skied elegantly down to me and stopped a few feet from the bothy. Elin came next, a little less gracefully but still in control. Christian managed the last ten feet or so on his bottom, without his skis, and Lyle came last, laughing, and retrieving Christian's equipment on the way.

"We've come calling," announced Lyle. "We thought we'd check on a few people. You know Andy Kullander and Christian. This is Elin, my second cousin. They live beyond Hunger Moor, in the bothy above the summer harbour, but they saw the storm out in the *fi'ilsted*."

I was delighted to see them. "Tea?" I offered. "Biscuits?"

Skis and poles were leant up against the bothy, boots and outdoor clothing dumped on the floor, and mugs arranged on the table.

"Wasn't it wild?" exclaimed Andy, talking about the storm. "I stayed up most of the night, the first night, watching the snow. Our whole house shook!"

Christian sounded almost disappointed. "I went to sleep before it started," he complained. "And by the time I woke up, everything was white. It was still snowing, though."

Elin was the youngest of the three children, a pretty little thing with mousy-blonde hair, in a tangle because of the way she had pulled her hat off. "Malchi and Petter took us outside to look, at midnight," she said, her voice earnest but her eyes sparkling. "I'd never seen so much snow. You couldn't even see the school from the *fi'ilsted!*"

Lyle grinned at me, enjoying the children's excitement as much as I was.

"Everyone's outside today," announced Christian, "the whole of Hus! Building snow houses and throwing snowballs!"

"Aren't you missing all the fun?" I enquired, although they gave every appearance of enjoying themselves with Lyle.

Elin looked serious. "We're helping Lyle check on outliers," she explained.

"And practising our skiing," added Andy. "I came down from our place to the village with Dad. He and Robert are checking round the northern coast."

"Can we go down to your beach?" Christian wanted to know, taking another biscuit from the tin. "I want to show Elin where you found that *un-fed* girl."

I looked at Lyle. "Not on your skis," he said. "Not without me. But you can go on foot if you want to give it a try."

The children were off at once. We could hear their voices as they followed the line of my footpath, past the old coal shed and down towards the sea.

Lyle sat in one of the rocking chairs. I sat opposite. I had left the bothy door open, and we could still hear the children, screaming and shouting as they encountered snowdrifts and, no doubt, fell numerous times on the snowy rocks.

"Christian seems fascinated by that wee lassie," I said. I found it slightly worrying.

"He is," agreed Lyle. "He talks about her quite a lot. It frightens him, a child getting lost and nobody knowing who she was. His parents have stopped discussing it in front of him."

145

"We might know," I said. "Malcolm and me. Know who she is – was – I mean."

You can't really sit up straight in a rocking chair, but Lyle sort of stiffened. "Really?" he asked, sounding cautious.

I was trying to remember what I had promised Frankie. Nothing about Marigold, I was sure. "Malcolm and I went over there again, to the old airport. Did you know?"

"*Aja*," answered Lyle. "The whole of Gamla Hus knows!"

I laughed. Of course, they did! "Well, I spoke to a little girl over there, and she mentioned a sister, Lavender. But when I tried to find out more, she clammed up."

Lyle looked thoughtful, swilling his tea round in his mug. "Did you show her the cross?" he wanted to know.

"*Nei.*" How could I explain why I had taken that little piece of jewellery over there twice, and now wore it around my neck, and still had not shown it to anyone? "It didn't seem like the right time."

Lyle was quiet, staring at the glow in the door of the range. "Is something going on over there?" he asked at last.

"Probably," I replied evasively.

Lyle was quiet again. Then, "My sergeant doesn't want to know anything about it, you know," he told me. "His instructions are to let sleeping dogs lie."

In the distance, we could hear the voices of the children, coming closer.

"The Stensens are really in with some of the *harkrav*," he said.

"But Sergeant Stensen wouldn't cover for them, if there are *harkrav* involved, would he?" I found the idea rather shocking.

"Well… not cover for them, perhaps, but decline to get involved, maybe. Just keep out of it."

"But Lyle…!"

"I know." He sighed. "It isn't right, I'm with you there."

The children were close now. "Got you!" we heard Christian shout.

"No, you didn't," called Elin. "You hit the shed!"

"I'll help, you know," offered Lyle, "if you and Malcolm would like me to. I don't believe in leaving things well alone when the truth needs to be uncovered."

At that moment the children burst into the bothy. They were covered from head to toe in snow, grinning from ear to ear, their faces pink and their noses red.

"There's a snowdrift right on the beach!" exclaimed Christian. "Touching the sea! It's amazing."

"It was great!" breathed little Elin.

"Well," said Lyle with mock severity, "it looks as if I'm going to have to return you to your parents soaking wet and freezing cold! They'll never forgive me. Come on, bairns! It's time we went! Elin, you've got another of Malchi's lunches waiting for you."

"Lucky thing!" grumbled Andy as they stamped their feet to lose the excess snow and put their skis back on. It seemed that even the children favoured Malchi's cooking.

"Bye! Bye!" they all called as they left, climbing the slope behind the bothy in that awkward sideways way of people on skis.

"Remember what I said!" Lyle reminded me, and then they were over the ridge.

"No so fast!" I heard Lyle call, and they were gone.

I mopped up all the half-melted snow on the tiles inside the door and shut out the cold air. *Lyle*, I thought, *would be a good man to have with us, if we were to do as Malcolm seemed to think, and set up a watch on the refugees.*

It was probably that night that I finished Malcolm's *gensi*. I had never used quite that combination of colours before (nor have I since), and I was pleased with the effect. The co-operative had printed labels to put in the back of our products, but this seemed too personal for one of those, so I left the jumper as it was. I decided to use the same variation of pattern on a *gensi* for Duncan and spent the rest of the evening sorting through my wool stock and deciding on colours.

The following morning, Malcolm phoned.

"There's a ferry coming in today," he told me. "My ponies will be on it."

"Is the pass open?" I wondered. "What'll happen to them if you can't be there to collect them?"

"*Nei!* The pass won't be open for a while yet," Malcolm told me. "I checked with Lyle this morning. Dougie'll look after them until I can get there. And maybe the cart'll arrive next week, and then I'll be able to fetch them both at once."

I thought it was time to come clean. "Malcolm," I said, a little hesitantly, "I spoke to Lyle a couple of days ago, about the refugees."

"You did?" He sounded surprised, but not particularly displeased. "How did that come about?"

So, I told him about our conversation.

"Mm!" he sounded thoughtful on the other end of the phone. "I think that's a good thing," he told me. "Do you know, I had wondered if there might be some sort of collusion going on, something a wee bit fishy about the treatment of those people, even before Verity said that she thought the refugees were being used. Didn't you?"

"Well…" I had obviously realised that the refugees were hiding something from us, something really bad involving 'bosses' who had some sort of control over them, but it hadn't occurred to me until I talked to Lyle that *harkrav* might be involved.

Malcolm laughed. "You're so trusting!" he exclaimed. "Do you ever think evil of anyone?"

I didn't answer that.

There was a pause in the conversation. Then, "I'm really pleased if we've got Lyle on board," added Malcolm. "We could use him."

"*Aja.*" I felt the same. It was as if Lyle might add some legitimacy to our rather ill-formed plans.

★ ★ ★

It was another fortnight before the pass was properly open. Lyle and Alf had been over once, just to test the conditions, but they had gone on foot, and came back with photos on their phones showing a totally white island and beautiful blue sea and sky. The weather forecast didn't suggest that any more severe storms were on the way, and the outliers who had seen out the worst of the weather in the village started to return to their bothies. Nobody had been hurt, although there was much talk about the wee bairn who had been born at the height of the storm, over towards Aeloff's Hill on the east of En-Somi. A few people had seen the snowy owl, too; the news of her appearance was even mentioned on national radio, as a sort of postscript to accounts of various snow-related disasters on the mainland. Jamie MacLoughlan had lost a few sheep in the snowdrifts, although most had survived in his winter sheepfold down by Odin's Inlet.

Petter and Malchi decided to organise a celebration at the *fi'ilsted*, to mark the occasion of the worst storm in five years, and possibly longer. We all gathered there in time for one of Malchi's amazing fish stews, and for some rather good whisky. The children had created a cast of snowmen and women, dressed to resemble village characters; they had barely started to thaw and caused much amusement and some disgruntlement. I was depicted wearing a blue woolly hat, which was realistic. Malcolm's snowman was very round, and someone had donated a bright red wig, which had seen better days. He laughed and laughed when he saw it.

Olaf had written a new song almost entirely in dialect, praising the *huldufolk* for keeping us safe, and describing the northern lights, which had been a token of their promise to us at the end of the celebration with the wee houses. As if to reinforce the message of his ballad, the northern lights appeared again that night, green and pink, swaying gracefully in the frosty night sky. It was, I remember, magical.

It was while we were all standing outside the *fi'ilsted*, each about to make our separate ways home, that Lyle came up to Malcolm and me and pulled us a little aside from the chattering crowd.

"The pass is more or less open now," he commented. "You'll be going over to Storhaven to collect your ponies, I suppose, Malcolm?"

"*Aja*," agreed Malcolm. "I've fixed up the barn where *Morimori* Cadha used to keep her goats in the winter. It makes good stabling. I'll have to keep the cart under a tarp until I can build something more permanent in the summer. So, I'm all set."

"You'll be walking over, then?" Lyle asked.

"*Aja*. There's nothing else for it, if I'm to bring the ponies home."

"Maybe I'll walk over with you?" offered Lyle. "I need to see Sergeant Stensen anyhow."

"Will you come, too?" Malcolm asked me. "We could call in on Verity."

"That's the wee minister, is it?" asked Lyle. I thought he sounded interested.

"*Aja*," we both answered at once.

Just then, there was a big cheer. Robert, who really didn't like the snowman that was supposed to represent him, had started to prise off great lumps of frozen snow and throw them at the children, who retaliated by hiding behind other snow characters and lobbing snow back at Robert.

When we could hear each other again, Lyle asked, "You grew up on the east of the island, didn't you, Malcolm?" Of course, he already knew that. He was leading up to something. "So, you know the moors above St Matthew's Bay?"

Malcolm sounded cautious. "*Aja*, a bit… They weren't too keen on us playing up there once the airport had been built."

Lyle was quiet for a moment. "So, you'd know if there was a place where we could hide out for a day or two? Where we could watch the airport without being seen?"

"*Aja*…" Malcolm was speaking very quietly. Instinctively, we all moved closer. "There're several ruined bothies," he said. "Or that's how I remember it. It's all *harkrav* land up there, just used for sheep. At least, it used to be."

"Are you up for a bit of exploring, then?" Lyle wanted to know.

"I am!" I announced. They weren't going to leave me out.

"*Aja*," agreed Malcolm.

"What's going on over there?" teased Petter, noticing our huddle. "Not planning to open a *fi'ilsted* in opposition to us, I hope?"

Everyone laughed.

"It wouldn't be fair to you," Lyle said. "You'd lose all your customers overnight!"

"So we would!" agreed Malchi, whose cooking was unbeatable right across the island.

★ ★ ★

Walking over to Storhaven with Lyle and Malcolm was very entertaining. Both were full of stories of the mainland, Malcolm from his years of social work in Edinburgh, Lyle from his training and a year in Aberdeen policing some of the less affluent neighbourhoods before his return to the island. We were carrying quite heavy backpacks, all three of us, because of our plan to see if we could hide out in a ruined bothy, but we were young then, especially Lyle, and I don't recall it being a problem.

I do remember, very clearly, stopping at the top of the pass where you can see down towards Storhaven, sitting where the rocks sheltered us from the wind and drinking hot soup from flasks. A very gradual thaw had set in, and the track between the ruined chapel and the town was a brown ribbon winding between white moorland. To our left, the steep, snow-covered cliffs at the north of the island drew a sharp line against the dark sea. Under his coat, Malcolm was wearing the *gensi* that I had knitted him; it looked great when the uphill climb made him hot and he unzipped his jacket, although really the red didn't go with his hair.

Already, the days had started to get longer. It was mid-afternoon by the time we arrived at Verity's, still light but not sunny, because Storhaven faces east, and the sun sets early behind Fyrtarn Fjell. Malcolm went off to check on his new ponies at the Frasers', but Lyle and I were invited straight up to Verity's flat, and I sat on her window seat looking down on the street below while Lyle and Verity went into the kitchen to make tea. Lyle seemed to have forgotten about the need to see his sergeant.

I saw Jean, the woman from the tea shop, stopping in the street opposite, talking to another person whom I didn't recognise. I could see Jean's face; she looked happy. At one point it seemed as if she was laughing out loud. Sergeant Stensen and two well-dressed men walked up the hill towards the city hall, apparently engrossed in conversation. A couple of bairns ran down the hill towards the harbour. Compared with Gamla Hus, it was quite busy.

Malcolm was away a while. Lyle and Verity brought in the tea and Verity turned on the lamps, creating a warm glow. I was aware of a spark between Verity and Lyle and sat back, watching and listening as they sounded each other out.

"I'm pretty disillusioned," Verity was saying. "I thought, you know, that my congregation would feel as I do. I mean, they've been very good to me, very welcoming, but it's as if their faith lives in a different compartment of their lives from their business."

"I've never had much interest in religion," said Lyle. "I joined the choir when I was at school in Shetland. I liked the ballads and the Scottish folk music, but when we sang religious stuff, it seemed to me to be just words. I went to the kirk a few times, my friend's father was a minister like you, but to be honest with you, if there is a god, I feel closer to him out on the moors. Or on a boat when I'm fishing in the summer."

When Malcolm came back, we discussed his ponies for a while. Dougie, who seemed to know about these things, reckoned that Malcolm had done well in his purchases. They were very small, about 70% Shetland ponies, Dougie had estimated. The cart was also fine, so Malcolm was truly independent, no longer needing to borrow transport from people in Hus.

We had planned to stay the night at Verity's. Lyle would need to sleep on the sofa bed in the sitting room, but, as he pointed out, that was luxury compared with the ruined bothy where we hoped to sleep the following night.

We discussed our plans over dinner. "We may only be able to check out the area tomorrow," Malcolm told Verity. "We've brought supplies enough to camp out for a couple of nights, but we don't know if we'll find anywhere suitable."

It was towards the end of the meal that Verity asked, a little shyly, "Can I come?"

I remember the three of us looking at each other. I don't know what expression was on my face. I wasn't really surprised at Verity's request. Malcolm looked calm and thoughtful. Lyle looked hopeful.

"Have you got what you'd need?" Malcolm asked. "Warm clothes, a winter sleeping bag, good boots?"

"Of course!" Verity sounded indignant. She may only have been on the island a couple of months, but she had acclimatised pretty quickly, and her pastoral visits sometimes took her to outlying bothies.

"Then come!" smiled Malcolm. "We'd love to have you."

"*Aja!*" agreed Lyle, enthusiastically.

I ngrid was still in her dressing gown when we called at the Frasers' the following morning, to tell them that we were collecting the ponies and trap. She took in our outdoor clothing and heavy packs, but only commented, "You'll be off on a jaunt, then?"

"*Aja*," Malcolm agreed. "When the summer comes, I'll drive over and take you and Dougie out for a picnic!"

"That'll be grand," Ingrid answered, grinning. "We'll look forward to it!"

There is only one track out of Storhaven, going north, the tarmacked road they call 'The Road Less Travelled', so we were bound to leave the town that way. Malcolm was trying to recall from his childhood which of the smaller paths leading off to the left were, in fact, just tracks to a single bothy or a *harkrav* dwelling, and which continued on, up into the moors. The owners of the larger homes had made the job a little easier for us, because they put signs at the turnings that said things like 'Private Road', or 'The Old Pottery. No Through Road'. Malcolm was sure there had been a track heading west before we reached the only easterly turning to the cemetery on Aeloff's Hill, and we did indeed find such a path and turned into it, but the track dwindled out after a few bends and a very steep incline, and we had to free the ponies from their harnesses in order to turn the cart round on a patch of narrow, rocky, flat land.

Florian's Croc faces east, of course. On the previous occasions when Malcolm and I had travelled this road, I had tended always to look to my right, at the sea. Only now, because we were searching for a track, did I take much notice of what lay to the west where the *harkrav* lived. Their homes were scattered across the moorland like bothies, but they didn't look like our simple homes. A couple, (like the Kullanders' place) were built in the

155

Norwegian style and painted dark red. They tended to have large picture windows facing the rising sun. One or two of them were stone-built like traditional bothies, but larger, and most of them had what appeared to be separate stable blocks. Like our homes, each had a wind turbine somewhere nearby.

"I've been in one or two of those," Verity told us. "They're very nice, but you could be anywhere once you get inside. Lots of imported wood and glossy tiles."

The road deteriorated after we passed the track up to the cemetery. Malcolm's new ponies were doing well. It seemed that Dougie had harnessed them to the cart every day and taken them out, so they were already operating as a team. The bench seat was really only wide enough for three passengers, so Lyle was sitting in the back with all our bundles of equipment, but he seemed quite happy with the arrangement. It was he who spotted the track we finally took.

"What about that?" he asked, pointing to a very narrow path sunken between two rocky outcrops.

"Oh!" Malcolm was frowning. "*Aja*, I remember that. We used to cycle up there," he told us. Then he grinned. "I kissed a girl for the first time on the moors somewhere along that track!"

"Is it wide enough for the cart?" Verity wondered.

Lyle jumped down from the back and measured the width by taking two paces. He estimated the size of the trap in the same way. "It should go through," was his verdict. "Do you remember whether the path gets any narrower, Malcolm?"

"*Nei*," Malcolm was very sure. "It widens out. I think this'll serve our purposes."

Lyle didn't climb back into the cart until we had made the turn and navigated that first rocky space. Malcolm had remembered correctly. Almost at once, the track widened. It was very rough, obviously not much used, but the ponies were sturdy, bred for this sort of terrain, and the cart had been built in the traditional En-Somi style, hard-wearing rather than elegant.

The ride up onto the moors that morning was fun. Having Verity and Lyle there, both still young people, made me feel younger too. It had been dawn when we left Storhaven, but the low morning sun was bright on our faces, and sometimes on our backs. There were sheep everywhere, looking shaggy and none too clean in their winter wool, and lots of black-backed gulls. Once, we saw a mountain hare, bounding away from us in a zigzag lope, white against the patches of green where the snow had completely melted. We saw one ruined bothy, nestling against the moorland and looking out to sea. Verity and I walked over to it, to check whether it would serve our purposes, but we were still too far south on the island, we couldn't see the old airport or St Matthew's Bay. It looked as if the track might take us north, so we drank some tea and then moved on again.

★ ★ ★

"So, what do we do if we don't find what we're looking for?" Lyle wanted to know. It was early afternoon, we had eaten some lunch, and already the moorland was in the shadow of Fyrtarn Fjell.

Malcolm removed his woolly hat and scratched his head. "It's a long way back," he commented.

"We've got enough food for a couple of days, at least," I pointed out.

"It would be a pity to go home now!" was Verity's verdict.

"Well…" Malcolm was thinking aloud. "What if we keep going forward while we can still see, and if it looks as if we're not going to find any ruins, we'll make camp for the night and head back tomorrow?"

None of us wanted to cut the expedition short, and so we all agreed.

We had made the right decision, too. We were in deep shade by mid-afternoon but out at sea, the water was still glittering and blue in the low sun, when Verity asked, "What's that?"

157

She was pointing to a sort of hollow higher up on the moors. It could have been just another rocky outcrop; it was hard to tell in the long winter dusk. Or it could have been an old bothy. From our track, there didn't seem to be a discernible track up to it.

"I'll go and check it out," volunteered Malcolm.

"I'll come too," I added, jumping off the cart after Malcolm.

It was a steep climb and the ground was boggy, but the closer we got, the more obvious it was that we had found another ruin.

"It's not much worse than *Mori-mori* Cadha's place was when I bought it," commented Malcolm.

We had found a neat little building with a door that was closed, but not locked, and broken wooden shutters that no longer protected two small windows, facing east. Inside, there was one room, bare stone walls and a stone floor, and a hearth at the northern end which had obviously been used for a real fire. There was no wind turbine outside, and no sign of there ever having been any electricity. There was, however, a sink in the south-west corner of the building, in traditional style, although when we tried to turn the tap on, nothing happened.

We stood in front of the bothy in the dusk, looking out at the bright sea. To our left we could just see the roof of the old airport, and a little patch of sand that was St Matthew's Bay. Directly ahead of us, looking almost straight down the marshy slope and beyond the road, was a second beach, smaller and, for all we could tell, inaccessible from the landward side.

"What a beautiful place to live!" I commented. "I wonder why it was abandoned?"

Malcolm gave a sort of grunt. "I can guess," he said. "This'll be *harkrav* land. What's the betting they evicted the tenants, intending to make this into a holiday cottage?"

"And then the airport closed," I finished the story. It was not a new one. "So, they just left it as it is."

It was perfect, or almost. After some scouting around, we found the track that the inhabitants of the bothy must have used, which avoided the marshy land below the cottage by circling round to the south and then up, so that in the end the ponies and cart arrived behind the building, where we also found a sort of shed and a broken-down outhouse. We settled the ponies, draped them in their blankets and fed and watered them, and then moved our stuff inside.

It could have been a snug little home with a fire roaring in the hearth, but the building had obviously been empty for a while, and it was icy cold.

"We can't light a fire," Lyle pointed out. "Someone might see the smoke."

We thought he was right. One of the windows had broken so we sealed it up with Malcolm's groundsheet to stop the wind blowing in, but it did nothing to warm the building. Malcolm produced a camping stove from his backpack and Verity made tea and then, afterwards, Lyle joined her in heating up tins of soya mince and beans. Malcolm and I cleared the floor of debris to make a place where we could sleep, then the four of us, still wearing all our outdoor clothes, sat on our bundles to eat our meal.

Afterwards, we went outside and stood in front of the bothy, looking towards the sea. Over by the old airport a light was flickering. We thought that the refugees must have built another outdoor fire. The sea was just a black mass. There was no moonlight and no stars, but out on the horizon there were two dim lights.

"How odd," commented Malcolm, pointing them out to us. "It looks as if there's shipping out there."

"That's not likely," was Lyle's response.

"Fishing boats, maybe?" I suggested.

"Perhaps." Malcolm sounded unsure.

"I don't think so." Lyle was, after all, our expert on the law. "Fishing's banned that far out, for conservation reasons. We're the only ones, the islanders, who can fish these waters, and then only as far as three miles out."

"A ferry?" wondered Verity.

"The ferry comes in on Fridays," I pointed out. "It's Tuesday."

We stood in silence. The lights vanished beyond the horizon. There was the faint, distant sound of cheering brought to us on the bitter cold breeze from the old airport.

"I think I'll be warmer in my sleeping bag," said Verity, signalling to us all that it was time to go in.

I 've always been a good sleeper. When I was a child, Granny used to stay with me until I had dozed off, and later, when I was in my teens, we used to leave my bedroom door open so that I could hear her, pottering around downstairs and watching TV, so sleeping was never a lonely business for me. I remember struggling a bit after Granny died so suddenly, but when I became pregnant with Duncan, my restlessness seemed to pass. Bjorn was different; he rarely slept through the night, and I often woke in the morning to find him dozing in one of our rocking chairs, an open book on the floor next to him. Duncan was like me, an easy baby, although inclined to wake rather early when he was little, before I was ready to surface.

That night in the deserted bothy, though, I slept badly. Of course, it was very cold, but I climbed into my sleeping bag almost fully clothed, and the sleeping bag itself was good quality and designed for our sort of climate. Perhaps it was the novelty of sleeping so close to Malcolm. After all, that sleeping platform back in my bothy had been my sole domain for a long time. Or it could just have been that it was a very odd thing to be doing on a February night, kipping down on the stone floor of a remote cottage.

I woke feeling stiff and disorientated. The two sleeping bags on either side of me (Malcolm's and Verity's) were empty, but Lyle was still lying there on his back, snoring slightly, and looking more than ever like his Viking ancestors, with his wild blonde hair and beard. The door was open but from floor level all I could see outside were rocks and mossy turf, and the grey clouds that were scudding across the sky.

I wriggled out of my sleeping bag, found my boots and jacket, and headed outside.

Malcolm was squatting on the ground watching the camping stove, where water was just coming to the boil. He looked up at me over his shoulder and grinned. "You talk in your sleep!" he announced.

"Do I?" Nobody had ever mentioned that before. Perhaps it was a new thing.

"Verity'll be back soon," he told me. "Shall I make porridge?"

"*Aja*," I agreed. "Just what I fancy."

I sat on a rock not far from Malcolm and the stove. When I was low to the ground like that, I couldn't see the old airport, but if I stood, I could see some of the damaged roof and the broken tarmac by the old control tower. As far as I could tell, there was no movement down there, but then it was quite early, hardly light yet. Directly in front of us, the cove we had noticed the previous evening looked quite inviting. There appeared to be steps down, cut in the rock to the right, the southern side of the cove.

After a few minutes, Verity returned. Her face was flushed a healthy pink from the wind and from exercise, and she looked happy. "There's a sheep track that goes round the hill," she told us. "There must have been another building of some sort once, but only two walls are still standing. You can see down to the airport much more clearly from there, although I don't think anything's happening right now."

"Good!" Malcolm seemed to be in his element. "Will you wake Lyle? I'm cooking breakfast."

★ ★ ★

Fortified with porridge and tea, and after checking on the ponies, we set off along the path that Verity had found. She was right: it was no more than a sheep track, but it took us where we wanted to go.

"This was a winter sheepfold," announced Malcolm, looking critically at the two remaining walls to which the path had led

162

us. "Quite high, but perhaps the crofters had no access to lower land. I suppose it served its purpose though. Look!" He pointed to the steep slope to the north of the ruins. "It's pretty sheltered, for all we're so high!"

Verity was looking slightly mystified.

"Ours are moorland sheep," Lyle explained. "They live outside all the year round, but when it snows, we like to protect them in these shelters." Turning to Malcolm, he added, "We have sheepfolds this high on our side of the island too. You ought to go over beyond Hunger Moor sometime!"

"It's a perfect place for watching the airport," I said.

"What're we looking for?" Verity wanted to know.

"Well…" Malcolm took off his hat and scratched his head, as he tended to do when he was thinking. (Actually, he still does!) "The refugees talked about working, and about bosses. They're pretty secretive, though. So, we want to find out what's going on. That's all."

Nothing at all seemed to happen at the airport all morning. There was a strong north-easterly wind that day, driving grey clouds across the sky. It was very cold. The best viewing spot was in one corner of the ruin, but it was less sheltered there and we only had one pair of binoculars. We took it in turns, in pairs, to keep watch, while the other two warmed up in the more sheltered part of the old sheepfold. We fell naturally into two couples, Lyle and Verity, Malcolm and me.

We had just begun to think about lunch when Lyle, who was on watch with Verity, called over to us. "They've got visitors!"

We left the spot where we had been crouching and went across to look. Sure enough, we could see two mounted ponies, not Shetlands. One of the riders was wearing one of those riding hats the English wear, the other wore a flat cap.

We watched as they arrived at the airport. We couldn't hear anything, but we saw people coming out of the building and walking over to the mounted pair. Lyle had the binoculars.

"They're talking to a woman, I think. I mean, it looks like a woman…"

"Let me see!" Malcolm took the binoculars from Lyle and held them up to his eyes. "Oh yes," he said, "it's Frankie. We've met her. She's the leader of the refugees."

He passed the binoculars to me. "She's handing something over to the taller man," I told the others. "A package. Not very big. And that man, Jarvis, is there."

"Let me see!" Lyle took the binoculars from me. "Interesting!" he said. "I don't think it's drugs, although it's hard to be sure. The package is too big. It's heavy, too."

Malcolm was screwing up his eyes against the wind. Although only Lyle, with the binoculars, could observe the detail, we could all see that Frankie turned towards the building. "She's calling someone, I think," Lyle added, giving us a running commentary.

Several more people came out from the building. The other rider, the smaller one who seemed to have held back until then, turned in the saddle and removed a bundle of some sort, throwing it onto the ground close to Frankie.

"Huh!" said Lyle. "They've done an exchange."

We watched the refugees dive for the bundle and Frankie raise her hand to stop them, just as she had done when we had delivered our gifts. The two riders turned their ponies and started to leave.

"Can I see?" asked Malcolm, reaching out for the binoculars. Just at that moment, the smaller rider turned and looked in our direction, although I'm sure we were well hidden.

"My God!" exclaimed Malcolm. "It's Jean!"

At that point, Verity grabbed the binoculars from Malcolm to see for herself. She focused them carefully and seemed to look long and hard at the two riders below us. Then she handed them back to Lyle.

"Yes," she said, slowly, as if thinking aloud. "Yes, it's Jean all right. And the other person, the man, is Dominic Fox-

Drummin. You met him, Marie and Malcolm. He's the bald-headed elder. Do you remember? The one who said that if we help the refugees, we'll encourage dependency?"

★ ★ ★

By mid-afternoon the wind had veered round so that it was coming from due east, and we were so cold that it seemed unwise to stay in the shelter of the sheepfold any longer. Nothing much seemed to have happened down in the old airport. A couple of the lads came out and kicked something between them on the runway for a while, and a few adults headed over the rocks to the bay, but they weren't there for any length of time.

Back in the bothy, Malcolm and Lyle went off to see to the ponies.

"Do you really think that if we lit a fire, someone would see?" asked Verity.

"They might," I replied. "I don't think the refugees would notice, but we haven't explored the moorland above us. There could be a bothy quite close, for all we know."

"But if we lit it inside," persisted Verity. "In the hearth, maybe? Once it's dark, nobody'd see the smoke."

She had a point. I rooted around in Malcolm's backpack. I had seen him put a lighter in one of the outside pockets. "Let's experiment," I suggested, looking around for something that might burn. "Oh, I know!"

Outside the bothy there were a few dead, stick-like plants. Perhaps someone who had once lived there had grown flowers around their home. I gathered a few and went back inside. Verity was watching me, bemused.

I scrunched the cold, dry stems with my hands and put them in the hearth. At first, when I lit them, I thought that it wasn't going to work. Then they caught, and the tiny wisp of smoke rose and seemed to lean backwards, into the chimney.

"I don't think it's blocked," I told Verity. "I don't think the smoke would look as if it were being dragged upwards like that, if it were."

"I'm impressed!" congratulated Verity.

The thin, dry stems had burnt away almost at once, leaving just a few smudges of ash.

"We need a supply of wood," pointed out Verity.

"*Aja…*"

Just then the men came in. "My God, it's cold," exclaimed Malcolm, stamping is feet. "We ought to do something really energetic to warm ourselves up!"

"Like going down there," I indicated with a toss of my head, "to the cove, to collect some wood?"

Verity laughed. It was almost a giggle. "Subtle!" she said.

"What are you two up to?" Malcolm wanted to know. "We were only away fifteen minutes!"

"We thought we'd make a fire in the hearth," I explained. "But we need some wood."

Lyle walked across to the chimney and looked down at our tiny pile of ash. "You tried it?" he asked. "The chimney?"

"More or less."

Everyone was quiet for a moment. I was beginning to think I'd go on my own if the others didn't want to come, but Malcolm said, "It's worth a try!"

★ ★ ★

We managed to avoid the marshy patch below the bothy by staying north of it, and actually the way down to the road was quite easy. None of the others were sure that what I had seen were actually steps down to the cove, and from the road, the beach seemed completely inaccessible, but we all headed south and, sure enough, I was right. In fact, not only were there steps, but someone had looped some rope from poles, making a sort of floppy banister.

"I wonder who comes to this beach?" said Lyle, voicing the thoughts of all of us.

"Perhaps all this was done when they were hoping for tourists?" I suggested. "If they'd renovated the bothy we're camping in, this would've been their closest cove."

"*Nei.*" Lyle wasn't impressed with that idea. "The rope's too new. This has been done recently."

"It's quite convenient for us, anyhow," said Malcolm, jumping down onto the sand.

By then, of course, it was late afternoon and the whole beach was in the shade. Even so, we could see that it was lovely – smaller than St Matthew's Bay – and the headland between the larger beach and this one curved round a little to the south, so that the cove was more sheltered and the sea less rough. Of course, that also meant there was less driftwood.

Since we had descended on the southern side of the cove, that was where we started our search. It was not entirely fruitless. We found some smaller sticks and a broken plank of wood with a rusty nail in it. Together we worked our way along, just above the tideline, finding mostly seaweed. Then we came to an outcrop of rock and had to walk closer to the cliffs to avoid it.

"Hey, look!" Verity sounded excited. We were walking shoulder to shoulder, and she was closest to the debris at the top of the beach.

We all looked where she was pointing and saw at once why she was excited. Just a few feet away from her, hardly visible in the gloom of the afternoon, was a fire pit, carefully delineated with a circle of stone. And next to it, neatly stacked, was a pile of wood.

For a moment, nobody said anything.

"Could have been left there, just for us!" commented Lyle.

"It's really odd," Malcolm sounded puzzled. "I don't remember knowing anything about this beach when I was growing up in Storhaven. I mean, us kids were all over the moors and the beaches in the summer holidays when we were home from Shetland. You'd think I'd know about it!"

"Maybe it's private?" I wondered. "The property of some *harkrav* landowner?"

"Perhaps…" Malcolm still sounded uncertain.

Lyle was walking on ahead, looking around him, seeming preoccupied.

"There's some sort of jetty here," he called back to us.

We all rushed to join him. He was right. A ledge of rock led from the beach to a small wooden pier. Even in the half-light we could see that it was in good condition.

"So, do you suppose people come here for picnics in the summer?" Verity wondered. "By boat from Storhaven, maybe?"

"*Nei!*" Lyle sounded severe. "That's not what I'm thinking! I'm thinking this is used for smuggling!"

B ack in the bothy, besides the roaring fire, we discussed the matter. There had been some disagreement about taking the neatly piled-up wood. Lyle was worried about giving away the fact that we had discovered the cove, but Verity was surprisingly insistent about not wanting to spend a second night as cold as the previous one, and Malcolm pointed out that the cove was open, so anyone might notice the steps and explore down there, particularly older teenagers.

Malcolm had been a bit concerned about us giving our presence away, even though our fire was inside, and he went out in the dark once it was lit and climbed the moor behind the bothy to see whether the smoke showed up. He came back with the news that he couldn't see the smoke but that he could smell it. "But I don't think there's anyone living up there," he told us. "There're no lights anywhere. I think we're all right."

"So, let's sum up what we know," suggested Lyle.

"We know there're about fifteen people down there," started Verity. "All ages, some born here, some brought by the authorities about ten years ago. We know they're English. We know they're climate refugees."

"We know they were tricked into staying," I added, "by some people they call their bosses. They believe they're in debt to them, because the bosses give them stuff – but not much stuff, judging from what Malcolm and I have seen!"

"We know that they're in touch with other people on the island – two at least. One is Jean, the other is Dominic Fox-Drummin," said Verity.

"An elder at the kirk," said Lyle, flatly.

"*Aja*," agreed Verity sadly, and I smiled to myself. It was the first time I'd heard her use a dialect word.

"And that somewhere, there is a workshop," I added. "Not the one on Frigg Moor…"

"And what can we guess, although we don't know for sure?" asked Lyle.

"Well, we can guess that there's smuggling going on," Malcolm pointed out. "We saw lights out at sea where there ought not to have been any shipping, and we've found the jetty where they could land their goods. We don't know if the refugees have got anything to do with the smuggling, but it's going on one inlet along from St Matthew's Bay, so there's a reasonable chance they're involved."

"There's something else we know," I added. "Or at least, we think we know: that Marigold had a little sister called Lavender and that she isn't in the camp any more. And she might have been the wee bairn I found on my beach."

For a moment we were quiet. The wood crackled in the hearth and a gust of wind blew a waft of smoke back down the chimney.

"I'm not sure I understand," Verity said. "I mean – are all these things connected? And why would anyone smuggle things onto En-Somi?"

Verity's question seemed to drift in the air like smoke. Malcolm scratched his head, Lyle looked uncomfortable.

Then, "I think I need some whisky!" announced Malcolm, and he stood up to go over to his backpack.

"Good idea!" agreed Lyle, and he stood too, then sat down again.

I held my Thermos mug out to Malcolm as he brought round the whisky. Lyle still looked uncomfortable. "I think I need to give you some background," he said.

Malcolm was sitting down again. "*Aja*," he nodded. "Tell us what you know, and I'll see if there's anything I can remember from my childhood, to fill in any gaps."

"Well… it's history, really," began Lyle. "You know that

170

at different times En-Somi has been Scottish territory and Norwegian?"

"And Icelandic," I interrupted. "And independent!"

"*Aja*," agreed Lyle. "Well, the trading agreements between Norway and other European countries are different from the regulations about trade between the UK and Europe."

"Well, yes!" I suppose that Verity thought this was not so much history as general knowledge.

Lyle continued. "So, back before the climate emergency had become the only political issue anyone talked about, there was a strong feeling here on En-Somi, and on some of the other islands too, that we'd do better to revert to Norwegian control. For better trade. But of course, it never happened."

I was beginning to see where this could be leading. "But do we trade with Europe?" I wanted to know. "I mean, us, here on En-Somi?" I thought of us as subsistence farmers and fishing folk, not as people who imported or exported many goods, other than for our own personal use.

"*Nei*," said Lyle.

"*Aja*," answered Malcolm at exactly the same time.

The two men exchanged glances.

"Okay," Lyle said. "Your turn!"

Malcolm took over the story. "Well," he warned us, "this bit is partly rumour. I was only a wee laddie when this was the talk of the *fi'ilstedi*, but my papa believed that the *harkrav* wanted Storhaven to be some sort of free port. They were planning some high-tech, micro-electronics business. They constructed that place up on Frigg Moor. But then we had a really bad winter, lots of storms, and the attempt to be granted free port status failed, and so nothing came of it all. But that place up on Frigg Moor is still there, with lights on in the winter, and *harkrav* riding up there at all times of the day and night. I saw it for myself when I was staying at the Frasers'."

"And," added Lyle, "the *nasyonii* used to report suspect

shipping off our coasts in the summer. I learnt about it when I was training, in the 'Island Law' module."

"Used to?" Verity wanted to know.

"*Aja*, used to," affirmed Lyle. "There haven't been reports of suspect shipping for years now."

"Since Sergeant Stensen took over, maybe?" I asked.

All three of them looked at me, their faces serious.

"*Aja*," agreed Lyle. "That's about right, I would say."

★ ★ ★

"Can we stay one more day?" Lyle was wondering, as we sat together eating breakfast the following morning. It had been a much more comfortable night; the bothy had been warm and we had all been too tired to be affected by the hard stone floor or our close proximity to each other.

"I think my chickens'll cope," I said, laughing.

"I'm off duty," Lyle told us. "Free until the weekend."

"If anyone needs me and they can't find me," Verity added, "I think they'd go to Ingrid Fraser. She pretty well held the fort until I arrived."

"And I'm a free man!" laughed Malcolm.

"So, can we do one more day of observation? I really want to know what's going on!"

"Me too!" agreed Verity. "It seems to involve my congregation!"

★ ★ ★

We spent a pretty pointless morning in the ruined sheepfold. There was a bit of action down at the airport, but it just looked like people living their ordinary lives. Verity and I walked further round the hill and saw that there was indeed some cultivated land which we hadn't seen before, so the suggestion that the refugees might be growing their own potatoes seemed to be borne out. There was some sort of building, too – stone and corrugated iron. It could have been left over from the days when the airport attracted islanders over to that remote coast, but there was no way of telling. By lunchtime, we were all cold and our vigil seemed rather pointless. There had been no visitors down there and even if there had been, seeing people coming and going wouldn't really tell us what was happening. It would only confirm that something was going on. We wanted the detail.

Then, just as I was beginning to feel like giving up again, Verity, who had the binoculars, announced: "I think there's another boat out there, right on the horizon."

We all crossed to the best viewing point and peered, squinting, into the low winter sun. I could see a vague shape, but nothing more. We passed round the binoculars. There was no doubting it – a boat, similar to one of those old North Sea fishing trawlers, apparently just sitting there.

"You know what?" remarked Lyle, "I think we've been daft, sitting here in the daylight watching the refugees. If it's smuggling that we think is going on, won't it happen at night?"

Verity laughed. "*Aja*," she answered. "Of course! We ought to be down at the cove after supper, if we really want to know what's going on!"

"And we should be watching the next cove along," I pointed out. "That's where the jetty is!"

"In which case," suggested Malcolm, "I think we should go back to the bothy; I'll cook one of my camp specials, and we can rest up until it's dark."

★ ★ ★

Malcolm's 'special' was delicious. Somehow, cooking on a single-ring camp stove, he managed to produce stew and potatoes which, admittedly, didn't rival Malchi's meals, but which tasted delicious. Since it was daylight, we didn't dare light a fire, so we all wrapped ourselves in our sleeping bags, and passed the time talking and drinking tea.

"So, what brought you to En-Somi?" Lyle wanted to know from Verity. "I wouldn't guess you're from any of the islands?"

"*Nei*," Verity agreed. "Kilmarnock. My family is all still there. I'm the adventurous one!"

"I don't think of Church of Scotland congregations as adventurous!" was Lyle's response.

"You'd be surprised!" grinned Verity. Then she looked more serious. "I think I'm more adventurous doctrinally than some people."

"You've lost me," remarked Malcolm. "Church doctrines aren't my thing."

"Exactly," answered Verity. "Mine neither! I don't really know if I'm interested in the formal theology. I used to know a group of Quakers once. They don't have any creed or agreed doctrines, they just trust the leadings of the Spirit. Now that is adventurous! Imagine not having recognised boundaries, so that you don't know who's in and who's out! I used to think it was a great risk. In fact, I couldn't see how the Quakers had even managed to keep any sort of identity over more than four centuries. But since I came to En-Somi…"

"We're not a very religious bunch!" teased Malcolm. "Don't say we've caused you to lose your faith, in less than six months."

"Don't be ridiculous!" exclaimed Lyle, and I realised that he was feeling protective of Verity.

He needn't have worried. She was more than able to hold her own.

"I think my faith is stronger," she said, "but different. I have faith in the Spirit, more than I did, but much less belief in the church."

"Is that going to be difficult?" I wanted to know. "I mean, if you have moved away from your faith community?"

"I don't know," was Verity's response. "Perhaps so. It feels good though."

We played all sorts of word games as the afternoon passed, and it felt very light-hearted, but the mood became more serious as dusk fell. We decided to head down to the cove to see if we could find somewhere to hide, so that we could see what was going on, if, indeed, there was some smuggling activity that night. Lyle had his *nasyoni* phone, so that he could take pictures in the dark without there being a flash of light, because of course he had to think in terms of evidence and potential prosecutions. It was interesting: we each seemed to have a different focus. Verity was worried about the involvement of her congregation, Malcolm was concerned about the slavery aspect, but I admit my concern was mostly for the children.

It was quite a calm night and the moon was almost full. There was a breeze, but not the usual gale that we so often experience. The stone steps down to the beach were dry, and the waves were making a gentle slurp and suck against the rocks. Lyle led the way around the cove to a place where he thought he had seen a useful hiding place, and we followed in single file, keeping just above the water line. The tide was low and on the turn; with any luck, our giveaway footprints in the sand would be washed away before anyone saw them.

The hiding place Lyle thought he remembered turned out to be better than we dared hope. There was a small, sandy inlet, more of a crevice really, between two steep walls of rock, the sort of place that would be useful for changing into swimwear during a summer beach party. Further back, though, we discovered there was actually a cave. The sand sloped upwards to the back of it, and there was space for two or three people at the most to sit down. There were no signs that anyone had been there recently.

From inside the cave, we couldn't tell what was going on in the cove, but at the front, where it was just a crevice in the rocks, if we stood, we could clearly see the little jetty which we had noticed on our last visit. We also had a clear view of the steps down from the road.

We had dressed in dark colours and Malcolm had brought a flask of tea. We settled down to wait, knowing, of course, that it was quite possible that nothing would happen at all. Without discussing it, we all seemed to have agreed that Lyle was in charge. He was *nasyoni*; criminal investigations were his business. Lyle and Verity stood in the little rock-enclosed space at the front of our hiding place, but Malcolm and I sat in the cave, very close to each other.

For a while, the moon went behind some clouds. We saw the lights of a plane high in the sky, no longer a common sight on the island. I wondered where it was going. From Norway to America, perhaps? Or would it turn south and fly into London? Who flies nowadays? Not diplomats or politicians any more – they do all their negotiations in virtual meetings. Relatives, going to visit family members who they can only see once a year, now that travel is so difficult, and only then if they are lucky? I was snug and warm, out of the gentle breeze and wearing all my good winter gear. I leant against Malcolm and felt his arm go round me, so I rested my head on his shoulder. I was not sleepy, but I know I was very comfortable and relaxed.

I don't know how much time elapsed. Lyle, who was keeping a careful record, later told us that we left the bothy at five in the afternoon, and that it was six, or thereabouts, by the time we were hidden among the rocks. By then, of course, it was pitch dark, but our eyes had adjusted and there were still things to see. If you live in a town or city, especially if you live on the mainland, you probably have no idea how the night sky glitters and glows when there are no clouds, and how, on a night like the one I am remembering here, the sky is forever changing. From the back of the cave, we could just see a small portion of the view that Lyle and Verity were watching, but even so, we saw shooting stars, and a dim red glow, which might have been a planet, but which might just as easily have been some sort of satellite, circling our world. There were a few high clouds in the sky, so sometimes our world went briefly much darker, but as the clouds drifted away, the sparkling resumed. We talked in low voices, remembering night-time escapades of our youth, laughing about skinny-dipping and how daring it felt when we were teenagers. I told the others about my summer on a Greek island, about seeing flying fish, and once swimming among them, and Lyle told us about going fishing at night with his papa on Loch Innsjen, the long, narrow loch just to the east of the summer harbour, and of sea creatures which glow in the night-time surf.

Then, just as I was beginning to feel dozy, we heard sounds. At first it was just voices in the distance, adults and children.

"It's the refugees," suggested Lyle. "They're in St Matthew's Bay, not here. It might not be anything to do with our investigations."

But the noises came and went, getting gradually louder. "It sounds as if they're coming this way," commented Verity.

"*Aja*," agreed Lyle. "I think so too. There must be a track of some sort over the promontory between their beach and this cove."

We all listened carefully. I know now that the path the refugees were following is steep and difficult to navigate, especially in the dark, and that it winds among the rocks on the St Matthew's Bay side. Back then we could only guess, but our guesses were correct. The refugees, or some of them at least, were heading in our direction.

Then, "Aha!" exclaimed Lyle softly. "Marie, Malcolm, you might want to come here."

We crept to the front of the cave. Lyle was holding the binoculars to his eyes, but passed them the Malcolm, and he handed them to me. Just at that moment, a larger cloud drifted overhead and I could see nothing, but then it passed and in the brittle coldness of the clear sky I could see a rowing boat, heading towards the cove.

"There must be a bigger boat somewhere," I hissed.

Lyle took the binoculars from me. "*Aja*," he breathed. "But we can't see it from here. I wish we could – maybe I could trace the owner."

It was at that moment that we heard another sound. This time it came from the track, the road to the airport. Several ponies were approaching from the Storhaven direction.

"Excellent!" hissed Lyle. He was, I suppose, excited to catch the criminals in the very act of smuggling.

We all stood very still, clustered in the rocky crevice, peering into the darkness, listening intently.

The first people to arrive in the cove were the refugees. We heard Frankie's voice, giving instructions as usual: "Kids, stay 'ere. No wandering down onto that beach! Eric, Charlie, Si, you need to be ready to take the 'eavier packages. Shirley and Marigold, I told you to STAY HERE!"

Lyle had the clearest view of the jetty. "There's only about half a dozen of them," he told us, whispering over his shoulder. "They've definitely come to meet the boat!" He raised his camera to his eyes and took a couple of photographs.

By then, though, other voices were approaching. The pony riders were using the steps that we had used, down into the cove.

"They'll have to walk right past us!" whispered Malcolm.

"So we stay hidden," hissed Lyle confidently, but very quietly, ducking down into the shadows of the rocks and pulling Verity with him.

"Back into the cave!" breathed Malcolm to me, and we huddled in the gloom, away from prying eyes.

The approaching voices were *harkrav*; Scottish, but not island Scottish.

"So, with this delivery we should be able to finish the Russian order," one man was saying.

"What about the other request?" asked a second voice. "The Turkish one?"

"No," responded the first speaker. "The Turks and the Syrians will have to wait. We can't complete their lists until we get the stuff from France, and the French are ridiculously security conscious."

The two speakers and a third person, silent until then, were walking directly towards us. The tide was much higher than when we had arrived. Our footprints would long since have been washed away, but my heart was thumping. Surely, they were bound to see us?

But they were engrossed in their business talk. The third person spoke for the first time when they were within a few feet of our hiding place. "I don't like dealing with the Syrians," she said, and I noticed the way she pronounced her 's's – almost, but not quite, as if the sound was 'sh', the way Icelandic sometimes sounds. "They don't pay on time." I wondered where I had heard that voice before. It seemed vaguely familiar. Or was I just imagining it?

"No," agreed the first speaker, "but they pay well. And we can afford to wait."

The three people stopped walking. They were only about five feet away from us, but with their backs to our sheltering rocks. They were looking out to sea.

"Did you check the work those clowns did last week?" asked one of the men. "The stuff you collected yesterday? Had they done a decent job?"

"Yes, for once!" answered the second man. Then he added scornfully, "*Sommy klingers!*"

"Peasants!" agreed the woman, and there was that slight thickening of the 's' sound again. Then I realised where I had heard her voice before – outside the Castle *fi'ilsted* in Storhaven,

179

when I had been knocked over by some *harkrav* coming out after Malcolm and me.

I wanted to nudge Malcolm, to whisper to him that I recognised the people, or one of them at least, but any movement at all when they were so close to us would have been dangerous. I could see that Lyle was holding up his phone, recording the conversation and itching, no doubt, to photograph the men, but not daring to run the risk. And would a photograph of their backs prove anything?

Hiding as we were, of course, we couldn't see what was happening at the jetty. It was clear, though, that the rowing boat must have reached it.

"Catch the rope, then!" I heard Frankie say. "Si, pull 'em in. Good. All right then, 'and us them packages!"

"Not so hasty!" came a new voice, and this time there was no trace of *harkrav* aloofness in the accent. This was an islander, *bondi* like Lyle or Malcolm. It was then that I remembered: Marigold had said that I spoke like a boat man, not like a boss. So, this was how she knew about *bondii* and *harkrav*?

We could hear the boots of the trio as they walked across the sand towards the jetty. Lyle stood cautiously, holding his phone just above the rocky ledge as he gathered the evidence that he thought he needed. Then he ducked again as the *harkrav* returned, heading back to the steps up to the road.

"Two hundred dollars for the electronics," the woman was saying. "That's a good deal. But twenty dollars for food? Honestly, are those peasants worth it?"

"Well, we can't get the work done in Storhaven," answered one of the men. "Too many people would ask too many questions. So we're stuck with them. It's better than nothing."

"They're just a bunch of freeloaders!" exclaimed the woman. "Some of them don't do any work at all, and we're still feeding them! And they smell!"

"Just leave it!" One of the men sounded angry. "All the while they're out here they're not harming us. They think they owe us,

180

and we've got to keep it like that. Imagine what would happen if they started visiting the town and telling people what they know."

"They won't do that," said the other man. "They don't have the brains! They really believe we own them, body and soul!"

"Well, we do!" pronounced the woman. "We just bought them with twenty dollars' worth of food!"

The three laughed as they started to climb the steps.

The refugees seemed still to be unloading the boat. They were making quite a lot of noise, and by the sound of it there must have been at least two oarsmen joining in the conversation too. It felt safe for us to talk more normally.

"Did you recognise any of them?" Verity wanted to know. She was sounding relieved. "I'm pretty sure none of them worship at St Andrew's."

"Hard to tell," answered Lyle. "Not the sort of people I've ever mixed with."

"We've come across one of them before," I said. "At least, I think so."

I could feel the others all turning to look at me, although of course I couldn't see their expressions. "The woman," I said. "Outside the Castle. Don't you remember, Malcolm?"

"Oh… *aja*, maybe." It was obvious he wasn't sure.

"I want to see if I can find the boat," decided Lyle. "Will you three stay here and keep an eye on the refugees? I want to go up onto the headland, to get a better view."

"Is there anything you particularly want us to look out for?" Verity wanted to know.

Lyle paused. "I just need to know whether anyone else is involved."

"Stay in the shadows," warned Malcolm unnecessarily, as Lyle crept out from the darkness of our sheltering rocks.

We were able to watch him, the black shape of him, as Lyle carefully manoeuvred himself around the cove. The three people who were obviously the organisers seemed to have gone by then – we had heard their ponies thudding along the track towards the town, but it was just as important that the refugees and the oarsmen didn't know that they had been watched. Over on the jetty the unloading continued, the noise greater now that 'the bosses' had gone.

For a while we all sat together at the back of the cave. It was a tight squeeze, but comfortable. The sand was dry and soft underneath us, although the rocks behind us jutted out uncomfortably if you leant against the wrong parts. We could hear the refugees talking, and at one point we heard footsteps crunching towards us on the sandy shingle, but then we heard Frankie's voice: "You girls! Come back here! Haven't you learnt anything from what happened to Lavender?"

I heard a sulky response. It wasn't Marigold's voice so I guessed it might have been the bairn called Shirley. "That were a big wave what got her! There ain't no big waves tonight!"

"They're getting bigger. Come back!" demanded Frankie's voice, and we heard the steps retreat again.

"Well, that proves one thing," murmured Malcolm. "That wee bairn on your beach was Marigold's sister. No wonder no regular islanders recognised her."

★ ★ ★

The unloading seemed to take longer than I might have expected, or perhaps, with the *harkrav* gone, any sense of urgency had passed too. We couldn't hear everything that was said on the jetty – the wind had become stronger and was snatching words away into the gusting air – but at one point we all clearly heard, "Hey! Pass us the bottle, mate! Don't 'og it all yourself!"

"I wonder who provides the drink?" asked Malcolm.

"Someone who wants to keep the refugees just content enough not to rebel?" suggested Verity.

It made me feel sick.

Finally, we could tell that there was movement. An islander's voice came clearly on the wind: "We ought to be heading back. The weather's turning and old Jacob won't want to hang around so close to the shore."

I couldn't hear the answer, the wind and the waves had become noisier, but from the sounds the refugees made, we could tell that they had started climbing the cliff path back to St Matthew's Bay. Malcolm crept to the front of the cave and peered over the rocky outcrop.

"The boat's rowing out again," he told us. "It's hard work for them – they're rowing against the tide and the sea's rougher than it was. Give them ten minutes to round the point and it'll be safe to go." Then he added, "The tide's quite high now, we'll have to paddle to get out of here."

"Is there any more of that tea?" Verity wanted to know.

"It'll be cold," Malcolm pointed out, and he was right, but we shared it anyhow.

I was weary by then. It must have been late in the evening, and the adventure seemed to be over for the night. I was thinking longingly of my bed, even if it was just a mat and a sleeping bag in the ruins of an old bothy.

Then, just as I stood to take off my boots ready to paddle out of the cave, and as Malcolm shrugged his backpack over his shoulders, there was a sudden bright light. Almost simultaneously, and seemingly right overheard, came a huge crack of thunder, which echoed and rumbled round the cove.

183

We all jumped. "Definitely time to go home!" remarked Malcolm. But just at that moment a huge surge of water rushed into the cave, foaming round our feet, leaving only a foot or so of dry sand at the very back of our shelter.

"*Certainly* time to go!" I agreed, tucking my socks into an outside pocket of my backpack. "Come on!"

Even as I spoke, however, another wave rushed into the cave. At almost the same time, there was more lightning, and thunder rumbled around overhead.

We all three moved towards the cave entrance. The slope down to the beach seemed steeper than when we arrived. I was in front, and stumbled against something, a piece of rock perhaps, and lost my footing. The next minute another huge wave broke against the rocks where only moments ago we had been able to watch the activity on the jetty. I lost my footing completely and fell sideways into the churning water.

"Marie!" I heard Malcolm call. I could see the dark shape of him standing in the cave, and then another flash of lightning lit up his anxious face.

"I'm all right!" I called, staggering to my feet while the angry sea tugged at my heavy, wet clothing. Another wave rushed in, breaking around my knees, pulling me over into the surf again. I half crawled, half swam towards the beach, feeling the tug of the undercurrent pulling me back towards the breakers. Another wave seemed to break over me. For a moment, I was completely under the water. I gasped with the cold and the shock, and my lungs filled with salty, suffocating water.

"Lose your backpack!" I heard Malcolm shout as I surfaced again. "It's weighing you down! Lose it!"

I was being pummelled and pulled by the dark water, the sea was foaming white, rushing up the beach away from me, sucking me backwards into the bay. I staggered to my feet, fell again as another surge of water threw me forward, and at last managed to disentangle myself from the straps of my pack. I felt it bump against me, then there was another flash of lightning, another rumble and crash of thunder, and I was groping forward up the slope of the beach until, at last, I was lying, gasping on the pebbly sand, high on the beach, close to the cliffs.

I looked back towards the cave. The sky was pitch dark now; I couldn't see anything until the next flash of lightning lit up Malcolm, standing in the mouth of the cave with Verity right behind him, both up to their knees in the surging sea. I could see at once that escape for them was impossible.

Malcolm was shouting something, but I couldn't hear above the thunder in the sky and the thunder of the waves. Did he call, "Get help"? I thought maybe he did, but where would I find help in this remote place?

From Lyle, of course. I realised that he must be up on the headland, on the Storhaven side of the cove, trying to identify the smugglers' ship. Surely Lyle and I, between us, could rescue Verity and Malcolm from the cave before the tide rose much further?

I had lost my boots, I had lost everything except the soaking clothes I was wearing, but I would have to go as I was. I waved in the direction of my friends, and turned, heading for the steps out of the cove.

The storm was massive. The lightning flickered and streaked across the sky, the wind howled, the waves crashed against the rocks and the sea rushed right up to the foot of the cliffs. I was paddling still, there was no more dry land. At one point I trod on something really sharp and realised that I was walking across the stone hearth that we had noticed earlier, the place where we had found the wood store. It was all under water now. I looked back towards the cave, but I could see nothing, no sign of Verity or Malcolm.

I staggered on. I must have been frightened, but that isn't what I remember. As if it were a dream, as if I were outside myself, watching my progress, I remember staggering around the bay.

Surely, I thought, *it must be high tide by now!* But then another wave came rolling towards me, not breaking until it reached the cliff, and I was struggling to stay on my feet, looking for something on the cliff face to hold on to, grabbing some little plant that came away in my hand, and then watching the churning foam recede, and realising I had survived another onslaught.

There was another flash of lightning. It seemed to light up the whole bay and, to my amazement, there in front of me was the rope that marked the steps to the road. Another wave came pounding towards me, rearing up, ready to break over my head, but I grabbed the rope with both hands, took a deep breath, and let the sea do its worst. There were wild moments, dark forces knocking me this way and that against the rocks, but I held on, the sea retreated to prepare for another attack, and I dragged myself onto the bottom stone step and climbed two, maybe three of them, clinging to the rope all the while.

I paused, catching my breath. For a moment I just sat there. Right at my feet, the sea was seething and roaring, foaming and cresting and smashing against the cliffs. There was an almost continuous flickering of lightning and rumbling of thunder, seeming to come by then from inland, from the moorland north of Storhaven. I vaguely remember thinking that the storm was moving away, hoping that Malcolm and Verity would survive the violent sea. Then I had turned and was climbing the rocky steps, clutching the rope, dragging myself upwards until, at last, I came out onto the road.

★ ★ ★

I stood, gasping, on the broken tarmac. I was soaking, seawater was dripping from my jacket and my trousers were tight against my legs. I had lost everything – my phone had been in my backpack so I couldn't contact Lyle, or anyone else. In any case, who was there to contact? The only other people who knew where we were, were trapped in the cave below.

186

I realised that I had to find Lyle. He was going, he had said, to the headland, to see if he could identify the smugglers' ship. I stumbled along the track, looking for some sort of path out onto the clifftop, but the only time I could see anything was when the lightning lit up the sky in sudden, fierce brightness.

At first, I found nothing, no way that looked safe. That part of the island was strange to me then; I had no idea where there were treacherous, sudden slopes or loose rocks. I felt panic rising up inside me. "Lyle!" I shouted, helplessly, but my call was lost in the ferocious night air.

Then I saw something. It was only a sheep track, but considering that our sheep spend all the year around on the moors, very few of them get into difficulty. They must have some sort of instinct about where it's safe to go. Anyhow, what choice did I have? I started to follow the path, stopping when there was nothing to lighten my way, taking advantage of every flash and streak that lit up the path ahead. At one point, the track took me very close to the edge of the cliff. I could see down into the cove, and when the sky lit up, I could see that the whole bay was a heaving, foaming mass of white. Could Malcolm and Verity possibly survive this? Then the path took me away from the edge, and suddenly I was at the very point of the headland.

I have been back to that spot many times since, and every time I go there, I am amazed that no harm came to me that night. The headland – locals call it 'Lyle's Lookout' nowadays, although on old maps it is called 'Paske Ekstrom', which only means 'Eastern Extreme' – is the easternmost point of En-Somi. There was nothing to shield me from the wind between the island and Norway, and the wind that night was powerful, gusting and roaring around me. Far below, the waves were crashing against the rocks, sending up mountains of spray as high as the clifftop. I thought, perhaps, that I could see the lights of a ship far out to sea, but closer, on the headland, there was no sign of Lyle.

"Lyle!" I called again. "Lyle! Where are you?"

I don't suppose that if he had been there, he would have heard me, but there was no sign of him. He must have got the evidence he wanted, I reasoned, and left. Where would he go then? He would return to us, to the cave, I decided. I must have missed him; we must have crossed paths.

I turned my back to the sea, looking inland. Again, the sky lit up, and in that fraction of a second, I saw that there was another path, better trodden than the one I had taken, leading back towards the road. No wonder I had missed Lyle. More confidently now, I started to return to safer land.

Even so, it was not easy going. The path I was following by then was well defined; it would have been easy walking in daylight, but I had to wait for more lightning to show me where to go after every hundred or so steps.

The storm was moving inland, by then. I could see the lightning flickering and flashing over the moors. I paused for a moment, yet again, for light to brighten my way ahead, and as the lightning came, I saw something bright in the grass, right at my feet.

I bent to pick it up. It was a phone. It was Lyle's phone, the initials 'N.I.' showing that it was police issue.

I must have been more tired than I realised. For a moment I held the phone in my hand, and my mind was blank. What was Lyle's phone doing on the headland? Surely, he wouldn't be so careless as to drop it? He was *nasyoni*, trained to deal with emergencies! And he would need that phone, it had evidence on it!

Then I realised. Of course, it had evidence on it, incriminating photographs of the smugglers on the beach, of the refugees, too, and perhaps of the ship anchored out to sea, and recorded conversations. Lyle would drop his phone if he thought he was going to be caught with it, discovered by the wrong people.

I assumed it would be locked, but I pressed a key randomly, not sure what to expect. At once a messaging page came up,

188

with an unsent message to a number I didn't recognise. 'In the hands of organised crime,' it read, 'send immediate assistance'. I pressed 'send' and saw the message change colour. I hoped I had done the right thing.

So now what? Malcolm and Verity were still in the cave – if they were still alive. For a horrible moment, I pictured their bodies, tossed around in the seething ocean, face down, dead. Then I took a deep breath. Lyle could not help. I could not rescue my friends alone. I had to fetch help from somewhere.

I knew of only two places where I might go. If I turned towards Storhaven, I would come across one of those turnings to the right, to a *harkrav* home. They would have communications and maybe manpower. But the smugglers were *harkrav*. If I called at the wrong home, I might so easily end up captured too, like Lyle.

Or I could head the other way, to the old airport. Would the refugees help? I had a feeling they would.

I stumbled back to the road and started running north.

It was a hell of a journey. The road was rough and stony against my bare feet. My clothes were wet and heavy, my whole body was weighed down. It was as if I were struggling through mud, or in a nightmare where I was running and running but getting nowhere. The slope up, before the bend which finally allows a view of the derelict airport, seemed endless. Twice I fell. The first time I struggled to my feet and limped on. The second time it seemed utterly hopeless. How much time had elapsed since I had left the cave? How could anyone have survived the swirling cauldron of the cove? I could imagine now what had happened to that wee bairn, Lavender.

Then I remembered that I was wearing her cross. I reached inside my cold, wet clothes and touched it, still safe against my skin. It made me think of Verity, of her talk about praying. What did she say the Quakers did? Just hold things up to God, like a child holding up a picture to an adult? It was worth a try.

I shouted out loud, unaware of how crazy I would have looked if there had been anyone around.

"Lyle has been captured!" I yelled at the God who might, or might not, be there. "Verity and Malcolm are trapped in the cave! Help!"

Then I struggled to my feet again and ran over the crest of the slope and down towards the old airport.

★ ★ ★

Despite the storm, they had a fire going outside, in the same place as they had lit the Hogmanay bonfire. I could see the silhouettes of figures against the backdrop of the flames, and when another flash of lightning came, I could see that there were children as well as adults gathered round the makeshift brazier. I thought I could see Frankie, with a bottle in her hand. With one last effort, I staggered down the slope and collapsed on my knees by the fire.

"Marie!" Wee Marigold was the first at my side, but only by a fraction of a second. At once, I was surrounded by people, the bottle was pushed into my hands, a coat was thrown round my shoulders.

From outside the circle I heard, "What the hell?" It was the refugee called Si, the father of Marigold.

"We need your help!" I gasped. "Verity and Malcolm! They're in the cave! We need to save them!"

"'O's Verity?" asked someone.

"*Your* Malcolm?" exclaimed someone else.

"Which cave?" Frankie wanted to know.

The alcohol had reached my stomach. My head was clearing. "The cave in the next cove," I said. "The tide came in… I just managed to get out… they're stuck."

"Lavender's cave," whispered Marigold, who was still squatting beside me. "They is trapped in Lavender's cave." Suddenly, she jumped to her feet and started shouting. "We gotta save Malcolm!" she yelled, and when the adults just stared at her, she stamped her foot. "Now! Now! We gotta save Malcolm!"

"Don't be so bloody stupid!" It was Jarvis, scowling in the firelight, swaying slightly as if he were drunk. "And tell that kid to shut up!"

I saw Frankie turn her head sharply, and Si broke into the circle.

"Marigold's right!" he shouted. "Now! There's no time to lose! Come on! Find some rope! Charlie, get them poles. Let's go! Let's go!"

"But what…?"

"Why…?"

"'Ow…?"

"Questions later!" decided Frankie. "We'll 'ave to go by the road; the cliff path's not safe on a night like tonight!"

191

Then she looked down at me, still sitting on the ground by the fire. "You'd better stay 'ere with Rose and the children," she told me. "This ain't no place for kids! And you's exhausted."

"*Nei!*" I exclaimed, staggering to my feet. "I want to come!"

"And me!" declared Marigold, grabbing my hand.

"Well… Charlie, find 'er some shoes for God's sake! And some dry clothes! 'Urry up, everyone, ain't no time to waste!"

"You're all flippin' nuts!" exclaimed Jarvis. "Fink you can look after other people? You can't bloody look after yourselves!" He spat into the fire and grabbed the bottle that they had been passing around.

Charlie reappeared with a bundle of clothes. I hesitated for a moment. Was I supposed to change here, in front of everyone?

"I think they'll fit," remarked Charlie. "Better 'n nofing."

So I found myself stripping off to my underwear by the fire, and since nobody was taking any notice, it didn't seem like such a big issue. It was no different from changing on the beach to go swimming, after all. I was down to my bra and pants, and about to put on a tee shirt of indeterminate colour, when I suddenly became aware of Jarvis, staring at me. For a moment I thought he was looking at my near-naked body, but then it suddenly occurred to me that he was looking at the cross, Lavender's cross, on the chain round my neck. I quickly pulled the tee shirt on over my head to cover it. The man gave me a calculating look, as if he were assessing me, then gave a sort of shrug and, still holding the bottle of hootch, walked away into the darkness.

I finished putting on clothes that were at least dry, and watched Rose, with baby Thistle on one hip, scooping up the pile of discarded garments and taking them inside through the corrugated iron door. I put Lyle's phone into the pocket of the trousers I had been given, trying to ignore the fact that there was already something left in there from the last wearer – a piece of string, I thought, and a shell. Then we were off, back up the track again, to crest the hill and follow the road down towards the cove. My heart was pounding. What if we were too late? But it helped to find myself surrounded by people who shared my urgency, and wee Marigold was again clinging onto my hand, tugging me forward.

Up at the front of the motley crowd, Frankie, Si and Charlie were making plans. I heard odd words and phrases as I struggled back up the slope, my legs heavy as if they had weights on them, Marigold's hand tugging me forward: "… down from the ledge…", "only the swimmers…", "take them poles!" I had a brief, reassuring moment. It sounded as if Frankie and the others knew what they were doing, but then we were over the crest of the hill and I could see down into the cove, into the foaming, turbulent sea. How could Malcolm and Verity possibly have survived?

"Stay 'ere!" commanded Frankie, and it didn't occur to me for a moment to question her. Charlie and Si were tying a length of rope around their waists, and Si, who was at the front, had grabbed an old tent pole, and was climbing over the edge of the cliff. I realised he was going to abseil down to the cove, and that Charlie was going to follow.

"Do you know a spell?" asked Marigold urgently. "We needs a spell, to keep 'em safe."

"I don't think spells would work," I answered. "And anyhow, I don't know any…"

"But we gotta do somefink," insisted the bairn. "We gotta 'elp 'em!"

"Then perhaps we ought to pray?" I suggested.

Marigold sounded scornful in the dark. "Won't do no good," she answered. "I prayed for Lavender, but the waves took 'er away. She was sucked out to sea, and we won't never see 'er again."

"I'm sorry," I said, feeling helpless to comfort the bairn. Then I added, "But I'm going to pray. You can pray with me, if you want."

Of course, I couldn't see her expression, but she was quiet. I did that thing Verity had described again. I pictured Charlie and Si making their way down the cliff face. I pictured the cave, and Verity and Malcolm, perhaps up to their armpits in freezing water. I held those pictures up to God and, in my mind, I said, "Look!"

It would be great to say that I felt a strange warmth creeping over me, or that I had a sense of having been heard, but to be honest, no such thing happened. Instead, Marigold tugged at my hand again, and said, "Go on, then! Say them words. The prayer words!"

"Oh, sorry," I said, suddenly wanting to laugh. "I said them in my head."

"That's no good!" Marigold reprimanded me. "'Ow's 'e going to 'ear? You 'ave to say them out loud!" Then, to my surprise, she started to recite the Lord's prayer: "Our father, who art in 'eaven…"

I think she got a bit muddled in the middle. Surely the original words said 'bread' not 'spuds'? And there's nothing in the Bible about 'lead us not into Stor'aven", but she had the basic idea, and when she had finished, she sounded satisfied.

"See!" She said, "That's 'ow you does it. Now we 'ave to wait and see if it works!" Then she added sadly, "It don't always work. It didn't work for Lavender."

I felt a sudden, great affection for the child. What a strange and incomprehensible world she was growing up in!

Then there was a shout from the cliff edge. "They've reached the cave!" It was Frankie, calling back to us.

We jumped to our feet and rushed to the grassy edge, where Frankie and two of the other men were standing. It was pitch dark, and there was less lightning by then. The storm was all behind us, up on the moors, but the sea was still churning and heaving below us. Everything seemed to be white foam and spray. Then, at last, there was a flash of light and an echoing roll of thunder, and for a fraction of a second, I could see the mouth of the cave, and the two rocks that had formed the crevice, and

Verity and Malcolm slumped, precariously, on top of them, just out of the water, like two old coats washed up by the churning sea. Si was standing up to his waist in water, right in front of them, looking up.

"Where's Charlie?" I asked, of no one in particular.

"At the bottom of the cliff," answered Frankie, still peering down into the cove. "'E'll 'ave stuck that pole into the sand, to 'old on to. Keep him secure. We should 'ave done that when we lost Lavender, but we didn't know, not then."

I could feel wee Marigold shiver besides me. "She's been all eaten by fish," she said mournfully.

"I don't think so," I said. "I think she had a proper burial."

"Don't fill the kid's 'ead with nonsense!" rebuked Frankie. "We 'as to face the truth, we does! No 'appy endings for the likes of us!"

I wanted to tell them what I knew, but that was not the time or the place. Anyhow, it was right at that moment that the man next to Frankie exclaimed, "They got one of 'em!"

Frankie seemed to forget her anger at me instantly. Suddenly she was all calmness and common sense. "Pull 'em up as soon as they're ready," she commanded. "'Ave them blankets ready." Then, to me, "Keep that kid away from the action. She don't need to see no more dead bodies!"

I pulled Marigold back onto the road. She was shivering, so I put my arms around her, holding her close against me. A frightened bairn is everyone's bairn. So, there we stood in the dark, and waited, and half heard the urgent instructions that Frankie was calling down to the men in the cove.

At last, the first body was hauled to the top of the cliff. "It's the vicar!" exclaimed Frankie.

"Is she alive?" I called out. "Is Malcolm there? Did they make it?" I felt that I couldn't bear it if all they had managed to rescue were two lifeless bodies.

"Yeah… oh, no! 'Old on!" Frankie called over her shoulder. Then, "It's all right, Marie! They've got your bloke."

195

Frankie's warning was still in my ears. Marigold didn't need to see any more dead bodies. I desperately didn't want to see any, either. I held the bairn tight against me and waited.

And then, there he was. Malcolm. Holding onto the rope, climbing up over the rim of the cliff, allowing himself to be pulled away from the edge, standing on his own two feet, gasping. "Thank you! Thank you!" he said, over and over again.

I felt Marigold wriggle out of my arms. "'E's safe!" she exclaimed. "It's your Malcolm! 'E's safe." Then she gave me a little push. "Go on, then!" she commanded. "You 'ave to go and kiss 'im! That's what people do!"

So, following the bairn's advice, I did just that.

B ack at the old airport, Rose had built up the fire, and had been busy organising some sort of strange concoction of hot soup. Verity, Malcolm, Si and Charlie all changed, as I had, into ragged but dry clothes, in front of the fire, while everyone stood around, some talking excitedly about the events of the night, others looking serious and withdrawn. I noticed how the children stayed close to their parents, with the exception of Marigold, who went between Malcolm and me, worrying that we were warm and dry, checking that we had enough soup.

Frankie came over to where we were sitting, perched on broken plastic seating ripped from the departure area. "We'll 'ave no rest tonight," she told us. "The kids'll all be thinking about our Lavender. I suppose you knows about 'er by now, does you?"

"More or less," I agreed. "She was washed out to sea one night?"

"Yeah… Not the first of our lot to die, but the youngest… and the most recent. Stuck in that cave, just like you." She looked away, towards the rocks that shielded the airport from the sea. "So, what was you doing there?" she finally asked. "Trying to catch us out?"

"*Nei!*" I said. "*Nei*, that wasn't it!"

"We were trying to find out what was going on," explained Malcolm. "We had guessed about the smuggling. We wanted to know who's behind it."

"So that you could do what?" asked Frankie, her tone a mixture of scorn and anger. "Get us thrown off this island? Put into some camp somewhere? 'Ave our kids taken away from us?"

"*Nei!*" I exclaimed. "*Nei*, none of those things! We wanted to free you. Don't you know you're being used? You're like prisoners here already. The *harkrav*, I mean the bosses, they're using you like slaves."

197

Frankie was quiet for a moment. All around us, people were talking. The storm had died down a bit, or moved further west, but the flames of the fire were still dancing wildly in the wind. Rose was hovering around Verity, treating her almost as if she were one of the children, wrapping a blanket round her shoulders, hugging her.

"Any'ow," Frankie wanted to know, "what can you do, now you knows?"

"Go to the *nasyonii*," I suggested. "The police. Get the smuggling stopped. Free you."

Frankie laughed. It was a bitter, hard laugh, and it told us how little we knew. "The pigs is in on it!" she said. "Much good that would do!"

"What do you mean?" Malcolm wanted to know. "We had a friend with us – from our side of the island. He's *nasyoni*, police, and he definitely isn't in on it. He was trying to collect evidence."

"Oh yeah?" Frankie was unimpressed. "But 'e conveniently vanished when things got tough, didn't 'e? Probably sitting by the fire in some boss's 'ouse by now, or in a pub, if you 'ave 'em!"

I felt rather than saw Malcolm turn to me. "Didn't you find Lyle?" he asked. "Or didn't you try? Did you come straight here, for help?"

Was it safe to tell Malcolm, in front of Frankie? But what did we have to hide? They knew so much of our side of the story already. I took Lyle's phone out of my pocket. "I looked for him," I explained, "but I couldn't find him. I found this." I tapped the phone to wake up the screen, and passed it to Malcolm, with the message glowing green in the night: 'In the hands of organised crime, send immediate assistance'.

"He sent the message," Malcolm said. "If the *nasyonii* are in on it, as Frankie says, he's played right into their hands."

I felt sick. "It was me," I groaned. "I pressed 'send' when I found the phone! What have I done?"

Frankie leant across me to take the phone from Malcolm. I saw that he passed it across willingly. As far as he was concerned, we were all on the same side. Of course, he was right.

She read the message silently, then gave the phone back to me. "And you're sure this bloke, this policeman, 'e ain't part of the scheme?"

"Certain," I answered.

"So," Frankie summed up the situation, "they've caught 'im, the bosses 'ave. They know 'e knows what they's up to. It don't matter that 'e messaged 'is boss, because they've got 'im any'ow. But 'e's in big trouble."

"Where would they take him?" Malcolm wondered. "If they didn't get rid of him at once, if they are holding him captive, where do you think that would be?"

"I knows," said Si, who must have been standing behind us for a while. "I went there once, to 'and over some work what we'd done. I could take you, but it's a long way. 'Alf way to Stor'aven."

"I fink," announced Frankie, standing, "that our night's work ain't done. Charlie! Eric! Rose! We needs to be making plans. Come over 'ere!"

★ ★ ★

"It were that time we 'ad to assemble them micro-screws. Remember?" Si told everyone. "A rushed job. That Jean were going to collect 'em from us, but the day before, she came over and said she couldn't do it. She told me where to take the stuff." He looked sad in the firelight. "I took Lavender. She were so excited. The big 'ouse and everyfing. And the 'orses."

I wanted to know where the refugees had assembled the electronics, but of course that wasn't relevant. Instead, I asked, "So how did you get there?"

"Along the road to Stor'aven," he explained. "Then up this long, steep track onto the moors. It took us ages – all day to get there and back on foot. I 'ad to carry Lavender. She was just a little kid. Do you remember, Rose?"

Rose just gave a sort of grunt.

"If we set out now," said Frankie, "it'll be broad daylight by the time we gets there, even in this godforsaken dark winter!"

Almost for the first time since being rescued, Verity spoke. Her voice was quiet, subdued, but so useful. "Your ponies, Malcolm!" she reminded us. "At the bothy!"

I have confused memories of the next part of the night. I was exhausted and, now that I needed to walk again, I realised how cut and bruised my feet were. Nobody had been able to find any shoes to fit me, and I had been barefoot since leaving the cove, so Malcolm tied strips of cloth round my feet with surprising skill. There was talk of taking Verity back to our ruined cottage, but as Rose pointed out, it would be freezing cold. She was in a bad way from being exposed to icy water for so long, and, reluctantly, she agreed to stay at the airport. The general opinion seemed to be that as many able-bodied people as possible should come with Si, Frankie, Malcolm and me, and in the end, there were eight adults plus Marigold. As well as Charlie and Eric, the other two were the young couple, Quincy and Mo. I was pleased to see them.

I remember being impressed with Malcolm. I only found out later how he and Verity had survived their bitter exposure to the waves, clambering up those almost-sheet outcrops of rock and singing children's songs with actions to keep their blood circulating. It was Malcolm, not me, who remembered the shortest way back to the bothy, and it was Malcolm who asked careful questions of Si, trying to work out where the *harkrav* house had been, where he and Lavender had delivered the work of the refugees, well over a year earlier.

Once at the ruined bothy, it became clear how wise Rose had been about keeping Verity at the airport. Despite our attempts to make the place weatherproof, the floor was wet and the whole place was bitterly cold. The ponies were pleased to see us, though, and Marigold, especially, was pleased to see them. Malcolm harnessed up the cart, and Malcolm, Si and Frankie sat at the front, on the bench seat. The rest of us huddled into the cart, our closeness doing something to keep us warm.

All this time the storm had been moving west. We could still see the lightning in the sky, and the thunder was rumbling over the moors. Malcolm took the cart back down to the main track, and we headed towards the town. Wedged between Charlie and me, Marigold went to sleep. The weight of her was gentle on my legs.

"She's taken to you," commented Charlie. "The kids're usually shy of strangers. Scared."

"That's not really surprising," I commented. "From what I hear, they haven't had particularly positive experiences of other people!"

"No."

There was a friendly silence, then, "So you worked for the bosses?" I asked, stating the obvious.

"Yeah – some specialist electrical stuff. To do with them long-distance drones. The one's what've been banned by the Europeans. We just assembles stuff. We never sees no finished articles."

"They use 'em as some sort of weapon," Mo butted in.

"You don't know that!" argued Charlie. Then, in a softer tone, he added, "Mind you, whatever they're for, them bosses is up to no good. Or why smuggle the components in? And why con us into doing their graft?"

"Mo's right," Quincy insisted. "It's for weapons. I over'eard them talking. They sell 'em to foreign countries. That's why me and Mo won't 'elp no more."

"So where do you work?" I wanted to know. I was no expert in these things, then as now, but I was pretty sure you needed a clean and tidy place to put together micro-electronic parts.

Frankie turned round. She had obviously heard our conversation. "There's a workshop," she said. "Beyond the runway. Over the ridge where that big 'eap of stones is, down from our spud field. We all works there, even the kids. Not the tinies, of course. Rose keeps them."

The wind had dropped a bit by then, and it seemed to me that the clip-clopping of the ponies and the scrunching of our wheels on the track was making quite a noise. Each time we came to a turning right, onto the moors, Malcolm stopped the cart and Si jumped off, to explore the track.

At last, he returned and said to Malcolm, "Yeah, this is it!"

I had started to feel much more awake. Marigold was still sleeping deeply, but Mo and Quincy had started talking to each other in low voices and I heard a subdued chuckle from Malcolm in response to something Frankie had said. *'We're beginning to wake up,"* I thought. *"It must be morning.'*

Mo rooted around in a bag she had brought. "Breakfast!" she announced, tearing off bits of bread and passing them to each of us. "And this'll keep the cold out!" A bottle followed the bread, this time passed from person to person.

But when the hootch reached Frankie, she spluttered, and turned round, looking at us angrily. "'O brought this!" she demanded. Then she reached across Si and poured the contents out onto the track. "We need to 'ave clear 'eads!" she said.

When she was looking forward again, Charlie leant over and touched Mo's hand. "It was a kind thought!" he said softly, and winked.

★ ★ ★

It was, I suppose, about eight in the morning. The track we were following was in good condition, obviously cared for by somebody with the resources to repair the endless damage done by our merciless weather. We were climbing steeply up onto the moors, but the road twisted and turned, following the lines of the hills, so that it was not too much work for the ponies. Here and there we saw stone benches on flatter ground beside the track – viewing points, I guessed, for walkers, although this was private land. When the road took us north, we could look to our right, towards the sea, where already, nearly two hours before sunrise, the sky looked lighter.

Frankie's action in pouring away the hootch had sobered us all, in more than one sense. We started to discuss what we were hoping to do.

"Them bosses is ruthless," Frankie told us. "Lavender's death was an accident, but Tracey's weren't. She told that Jean that she were going to report the bosses. Next thing, she's lying on our beach with 'er 'ead caved in."

"Yeah," Si agreed. "That time me and Lavender went to the bosses' 'ouse, 'e told us that we was disposable. More where we came from. 'E was warning us not to tell anyone where 'e lived."

"You're taking a risk," suggested Malcolm, "just to help us rescue our friend."

"Yeah, well…" Charlie sounded resigned.

"We been wanting to do somefink for a bit now," put in Quincy. "We bin living like animals for ages. Time we got ourselves free."

"Don't count no chickens!" warned Frankie. "Even if today's activities turn out well – and we don't know they will – we still don't know what'll 'appen to us. It weren't that much better before we came 'ere, remember."

At that moment, Malcolm turned and looked at me. Neither of us said anything, but I was sure that we were thinking the same thing. These refugees would not be sent away from the island, not if we had anything to do with it.

T he glow on the eastern horizon was bright, with red and yellow streaks across the sky, by the time Malcolm halted the cart at Si's suggestion.

"I think we're almost there," he warned us. "We don't want to be seen."

We all looked around us. Already it was light enough to see the lie of the land. We were at the foot of a steep rise. It looked as if a stone wall had been built to make the slope secure, to prevent the thin soil from being eroded. Along the foot of the wall was a flat area extending south, with another of those stone benches at the end.

"A good place to come and watch the sunrise!" commented Charlie.

"A good place to hide the ponies!" was Malcolm's reaction.

I gently woke Marigold, who looked confused, then we all climbed down, feeling stiff and cold, and stretched our legs. Malcolm drove the cart round as far as the bench and settled the ponies under their blankets. Then we all gathered beside the track again.

"So now what?" Quincy wanted to know.

Malcolm suggested, "Perhaps a couple of us should go up to the house? Is it far, do you think, Si? We need to find out whether Lyle is here, before we can decide what to do next."

"Not much good any of us going," pointed out Frankie. "This mate of yours don't know us."

"You're right," agreed Malcolm. "I could go on my own?"

"Oh no!" I was not having that. "I'm coming with you!"

Frankie looked at my feet, still bound with rags. "Is you up to it?" she wanted to know.

"*Aja,*" I insisted. "Of course I am!"

★ ★ ★

To begin with, we followed the track. It was easy walking, and already it was quite light. When I first saw my shadow, I turned and looked behind me. "Oh, Malcolm," I whispered.

He turned too. The tip of the golden ball of the sun was just emerging from below the black horizon of the sea. It was stunningly beautiful. Of course, we never see a proper sunrise on the west of the island, and the sight took my breath away.

"*Morning has broken, like a new morning,*" murmured Malcolm, remembering a song the children sing at school on the island, a song Duncan had taught me. "Let's hope it brings a blessing."

"Do you believe in blessings?" I asked. His remark had surprised me.

He reached out and took my hand. "I do," he said. "I really do."

The house, when it appeared, was like a sort of imitation bothy. The pitch of the roof, the stone walls, the height of the door, were all exactly like any other cottage on the moors, but the house was long, like two bothies attached, and there was a separate stone building to one side, large enough to stable several ponies and to provide storage for a cart or two, and who knew what else. Behind the house, and further up the hill, their wind turbine was turning gently in the breeze that followed the storm. It was a peaceful scene.

We stood still in the shadow of some rocks. There were no signs of life.

We were high on the moors. From our position we couldn't see the coves or inlets far below, but as the world woke up, we saw sheep spread out over the grasslands, and black-backed gulls wheeling and diving over the sea.

"How beautiful," I breathed.

Malcolm squeezed my hand. "This is how the rich live," he said. "But I'd rather have my bothy – or yours."

We stood a little longer. The sun had topped the horizon now and it was hard to look directly at it.

"We'd better scout around," I suggested, "before the household wakes up."

Once we left the shelter of the rocks where we had been standing, there was no more cover. The four windows looking east had shutters, but they were open, and it was impossible to see in, to know whether anyone was watching us. Rather than cutting across in front of the house to the outbuilding, we crept further up the hill to the north of the bothy, and ducked low below the small western windows on the uphill side. The area had been paved with stone, like the uphill side of my bothy, but where I had my chicken house, the owners of the cottage had built a small timber hut. "A sauna!" said Malcolm. "Very nice!"

There were no windows on the western side of the long, low outbuilding, and the ground under our feet was rough. My right foot was painful, I was suffering from a hectic night without shoes, but I didn't want Malcolm to know, so I gritted my teeth and led the way.

The outhouse had been built right into the southern hillside. For a moment it looked as if we couldn't get round the building that way, but then Malcolm started to scramble up the slope. He held out his hand to pull me up, and we slithered down a rocky face until we were at the front of the building again.

There were three stable doors, all closed, nearest to the house. Closer to us, there was a small window, its shutters closed, and two heavy-looking wooden doors.

We walked to the first door. It was locked with a metal padlock fixed to the old-fashioned catch; there was no way we could get in. We tried the second door – also firmly closed.

"Try the shutters," I suggested.

We walked back to the only window. The shutters were on the outside of the building, and it was simple to open them. I stood on tiptoes to peer in.

"What can you see?" whispered Malcolm.

"Nothing… wait a minute. Yes, I think there's someone in there. It could be Lyle – I'm not sure."

Malcolm edged me to one side and peered in. "It's hard to tell," he agreed. "It's so dark in there. It could just be a bundle of rags." Then he did the obvious thing and tapped gently on the dirty glass of the window.

It seemed as if nothing might happen. We stood in the stillness of the morning and there seemed to be no movement anywhere, except sheep lazily grazing and gulls soaring on the Arctic thermals. Then, "Yes! It's a person!" exclaimed Malcolm. "It's Lyle!"

He stood aside for me to peer in. A ray of sun suddenly streamed in, and I could see him, our friend, slumped on the floor in the far corner. He raised one hand, very slowly, and gave a sort of wave, then dropped his head.

"He's in a bad way," I said, making way for Malcolm again.

But just then we heard a new sound, the noise of a door opening, the manicured voice of a member of the *harkrav*.

"It's a beautiful morning," commented a man.

"That's often the way," agreed the equally sophisticated voice of a woman, "after a storm like last night's."

"Will you make breakfast?" asked the first voice. "I'll wake the others."

"What about him?" asked the woman.

"Let's decide about that after we've eaten," suggested the man. "He won't come to any mischief where he is."

"Shall I give him something to eat?" wondered the woman.

"There's no point," answered the man. Then we heard the door close.

"We need to get help!" I whispered. "Let's go for the others."

"One of us ought to stay here," Malcolm answered. "They might move him or something."

I didn't like to think what the 'something' might be. "I'll

stay," I volunteered. "You'll be quicker getting help." I looked down at my rag-covered feet.

"*Aja*," whispered Malcolm and, at once, he was on the move, not trying to find the way we had come, just slithering down the grassy slope and out of sight.

I looked for a place to hide. Closer to the main dwelling there was a low wall, creating a sort of veranda where, I supposed, in the summer people might meet and drink their coffee, or their cocktails. The ground sloped away steeply on the other side of the wall, but there were places where I could crouch and stay out of sight, but within hearing distance.

For a long time, nothing seemed to happen. The breeze, tugging at my borrowed clothes and my dishevelled hair, was cold, and my feet were hurting. I was so still that a huge, black-backed gull glided to land on the wall, just a few feet from me. He looked at me with his head sideways, a malicious glint in his red-rimmed eye. I remembered seeing gulls pecking at dead creatures on the shore, and diving down towards newly born lambs, and I feared for my eyes, but after studying me for a moment or two, the bird gave a squawk, and flew away. From a distance came the sound of a cock crowing, and for a moment I wondered how my chickens were getting on without me. I thought I heard a low groan coming from the outhouse, but I didn't dare climb back up onto the paved area to peer in through the grimy window. And anyhow, what could I do to help? I stayed hidden and waited.

I have no idea how long I waited there. The clothes that the refugees had lent me were not as weatherproof as my own winter outfit, and I started to shiver. Over to the east I could see a roll of grey-black cloud approaching, blotting out the promise of the blue sky. I wondered where the others had got to. Surely the *harkrav* must have finished their breakfast by now? Would they then turn to decision-making, concerning Lyle? We had no time to lose!

Then, at last, and to my great surprise, I heard a hissing sound a little further down the steep slope, just out of sight.

"Marie, are you there?" It was Frankie. "'As anything 'appened?"

"*Nei*," I whispered back. "They're all in the main house, the bosses. Having breakfast. Where are the others?"

"Malcolm's taking 'em round the back," she murmured. I still couldn't see her. "They's looking for something to help 'em break down the door. 'E says your mate's in there."

"*Aja*," I agreed. "But he's in a bit of a state. They must've done something to him."

"Yeah," hissed Frankie. "They would. Beat 'im up, I s'ppose."

At last, I heard them. Not their voices, but a slithering, slipping sound, and one by one the rest of our group crept along to hide with me, behind the wall: Malcolm, Charlie, Si, Eric, Quincy and Mo. And gripping Mo's hand, looking frightened, was little Marigold.

"We couldn't leave 'er alone," whispered Mo to me.

"We shouldn't never 'ave brought 'er!" sulked Si, but then he grinned at his daughter, and I saw how proud he was of her.

"So, what now?" I wanted to know.

"We couldn't find nofing to 'elp us break in," Frankie explained, "so we fought the best fing might be a rock."

"To break the lock," added Malcolm.

"Won't it make a lot of noise?" I worried. "They're all awake now, and it's a still morning."

We were all quiet, considering the problem.

"We need to get them away from here," Malcolm suggested.

"But 'ow?" Charlie sounded doubtful.

"I can do it!" It was Marigold, suddenly sounding very alert. "I's small, they won't suspect me! Let me 'ave a go!"

"No!" It was Si, protective of his daughter. "You know what they did to Tracey! They wouldn't 'esitate…"

"But Marigold's right," Frankie interjected. "And we's here to protect 'er. We won't let nofing bad 'appen to 'er."

"Please! Let me!" Marigold was appealing to her father. Then, taking matters into her own hands, she started to climb the low wall that marked the edge of the patio.

"Marigold…" Si sounded desperate, but Frankie stopped him.

"Shh!" she whispered. "You've got a brave one there!"

★ ★ ★

I desperately wanted to peer over the wall, to see what Marigold did, but the risk of being seen from the house was too great. We all crouched there and listened.

Marigold knocked on the door, loudly, urgently.

"What the hell?" The first man we had heard seemed to have answered the knock.

"Who is it?" called a voice from inside the house, the same woman I had heard earlier. "Duncan, who's there?"

'*Ah,*' I thought. Marigold had told me, back in the old airport when I was just getting to know her, that Duncan was a boss's name. Now I knew how she had come to that conclusion.

"It one of those kids!" called back Duncan. "From the pit!"

Immediately, we heard another voice. I recognised the slightly pompous sound of Dominic Fox-Drummin, whom I had first heard at the *domstol*, the court or gathering of the elders of the kirk, and who Verity had recognised down at the old airport, with Jean, doing some transaction with the refugees. "What the hell is she doing here?" he asked, sounding more English than Scottish. "How do they know where you live?"

Duncan answered. "Oh, one of them came here once, a man and a kid. What do you want, you little brat?" he added.

"Come quick! Come quick!" Marigold cried. "Them police 'ave come. They came on a boat! Quick! Quick!"

I was impressed by the child's acting.

"What police?" I could hear something other than irritation in Dominic Fox-Drummin's voice. Concern? Even fear?

210

Marigold was doing well. "The filf! Police!" she insisted. "They came on a boat! They's looking for the workshop!"

"Hell and damnation!" It was the voice of the man Duncan. "Sounds like mainlanders. How the hell could they have found out?"

The woman joined in. "Where are they?" she shouted, and I heard Marigold's voice.

"You're 'urting me!" she complained. "Don't 'urt me. I come and warned you, didn't I?"

"She's right." It was Duncan again. "Where did they land?" he asked.

"I don't know the names of places," complained Marigold, sounding convincingly sulky. "That beach where them thistles grow."

"Oh, for heaven's sake!" The woman was obviously not blessed with great patience.

"Can you show us?" Duncan asked. "Is it far from here?"

"Not that far!" answered Marigold. "I'll show you. Come on! Quick!"

"I'll follow 'er," whispered Si, obviously desperate to protect his little girl, and at once he turned to slither down the lichen-covered rocks to a place where he could see the track.

"She's a clever bairn!" Malcolm commented to nobody in particular. Then, as soon as the bustle of the departing *harkrav* had become more distant, "Come on! Let's get Lyle!"

211

A rock was not a very convenient or efficient tool for breaking into Lyle's prison. Malcolm tried first to break the padlock, but it was difficult to get a good angle on it, and it was not long before he had thumped his hand, dropped the rock and started hopping around, massaging his fingers. Charlie had a go too, but with no more success.

"What about smashing down the door?" suggested Frankie.

"Worth a try," agreed Malcolm, and he, Charlie and Quincy lined up and barged into the door, shoulders first.

It didn't even shake.

"Now what?" Mo was looking worried.

I suddenly had an idea. "Try the house!" I suggested. "They must have keys!"

"*Aja!*" Malcolm sounded excited.

We all raced to the doorway. Sure enough, in their rush to leave, the *harkrav* hadn't locked it. Well, why would they, living up on the moors?

Verity had told us that, when you went inside their houses, the homes of the *harkrav* didn't look like En-Somi buildings, and she was right. Although the house was built of stone, the walls inside had been lined with something that made them flat and smooth, and they were all painted white. Along the opposite wall, as we burst in, were rows of shelves with books and ornaments arranged in a manner which, I suppose, was considered tasteful. There were deep red rugs on the polished slate floors, and far more furniture than you will ever see in one of our bothies.

"My God!" It was Frankie, standing behind me. "So, while we bin slaving away down there, they've bin living like this?"

"We need to find those keys!" It was Malcolm, standing in the middle of the room. "Charlie and Eric, try those rooms!" He pointed to a door on the left. "Mo and Quincy, try in there. Marie and I'll look in here. Grab any keys you see. Frankie, will you keep watch?" Then he called after them, "And don't steal anything!"

I could hear Charlie and Eric talking as they searched the rooms Malcolm had allocated to them. Malcolm and I started systematically looking in every cupboard and drawer, even checking inside food containers. We found some beautiful things: a coloured glass paperweight with a Scottish thistle encased in the glass, a leather-bound address book, a tracker watch that seemed to be made of pure gold.

Mo and Quincy reappeared. "Ain't no keys in there," Mo said. "Just clothes and shoes and books. And a television for each bedroom!"

Charlie and Eric returned too. "No luck," agreed Charlie. "Just posh people's stuff!"

We had finished checking the main room, and had found nothing.

Frankie peered in, from the front of the house where she had been standing. "Found 'em yet?" she wanted to know.

"*Nei!*"

"No!"

"No luck."

We all looked glum. "Perhaps they took 'em with 'em?" suggested Mo.

"So we'll have to prise the door open," was Malcolm's response. "Has anyone spotted anything we could use to do that?"

We all stood and looked at each other. The house was full of comfortable, luxurious items, and what we wanted was something like a metal bar.

"We need to look outside," suggested Frankie, and left the building. The others followed. I was the last to go. '*Might as well close the door,*' I thought. '*No point in advertising that we've been in here!*'

Then, suddenly, a picture came into my head. It was of Granny's house. We came and went by the kitchen door, but there was a front door, never used. And besides the front door there had been a row of small hooks – and on the hooks there had been keys. All the time we had been searching the room, the door had been open. I closed it, and sure enough, there they were: two bunches of keys.

I grabbed both and ran out into the fresh air. "I've found them!" I called. "They were on hooks behind the door all the while!"

At once the others all gathered round me. "Brilliant! Well done!" It was Malcolm, smiling warmly at me. "Come on, everyone!"

We clustered round the padlocked door while Malcolm tried one key after another. At last, he found the right one, and the heavy door swung open.

Lyle was lying in a crumpled heap in the far corner of the shed. Malcolm went over to him in two big strides and squatted beside him. "Lyle! Lyle! It's us – it's me, Malcolm. Come on, Lyle – can you move? Can you stand up?"

Lyle looked at Malcolm through one swollen, puffy eye. The other didn't seem to open at all. He groaned.

"Charlie!" Malcolm was taking control. "Come here! We need to get him out of this hole. Gently does it, now. That's right! Charlie, put your arm around his back. That's right! Now lift! Easy! Take it easy!"

Lyle was groaning, hanging limply between the other two men as they manoeuvred themselves and their burden out into the daylight. He was in a terrible state, obviously badly beaten up and barely conscious.

"Lock the door again!" suggested Mo. "Let's put them keys back where we found 'em! Leave 'em wondering!"

Quincy and Frankie chuckled, but their mirth came to an abrupt halt.

"No need for that!" said the sneering voice of Dominic Fox-Drummin. "I'll have those keys now, thank you!"

We all whirled around. Standing at the far end of the patio were the *harkrav* trio looking supremely satisfied, and Marigold, looking tearful. Behind them, his face gloating, stood the refugee called Jarvis.

"Perhaps you will be so good as to carry your misguided friend back into the barn," said the man called Duncan. "He's not too well, and we don't want to leave him out in the cold! And then, I think…" he was looking at the other two 'bosses', "we need to sort out this situation. Wouldn't you agree?"

The woman and Fox-Drummin were smirking. Lyle groaned again. Over to the east, more dark clouds were rolling in. The rest of us were silent.

"Perhaps they should all sit down?" suggested Duncan. Then, when Lyle groaned again, he added, "Oh! For God's sake take him back into the shed! Now, on the wall, all of you! Hands in front of you, where I can see them!"

There didn't seem to be anything else to do but obey. Malcolm and Charlie returned Lyle to the place where we had found him. A cold wind was blowing from the east. I thought that the *harkrav* were right – Lyle was better off in the shed. The rest of us sat in a line on the wall at the edge of the patio.

"Oh, stop snivelling!" exclaimed the woman, and slapped Marigold's head. Malcolm came back from the shed and squeezed in between Eric and me. The feel of his bulk alongside me was comforting.

"She has a right to cry," remarked Fox-Drummin. "Give the brat credit for that. After all, if these fools hadn't meddled in our business, she'd be back at the pit now, playing with her damn-fool friends. Whereas now…"

"We ain't done nothing wrong!" Frankie interrupted. "We come 'ere to rescue some bloke what you beat up! We never beat 'im up. That was all your doing!"

"Ah," drawled Fox-Drummin, "but there you're wrong, you see – that's what happens if you only know half the story! Took you in, did they, these peasants? Told you a pack of lies? I suppose you think they're trying to help you?"

"They is!" Marigold was a brave wee bairn, but all her remark got her was another blow from the woman.

"Oh no!" smirked Fox-Drummin. "No, you couldn't be more wrong there! These two…" and he pointed to Malcolm and me, "they're from the other side of the island. Very old-fashioned, they are, over there. They have no love of strangers. I'll tell you what they want. They want to get you off the island. That's what this is all about. Help you? Not a bit of it! Help you to be gone, more like!"

Jarvis chipped in at that point. "Yeah!" he agreed. "And that geezer in the shed, 'e's the filf! 'E's only 'ere to arrest the lot of us!"

"Not all the *nasyonii* are corrupt!" Malcolm said, looking along the row of refugees to our left. "Lyle's as honest as they come. Just because the sergeant in Storhaven's hand in glove with criminals, it doesn't mean everyone is! And the last thing I want is to have you thrown off the island!"

"Oh, yeah!" Jarvis had stepped forward, hate glaring out of his eyes. "Is that the case? So why don't you tell us what 'appened to Lavender?"

"What do you mean?" It was Frankie speaking now. "Lavender was washed out to sea when we was unloading supplies! You know that!"

The other refugees nodded. Marigold said, "I saw 'er go! I saw 'er roll over and over in the waves and under the water. It weren't nofing to do with Marie and Malcolm! We never even knew 'em then!"

"That's as maybe," sneered Jarvis. "But they did 'ave somefing to do with it! Else why's that woman got Lavender's cross round 'er neck?"

"Don't be daft!" Frankie sounded scornful.

The *harkrav* were standing there, watching us all, saying nothing.

"Go on then," Jarvis came towards me. He grabbed me by the shabby coat I had borrowed and hauled me to my feet. "Show 'em that cross!" He ripped the garment from my shoulders and tore away the tee shirt. Then he whirled me around to face the other refugees. "So, tell me!" he demanded. "Is that Lavender's cross, or ain't it?"

Charlie frowned. "It's similar," he agreed.

"Could be," agreed Eric, looking worried.

"Must be 'undreds of crosses like that!" tried Frankie. "This don't prove nofing!"

Jarvis shook me violently. "So, tell 'em!" he demanded. "Tell 'em where you got it! Buy it, did you? Or did 'e give it to you?"

"I found it," I said.

"Found it, you say?" Jarvis shook me again. "Took it off some corpse, more like! Stole it from a dead child!"

He threw me down, so that I half fell onto Malcolm's lap, and whirled round to face Marigold, who was still standing with the *harkrav*, eyes round with fear.

"So, this is your friend, is it? This woman what stole from the body of your little sister? This is who you was working for when you tried to lure the bosses away?"

"Let me see that cross!" Marigold's voice was scared, confused.

The woman pushed her towards us. Marigold staggered a little with the force of the thrust, then found her balance again. She stood in front of me. "Can I see?" she asked in a small voice.

I was holding the torn coat together at the neck. I let go, so that Marigold could look at the cross. Gingerly, she held her hand out and cupped the little piece of jewellery.

"Hold on a minute," I said. I put my hands behind my neck and undid the clasp, then I handed the cross and chain to the bairn.

She looked at it closely. She turned it over and looked at the back where the scratch marks were, then she looked up at me. Her face registered utter betrayal.

"See!" Jarvis sounded bitterly exultant. "They ain't no friends of ours!"

Fox-Drummin, who had been watching carefully, also took a step forward.

"Time for a few explanations," he said, his smooth voice sounding almost gentle. "You've been well and truly taken in, I must say, but to be fair, it isn't entirely your fault. These peasants can be very plausible. If I didn't know better, I might have trusted them too. But Jarvis here is right. Their only desire is to get the lot of you off the island. They don't care where you go, or what happens to you – any old camp in some barracks in Northumberland, or a work camp, building sea defences in Kent – they're not bothered. You think things are hard here, but face it – compared to refugees on the mainland, you're free! Don't we bring you food? Don't we bring you medical care when you need it? Haven't we given you gainful employment? Don't you know that you're better off here than you'll ever be if you go back to the mainland?"

The refugees were silent. Charlie was kicking one foot against the wall we were all sitting on. Marigold moved towards Mo and buried her head in Mo's shoulder. Malcolm put his hand over mine.

Duncan spoke then. "So, we can call this a day, let you go, let you carry away that wimp in there…" he nodded his head towards the shed, "and let things take their course. I reckon that'll give you about five days more before you're all shipped off to God knows where. Or you can go home and leave these three with us. We'll sort it out from here, so that no harm comes to you."

The woman gave a subdued laugh. Everyone else was quiet.

"So, what will it be?" Fox-Drummin wanted to know. "Forget about this little interlude, let everything get back to normal, or take a chance with the authorities? When all's said and done, it's up to you. We've never kept you here by force before, and we don't plan to now."

Again, there was quiet – or almost complete quiet. I could just hear the soft sobs of Marigold, held in Mo's tight embrace.

Then Eric stood. "I'm for 'eading 'ome," he said. "Looks like we finished 'ere."

"Yeah," agreed Charlie, also standing. "Looks like we made a mistake."

Frankie stood. "Seems to be decided." She commented. "I, for one, don't fancy no work crew building sea defences."

Then they were all standing, not looking at Malcolm or me, embarrassment written all over their faces.

"Very sensible." It was Fox-Drummin at his smoothest. "And to show there's no ill-will – after all, any of us could be taken in! – we'll send down something good to drink, to help you to recover from your adventures!"

The refugees turned and, single file, they walked along the paved area to the track. They didn't speak. We watched them turn the corner by the rocky outcrop and then we could see them no more.

Malcolm and I sat on the wall, facing the *harkrav*, and behind us the dark clouds rolled closer.

★ ★ ★

"I'll let you gentlemen sort them out!" It was the woman, who turned and went back into their dwelling.

The two men looked at each other. Inside the shed, Lyle groaned.

"You realise, of course," said Fox-Drummin, approaching us, "that your friend might not have become quite so…" he hesitated, "unwell, if he had cooperated with us a little more?"

The man called Duncan added, "We offered him a good chance. All he had to do was to stay quiet, get on with policing the west of the island, mind his own business, and he would have found himself just a little better off every month. After all, his sergeant sees no harm in turning a blind eye!"

"When all is said and done," added Fox-Drummin, "we might be breaking the law, but only because it is a ridiculous law! We're not doing anything immoral! We're providing gainful employment for people who – let's face it – are virtually unemployable."

"And selling weapons to countries that are already torn apart by conflict!" I unwisely interjected.

Fox-Drummin scowled. "Oh, so you've worked that out, have you?" he wanted to know. "But I wonder if you've thought of this: if we didn't make and send them weapons, some other arms dealer would – probably some despot in a Third-World, tin-pot republic. Do you seriously think that if we turned our hands to making... shall we say... smart meters for hydrogen boilers, that there would be less war?"

Duncan spoke then. "I suggest," he said slowly, "that you join your friend in the shed. I'm sure he'd like some company! And consider your options. If you choose, you can walk away today, back to your ordinary lives. Forget all this. No reason you shouldn't all live to a ripe old age."

"Or," Fox-Drummin added, "if you feel that choice isn't for you... well, this is a hard island. Stormy. Dangerous. Accidents happen. You've been exploring a part of En-Somi you don't know. It's tragic when people get caught in storms, fall off cliffs, get washed out to sea... I am sure you would all be mourned, but life would go on."

Duncan chuckled. "Well," he suggested, "some life would go on, anyhow!"

"So, you join your friend in the shed, and think it over," suggested Fox-Drummin, "and we'll talk it over later, when you've had the chance to come to a sensible conclusion. In the meantime," he consulted his watch, "it's time for some lunch. And I do believe another storm is on its way!"

We had no choice. Either we went into the shed on our own two feet, or it was clear we would be forced. And just at that moment there was a dazzling flash of lightning and a crack of thunder. We needed to be under shelter.

The key turned in the lock behind us. Things were not looking good at all.

M alcolm went over to Lyle at once. Our friend was barely conscious, and cold to the touch.

"It's concussion, I think," muttered Malcolm. "The best we can do is to keep him warm and still – and try to stop him worrying."

He looked around the shed. In one corner there was a pile of old potato sacks, such as you find in the outhouses of every bothy on the island. "Here, Marie," Malcolm said, "help me to make a bit of a bed for Lyle."

We spread the hessian out on the stone floor and helped Lyle onto it. Malcolm took off his jacket and spread it over the man. I was about to take my coat off too – it was torn, but it would help. But *"Nei!"* insisted Malcolm. "You need to stay warm. There's no point in you getting ill!" Then he leant over Lyle and spoke gently to him, as if he were talking to a child. "It's all right now, Lyle," he comforted him. "We're with you. Just rest now and wait until help comes. We'll take care of you."

I looked at Malcolm. Until help comes? What help could we expect? Nothing from Lyle's sergeant. Nothing from the refugees. Verity was resting up down at the old airport after her earlier ordeal; she couldn't help us. And nobody else knew where we were. Malcolm scratched his head and pulled a face, as if to say, *Well, I had to tell him something!* Then he sat next to Lyle, wedged between our friend and some sort of workbench.

There was a lot of clutter in the shed. It's something you don't often see in or around our bothies. We live simply, and if something is no longer useful to us, there's usually someone else who can use it – or repurpose it. I had Malcolm's unwanted three-legged stool in my house, the bike Duncan grew out of had been used by Elin for several years, and the benches in the *fi'ilsted* had been made partly out of wood from two boats that, one winter, had been smashed by the waves in the summer harbour. Here, though, there were two cane chairs, the raffia around their legs unravelled, the cushions stained and watermarked. They were piled on top of each other. I managed to lift the top one down. There was very little floor space, but I edged it in between some cardboard boxes and an old suitcase, and the locked door. At least I had somewhere off the cold floor to sit.

There was another flash of lightning, and more thunder.

"Two storms, so close!" I said to Malcolm. It seemed strange, not the sort of wild weather we would normally expect on En-Somi. We are such a small rock in such a large ocean that the wind sweeps over and round us, unhindered by high mountains, and is gone. Thunderstorms only circle around in inland areas.

"Climate change," answered Malcolm. "No wonder they couldn't make a go of the airport!"

The wind was howling around the shed by then, and a draught was blowing steadily onto my feet. I pulled them up under me and wondered what would happen next. Would we have to give in, promise to keep quiet, go back to Hus, and forget the refugees? Was there any point in any other course of action? Were these apparently respectable people actually murderers as well as smugglers and arms dealers?

Then my mind drifted to Marigold. When she had realised that the cross I was wearing was indeed Lavender's, she had looked bereft. How could we go back to our side of the island and pretend that nothing had happened, leaving Marigold more convinced than ever that she could trust nobody? But would we achieve anything by refusing to cooperate with the *harkrav*? It seemed as if it were impossible to do the right thing.

She was such a sweet child, wee Marigold. I smiled to myself as I remembered her version of the Lord's Prayer: *Lead us not into Storhaven…* Of course, it made sense to her. She was convinced that the town was dangerous. It was that belief, that fear of

223

the islanders and of what they might do to them, that kept the refugees from straying far from the airport, that kept them out of sight and mind. To Marigold's young mind, it must entirely make sense.

She had wanted me to pray, though. She had been insistent, while Charlie and Si were rescuing Verity and Malcolm, that I either cast a spell or pray. I smiled to myself again, at the memory.

Then I realised. Of course, there was one course of action I could still try. I could pray. They say there are no atheists in foxholes. Perhaps there are none when people are locked in sheds, either.

I looked across at Malcolm. He looked exhausted, leaning against the shed wall, his eyes closed. When had any of us last slept? I decided to leave him to rest. This was an experiment to try on my own.

I closed my eyes. I listened to the gale blowing around the barn. I thought of what the bay would be like now. Would the tide have gone out, and come back in again? Would it be a cauldron of heaving water, the way it had been when I had last seen it? It didn't matter now; there was nobody trapped down there anymore. I thought of the refugees. Would they have made it back to the old airport before this new storm broke? I thought of the huge ocean, of that part of the ferry trip when you have left Lerwick or Bergen, and before Storhaven is in sight, when all you can see is water and sky. And that is just a small distance across a mighty ocean, a dotted line marking a ferry route in a mass of blue on a map. The world is so big!

And is there a God? If the ocean is big, and it is just one ocean, on one world, how big would God have to be? And if the waves in the cove were powerful, so that it was impossible to stand – powerful enough to sweep wee Lavender out to sea, powerful enough to pull down the cliffs and destroy the village where Jean used to live, how powerful would God have to be? And I thought of the snowy owl, and the orcas out in the bay, and the way Duncan had looked at me with unfocused, trusting eyes when the midwife had first put him into my arms, and I felt, suddenly, a surge of hope. My eyes were closed. I didn't see or hear anything other than the wind against the shutters and the small whirling of a wind turbine not too far away. And yet I did hear something. How can I explain it? A voice that was in my head – *nei*, in my heart. An affirmation. A promise. *It'll be all right.* Just that. No explanation. No suggestion of what we should do, Lyle, Malcolm and me, locked in a shed on the moors in a storm. Yet, at that moment, I knew, I absolutely *knew*, that it would be all right.

I opened my eyes. I uncurled my legs and winced as I put my injured foot onto the ground. I limped across to Malcolm. He opened his eyes and smiled at me.

"All right?" he asked.

"Yes," I said. "Yes, I really am! It's going to be all right," I told him. "It's going to work out!"

I saw that Malcolm was holding the hand of the sleeping Lyle. He held out his other hand to me. "Is that so?" he said, and he smiled. "That's really good news." He closed his eyes again.

I waited until he was asleep, then loosened his grip and went back to my broken chair. Then I waited, with a deep feeling of concentrated peace, to discover how our impossible situation was going to work out.

★ ★ ★

I dozed. Not peacefully, not with that sort of refreshing, dreamless sleep that I enjoy on my sleeping platform, in my own bothy, but I did sleep. So much had happened since we woke up in that ruined bothy – when was it? – two mornings ago. I was exhausted. I was aware of being cold. I was aware of my foot throbbing. I was aware of the thunder rumbling around outside. Then, later, I was aware of Malcolm standing over me, of his gentle voice coaxing me to stand, half carrying me over to the place where he had been sitting. It was dark again. Another night had come. After that I wasn't so cold, and I slept more deeply. I dreamt of Granny, of her sitting by my bed and stroking my hair, and I woke at last to find myself held tightly in Malcolm's arms, the warmth of his body curled into my back, his chin resting on my head.

"We've slept in some unlikely places!" It was Lyle, his head only a foot or so away from me on his makeshift bed. He was smiling, a little lopsidedly because of his injured face.

I smiled back. "That's rather an understatement!" I answered.

I could feel the steady rhythm of Malcolm's breathing, of his chest rising and falling against my back. He was obviously still asleep.

"Marie," Lyle was looking worried. "What's happened to Verity?"

"Oh!" Of course, I thought, the last thing Lyle knew was that we three were hiding in the cave. Everything that had happened since would have to be explained sometime, but not now. "She's fine," I told Lyle. "She got very cold and wet in the storm. She's down at the old airport."

Lyle seemed to give a little sigh. I thought it was relief.

I had no idea how much time had passed. My stomach gurgled, and I realised that I was very hungry. The shed was dark – but not pitch black. I could see Lyle's face, and there was a small streak of dull light high up on the wall above his head, reflecting the daylight that was creeping in through the one dirty window.

"How long have you been awake?" I whispered.

"I'm not sure. Half an hour, maybe. They gave me quite a beating, you know… and I lost my phone, with all the photos on it – all the evidence."

I gently moved one of Malcolm's hands so that I could feel in my pocket. "You didn't, actually!" I told him. I passed it across to him. "I found it when I went looking for you."

Lyle reached out and took the device. Clumsily (we later found that he had three broken fingers), he clicked here and there, and then gave a slow, satisfied smile. "Better hide this!" he said.

By his head there was a bag labelled *Potting Compost – indoor plants. Better results than nature alone can give!* It had been opened and was partly empty, the top just folded over. With difficulty, he opened the bag and dropped the phone into it.

Right at that moment we heard the *harkrav* approaching – the bang of their main door closing and a moment later the rattle of a key in the lock of our door.

"I'm too ill to talk!" whispered Lyle to me, and closed his eyes.

Behind me, Malcolm murmured into my hair, "And we don't know much at all. We came at Lyle's request. The whole thing is a bit of a mystery to us."

"And there were only the three of us," said Lyle out of the corner of his mouth. "Keep Verity right out of this."

Fox-Drummin came in first, a torch in his hand. He swept the light across the shed until he came to the three of us. "Very cosy!" he said in his usual voice, dry, verging on the sarcastic.

Duncan was right behind him. "Taking it easy, I see," was his comment.

Behind him was the woman. She was dressed for the outdoors, in a warm jacket and a woollen hat. She was carrying something that looked like a saucepan.

Malcolm and I sat up. Lyle lay still, his mouth a little open, his breathing sounding heavy.

"So," said Fox-Drummin, putting the torch down on the chair where I had started out, "we've given the matter some thought."

"A lot of thought," agreed the woman. Duncan laughed.

"This is the plan," Fox-Drummin continued. "We really don't think we can let you go. What's to stop you promising us that you'll keep quiet and then changing your mind later? So, I'm sorry to break the news to you, but you two," – he kicked at Malcolm's feet while he said that – "are going to leave the island. For good."

"What?" I exclaimed. "You can't make us do that!"

The woman laughed. "We can do more or less what we want!" she said, although I didn't think she was talking particularly to us.

"Try us!" suggested Duncan.

"Patience! Patience!" came Fox-Drummin's smooth voice. "They don't have the full picture yet!" He came a little closer and looked down at the apparently unconscious Lyle. "Hm!" he said to himself. Then he looked at Malcolm and me. "So, this is the situation," he explained. "You three islanders decided to go exploring in the middle of the winter. We'll never know why. It was a crazy thing to do – out of character. Strange. You two will have vanished from the island. We can only assume that some terrible accident occurred. We found this chap," and he glanced at Lyle again, "unconscious on the beach. We rescued him. But he'll never be the same again. He might tell rambling stories. He might come up with all sorts of conspiracy theories. But his sergeant will check everything out. If he recovers sufficiently, if his head clears enough and he stops talking about smugglers and plots, probably his sergeant will allow him to keep his job. It would be the compassionate thing to do. Your side of the island is pretty remote, after all. But of course, he'll never be capable of taking more responsibility. There'll be no promotion for him on the cards. It's a shame, really – such a promising young cop!"

Again, the woman laughed, a strange sort of giggle. It occurred to me briefly that she might not be entirely comfortable with what Fox-Drummin was saying.

"We're expecting another shipment," Fox-Drummin continued, in a matter-of-fact manner. "Probably next week. They'll take the two of you and drop you off somewhere. You can start over again. But if you ever, *ever*, say anything about what has happened here, I'm afraid – I'm very much afraid, that this chap here will have a relapse. And this time, he'll never recover."

★ ★ ★

We were all quiet. After a minute or two, Malcolm said, "My whole life savings are in that bothy of mine." I knew at once that he was acting. He intended to sound defeated.

I followed his example. "I raised my son on this island," I said.

"That's very sad," Fox-Drummin answered, not sounding sad at all. "But you're both young – relatively young. And a fresh start is better than the alternative."

"What's the alternative?" I asked, trying to sound frightened.

"Ah, well…" Fox-Drummin was almost gloating. "It could be that we find all three of you at the bottom of the cliff, and not even the cop survives. Now that *would* be sad!"

"I see." Malcolm sounded as if he had capitulated. "It doesn't seem as if we have much choice."

Duncan chuckled. "You haven't given *us* much choice!" he remarked, almost gleefully.

"If we're agreed?" Fox-Drummin wanted to know. "Then we can make a few arrangements."

Malcolm managed to sound sulky. "Agreed," he muttered.

"*Aja*," I muttered.

"Good. Well then, first I just want to check that you don't have anything on you that could cause us – or you – any difficulties. You first, come here!" and he pointed to me.

I struggled to my feet and limped towards him. He patted me down, felt into my pockets, and sneered at my torn tee shirt. "What's in that bandage?" he wanted to know and insisted that I unravelled the cloths that were tied round my feet. I was so grateful to Lyle for having hidden the phone.

When he was done with me, he pushed me roughly back towards Lyle and called Malcolm over. Malcolm appeared to be completely cowed. His shoulders were stooped, his head down. Anyone who knew him would have seen at once that he was acting, he was like a caricature of a defeated man. If it hadn't all been so grim, I might have laughed. Of course, Malcolm had dealt with all too many defeated human beings during his life as a social worker. He knew the look.

"Good! Good!" exclaimed Fox-Drummin when he was done. "So, all that's left now is to feed you!" He reached over to the woman and took the saucepan from her. "Here you are!" he said as he passed the pan to me. "There's only one spoon, but I'm sure you'll cope!"

"And water, please?" I asked, sounding timid, and Duncan passed over a glass bottle.

And with that, they left, locking the door firmly behind them.

The pan contained some sort of stew. It was lukewarm and rather salty. As soon as we heard the house door close, Lyle sat up. "I'm conscious now!" he proclaimed. "You're not having my share of that!"

We ate it, a spoonful at a time, taking turns. There wasn't enough to satisfy our hunger – Malcolm and I hadn't eaten since that picnic breakfast on the cart twenty-four hours earlier, and as for Lyle – but it was better than nothing.

"Now what?" I asked. "Are we really going to allow ourselves to be shipped off En-Somi?"

"Oh, I don't think so!" answered Malcolm, sounding very calm.

"But how," Lyle wanted to know, "can we stop them?"

"I don't know," responded Malcolm, scratching his head in that characteristic way of his. "Or not yet, anyhow. But it seems as if we've got a few days before their next boat is due. Something will happen!"

"You're such an optimist!" commented Lyle, but he sounded amused. I was feeling quite cheerful, too. Perhaps, I thought, it was the result of having some food inside us, or maybe relief because Lyle seemed so much better than when we had first found him.

After that we spent some time making practical arrangements. We took the cushions off the cane chairs and rearranged the sacking to make a more comfortable place for us all to sit, and where we would be able to sleep. We designated the far corner of the shed as a place to piss, and not for the first time in my life I thought how much easier life is for men than for women. Malcolm was wearing a solar-powered watch, but it had stopped working, so we could only guess at the time. The sun had risen by then, it could have been 10.00 or 11.00 in the morning, but we were all unused to the light on the east of the island, so it was difficult to be sure. Malcolm and Lyle checked over Lyle's injuries. We knew there was something wrong with one of his hands and they both thought Lyle might have one or two broken ribs, but his head seemed to be clear and he promised us that he didn't have a headache, or feel dizzy. Malcolm re-bandaged my feet and checked some grazes he had acquired climbing the rocks to keep clear of the waves down in the bay.

★ ★ ★

We sat, then, in the dim light, and talked. Malcolm and I had shared a lot by that time, about our families and about our experiences of Edinburgh, but neither of us knew Lyle as well as all that. He spoke of his dreams of how, as a child, he had wanted to be a footballer, of his mother's good cooking and the skills his father had as a fisherman. He told us of his love for children, of how he had briefly wondered about becoming a teacher until he realised that he would need to study for four years on the mainland, and even then, there was no guarantee of getting a job on the island. "I don't want to live away from here," he told us. "I'm my parents' only surviving child. I'd like to raise their grandchildren close by, the way I was raised, close to my *pari-pari*."

We took some exercise, running on the spot and then doing press-ups. I was hopeless at them. Malcolm said I let my back curve too much, but after half an hour or so I was at least warm. Lyle wanted to join in as well, but Malcolm wouldn't let him. It wasn't safe, he said, until we knew the extent of Lyle's injuries. Malcolm sounded so calm, so certain that at some point we would be in a situation where Lyle's injuries could be checked out, that I didn't feel any fear. We talked on and off all day. In the late afternoon, the three of us stood at the grimy window and watched the sun setting. The man, Duncan, brought us a loaf of bread and two bottles of Bokko beer. "No point in bringing anything for him!" he announced, standing over Lyle, who was again pretending to be unconscious. As with the stew at breakfast time, we waited until the *harkrav* were out of the way before sharing the food and drink between us. To this day, whenever I drink one of the stronger Norwegian beers, I am always reminded of sitting on the floor in that shed.

For a while, Malcolm and Lyle compared notes about their schooling in the two schools on En-Somi, and about their nervousness when, at aged eleven or twelve, they first caught the ferry to Lerwick to board there. Both of them thought the Kullanders were right to allow Andy to stay at home until he felt ready to go. I described the enthusiasm Duncan had displayed leading up to his first term away from home, and how I had been a little hurt by it. Malcolm, of course, had not met Duncan at that time, but Lyle knew him. "With parents like you and Bjorn," he said, "what did you expect? That laddie was born confident!"

After an hour or more of sitting in the dark, the conversation ran dry. I felt strangely peaceful. It might have been partly exhaustion, of course, but also the effect of praying, and the security of snuggling up to Malcolm. I suppose, too, that we were in a sort of emotional limbo. There was nothing we could do. The next few hours or even days, while we were locked in the shed, were decided. Why think beyond then?

Lyle started to doze again. By then we were all lying down, and I realised that he had started snoring, a light, gentle sound. Then Malcolm wrapped his arms around me, and started kissing me, not passionately – softly, almost comfortingly. I held him close and kissed him back, and a sense of peace, of wholeness, seemed to creep through my body.

Crack! Something had smashed against the shed window.

We all three started – Lyle out of his sleep, Malcolm and I out of our embrace.

"What?" exclaimed Lyle, struggling to get his bearings. I was suddenly wide awake. "Someone threw something at the window!" I said, jumping to my feet. And I was right. The glass was cracked, and peering through the window, lit eerily by a torch held somewhere out of sight, was the welcome, care-worn face of Frankie.

"Is you all in there?" she wanted to know. "We've come to rescue you!"

"We're all here," I confirmed. "Lyle's much better. But how are you going to get in?"

"Just wait quietly, away from the door!" This time it was Charlie.

Malcolm and Lyle had joined me at the window by then. "Back into our corner!" instructed Malcolm, and we all three did as we were told.

We could hear movement outside – some whispering and then a strange, whining hiss.

"They've found some sort of metal grinder," suggested Lyle.

"But a small one," agreed Malcolm, "judging by the pitch of it."

"Where would they lay their hands on something like that?" Lyle wondered.

"Oh!" It had suddenly occurred to me. "From their workshop. Some tool they use when they're assembling those weapons, maybe?"

"It's going to wake the *harkrav*," worried Lyle.

"So, we'd better be ready," agreed Malcolm, looking around the shed in the dark. But we had investigated earlier, and only found…

"Garden tools!" I exclaimed and limped across to the corner. There was a spade and a garden fork, both with long handles. The men each grabbed one. I took hold of the only remaining item which I thought could be useful: a long-handled yard brush.

The pitch of the whining, hissing grinder seemed to have risen. "We've nearly cut the lock," Frankie told us through the broken window. "Be ready to run!"

But of course, it was inevitable that someone in the house would have woken.

"There's a light on!" I heard Si say, and then, "'Ere they come!"

From where we stood, we could hear movement, the noise of running and scrabbling, and then an all-too-familiar voice.

"So, what do we have here?" sneered Fox-Drummin.

There was no answer, no sound coming from the refugees at all.

Then came Duncan's voice, from further away. "Oh, for goodness' sake, Dominic! You're getting paranoid about those refugees. There's nothing going on out here!"

"You think?" came Fox-Drummin's voice from just beyond the shed door. "Come and look at this padlock!" Then, "Ouch!" he yelped. "It's still hot!"

"Lie down!" whispered Lyle. "Quickly!"

We were back on our makeshift bed in no time. Outside, a light was moving around, casting shadows on the walls of the shed.

"This window's broken," said Duncan. "Someone's tried to break in."

"Or out," answered Fox-Drummin. "I'm more worried about this door. Look! The lock's almost completely cut through. Ten minutes later, and we could have lost them."

We lay still and listened.

"Are they still in there?" came the voice of the woman.

A torch beam shone in through the broken window and found us where we lay. "Yes," came Duncan's voice.

"Do you think this is the work of those dammed refugees?" asked the woman. "I thought we'd got rid of them, back to the pit."

"Could be!" Fox-Drummin must have known that we could hear every word. I suppose he was so sure of their ability to keep a lid on things that they just didn't care what we knew, or what we thought. "Or would someone in the town try to help our three musketeers?"

"But who?" Duncan wondered. "You're right about this lock. It's cooling down now, but whoever was trying to cut it open was working on it very recently."

"Could it be that bitch with the tea shop?" the woman asked.

"Jeanie? No!" Once again, Fox-Drummin sounded supremely confident. "She owes us too much, and she's in it too deep! If she brought us down, she'd bring herself down too."

"And she hates the refugees," added Duncan.

"Best to phone the sergeant, I think," suggested Fox-Drummin. "We need a bit of support out here."

"I'll do it." It sounded as if the woman had gone back inside.

"Wha…!" Suddenly Fox-Drummin let out a sort of muffled yell. At exactly the same time there was the sound of a scuffle and a thump.

I heard Frankie's voice, very calm and very threatening, saying "Now, gents! You better just stay 'ere and keep quiet. We've 'ad about enough of you!" Then she instructed someone, "Get your act together! Gag 'em!"

"Time for action!" Lyle said. "Come on, let's see how strong that lock is now!"

As if they had rehearsed it hundreds of times, the two men lined themselves up shoulder to shoulder and charged at the door. For a second, I thought that they were going to be no more successful than when Charlie and Quincy had tried to break in using the same manoeuvre. This time, though, the door shook at the force of the men against it.

"One more try!" exclaimed Malcolm. "We're nearly there."

They stood back, looked at each other and grinned, then charged.

It was almost anticlimactic. There was a sort of high-pitched squeal and the door flew open. Lyle fell right over, Malcolm staggered but stayed on his feet, and I rushed out after them, into the blustery night air.

"Nice to see you!" said Frankie. "I fought, when you appeared on the scene, that you was going to 'elp us! Seems like it's all the other way!"

"*Aja!*" I could hear the grin in Malcolm's voice. "It does seem that way!"

I could see the shapes of people behind the wall, where we had all hidden earlier, and Si climbed over it, and came up to us. "Best get away quick," he said. "That sergeant's on his way, an' 'o knows who else 'e'll bring to back 'im up."

A grunt came from Fox-Drummin, who was by now sitting on the slate slabs, gagged and with his hands tied. Even that muffled noise sounded scornful.

"Where can we go?" I asked. It had just occurred to me that the sergeant would head straight for the old airport when he discovered how things were at the *harkrav* house.

"Just come wiv us!" insisted Si.

We left the two men tied up and gagged in front of the building. Someone had grabbed the keys of the bothy and locked the woman in, which seemed like a pretty good idea to me. We took the keys with us.

"The sergeant'll be 'ere in no time," Frankie commented. "We needs to do what Si says. Come on! Lyle, can you walk?"

"*Aja,*" confirmed our friend, and we all set off.

★ ★ ★

The refugees seemed to know just where they were going. When we left the bothy, we didn't follow the track down towards the Storhaven road, the way we had approached it with the pony and cart. Instead, we climbed uphill, past the *harkrav*'s wind turbine and on up to the moors. We didn't seem to be following any path, although of course it was pitch dark and difficult to tell. Quincy was in the lead and seemed to know exactly what he was doing.

"Knows these moors like the back of 'is 'and," commented Frankie, who was walking just behind us. "'Im an' Mo, when they was kids, they used to play up 'ere. We never liked it. The bosses, they said if the kids was caught, we'd all be in the soup, but there weren't no controlling 'em. No parents, you see."

The weather was typical of En-Somi: a strong, blustery wind and clouds scudding across the sky. Every now and then, briefly, we could see the moon, but as quickly as it appeared, more clouds streamed between us and the light. The bandages on my feet were soaking wet, and I felt weak. Lyle was staggering a little; his breathing hurt and Malcolm was helping him with one arm round him and Lyle's arm across Malcolm's shoulders. Quincy was moving more quickly than us; every now and again he had to stop and wait.

"Not far now," encouraged Frankie, behind me. "Is you goin' to make it?"

"*Aja*," I answered. "Yes. I'm sorry if we're holding things up."

At last, we stopped climbing. For a little while, we walked round the side of a hill, rocks on one side of us, a steep uphill slope on the other, and then we started to wind our way back down a little sheep track. I didn't realise as quickly as Malcolm where we had come.

"It's our bothy!" he exclaimed. Then, to clarify what he meant, "It's where we were hiding a couple of days ago!"

He was right. We had approached it from above, where the outbuildings were more evident than the bothy itself.

Quincy led us round the side of the building. "Your ponies is safe in there," Frankie told us. "The others brought 'em up 'ere while we was rescuing you."

Then we were at the front of the bothy, and I could smell smoke, and there was a dim, flickering light showing through a window that was not properly covered.

We staggered inside.

And everyone was there: Rose, cooking something over a fire in the hearth, Marigold holding the sleeping Thistle, Eric and the boy, Shawn, the little girl called Shirley, and one or two others. Not Jarvis. Mo was sitting talking to Verity, but when Mo looked up and saw us, she jumped to her feet and ran to Quincy. Lyle gave a sort of sigh of relief and knelt beside the seated Verity.

"Oh, I'm so glad to see you!" he said and hugged her close.

Malcolm looked across at me and winked.

"Time to eat!" proclaimed Rose, and the usual array of plates and bowls appeared. I have never appreciated potato soup so much in all my life.

Over the meal, we caught up on what had happened. "I never s'pposed you 'ad stolen from Lavender!" Marigold reassured me. She was sitting right next to me. "'Cept for a minute or two, till Dad told me you wasn't the sort!"

Si was beside Rose, who was feeding baby Thistle. "When I saw 'ow things was," he told us, "I moved them ponies so's the bosses wouldn't find 'em. Then I just kept an eye on fings till the others started walking down the track, looking like they was going 'ome."

"We *was* going 'ome!" Frankie admitted. "We was a bit confused. Seemed like there was more to all this than we understood!"

"And we didn't want to be sent back to no barracks!" Quincy agreed.

"But Si 'ere, 'e told us to use our 'eads," Mo butted in. "Them bosses, they got us where they wanted us. Free labour. And we lost our little Lavender and I don't think they cared!"

"And we seen 'ow they live," added Charlie. "Mo, Quincy, Eric and me – when we was searching for them keys. Like pigs in clover. And us like London 'omeless, living in a building what's slowly falling down."

"So, we reckoned we got to pick our side," Frankie went on. "And we gambled on you."

"Thank you." I was deeply moved and resolved that we would never let them down.

"So we split up," Frankie went on. "Quincy knew of this old 'ut on the moors, and 'e reckoned it would be a good place to 'ide, but only 'e and Mo knew where it was."

"I came back up to the bosses' 'ouse wiv Frankie and Charlie," said Quincy. "Eric ran all the way down to the workshop to

240

find 'is tools, and everyone else went back to the airport to get everyone moving, as quick as possible."

"I was dead scared," Mo told us. "I 'ad to bring everyone up 'ere. What if I couldn't remember the way? Me and Quincy, we used to come up 'ere when we was kids, but it 'ad been years. We 'ad sort of given up dreaming…"

"But 'ere we is!" Rose remarked, holding the baby against her shoulder to burp her.

"What about Jarvis?" I wanted to know.

"'E weren't nowhere about," said Frankie. "Goes off by 'imself all the time, that one. Up to no good, I bet!"

"And now what?" I asked. It felt to me as if the refugees had taken control, and I vaguely hoped they had some ideas about what to do next. I didn't, and Malcolm and Lyle were very quiet.

"We 'oped you'd tell us!" chuckled Frankie. "We spent the last forty-eight hours not doing as we was told! It's wore us out! First time we's 'ad to fink for ourselves for years!"

I laughed, but I made a mental note to ask Malcolm later. If people are left with no freedom, do they lose the ability to think for themselves? Can that happen to anyone, or only in extreme situations?

For a few minutes we were quiet. The refugees had raided our store of wood – I later discovered that they had brought some of their own, too, and the fire was hissing and crackling, sending plumes of smoke into the room as the wind blustered in the chimney.

"We don't know how many people the sergeant'll bring out from Storhaven," Malcolm commented.

"Or what they'll do," I agreed. "If they decide to search the moorland, it wouldn't take them long to find us, would it?"

"'Specially if they 'as dogs," added Charlie.

"We need to get someone over from Lerwick," Lyle suggested. "The *nasyonii* over there are as honest as they come. My second cousin used to work with them."

"*Aja*," Malcolm was frowning in the firelight. "Or even the mainland."

"But 'ow?" Si asked.

We all looked at each other. "We needs a phone," suggested Frankie. "Doesn't you 'ave one?"

"I lost mine in the sea," said Malcolm.

"Here's mine." Verity was holding out a slim, battered object. "But it doesn't work anymore. I think it got too wet."

Lyle suddenly stood up. "Oh no!" he exclaimed. "Oh no! Do you know what I've done? I've left my phone in the shed, down at the *harkrav* house!"

"Well, t'ain't the end of the world," Frankie remarked.

But Lyle was still looking desperate. "It is!" he exclaimed. "It's got all the evidence on it! My photos of the ship, and of the smuggling. Video of unloading the cargo. A recording of conversations! Oh hell!" He sat down, looking miserable. "I'm a useless cop! That's twice I've lost it, and without it, we've got no evidence at all. Absolutely nothing!"

Malcolm, Lyle, Verity and I looked at each other, stunned. I'm not sure to this day that the refugees realised the implications of the lost phone. A justice system that could bring criminals to heel, especially wealthy, well-connected criminals, was way beyond their experience.

"Where is it, your phone?" asked Malcolm, sounding very calm.

"Hidden in a bag of potting compost!" Lyle groaned.

"But they don't know you had it!" I pointed out. "So will they even think to search for it?"

"That's right!" Lyle brightened up. "They searched me head to toe when they caught me, and took it in turns to try to get me to say what evidence I had, but I didn't say anything! They know for sure I didn't take a phone into the shed!"

"And they searched us, so they know that neither of us had it. It was hidden by then!"

242

Again, we were all quiet for a moment. I became aware that wee Marigold was asleep with her head resting against my arm. I looked across at her mother, and Rose grinned at me. Thistle was sleeping too.

"Seems to me," said Frankie thoughtfully, "that first of all, we needs to rescue that phone."

"It's got pictures of us smuggling," pointed out Charlie. "It's evidence against us too."

"Yeah," Frankie agreed. "But we can't do nofing about that. Fings can't go back to what they was. We'll 'ave to see what 'appens to us…"

"So 'ow'll we get that phone back?" Quincy wanted to know.

"We needs more people," said Frankie. "You needs to phone the mainland or whatever, and we needs to get that phone back." She looked across at Verity, sitting close to Lyle. "Is there anyone in Stor'aven what'll 'elp us?"

Malcolm and Verity spoke exactly in unison. "The Frasers!"

"Friends of mine," explained Malcolm, "and all round *bondii*!"

"I s'ppose that means good guys?" commented Charlie. "Do they 'ave a phone?"

"Everyone on the island has a phone," I explained. "And the people in Storhaven have a much better connection than us."

"But will they be able to bring 'elp?" asked Frankie.

Verity looked serious. "I've only been on En-Somi a few months," she explained. "I don't know who might be involved with the smugglers, and who isn't…"

"But we do!" exclaimed Malcolm, sounding excited. "Marie and me. Nobody on our side of the island has anything to do with all this. I'm sure Petter and Malchi would help!"

"And the Kullanders!" I added.

"Oh, and Robert, whose ponies we borrowed, and Patrick and Shona at the shop!"

"So, 'ere's a plan," said Frankie. Looking at Verity, she suggested, "You goes back to Stor'aven and finds your mates and phones the cops on the mainland – somebody'd better go wiv you – and then you two," nodding at Malcolm and me, "you go over to your 'ome and bring back them people you talks about, and we meets at the bosses' 'ome, and we finds that phone wiv all the evidence, and we keeps 'em there till the cops from the mainland come, and we 'opes for the best!"

"It's a plan," agreed Si, frowning.

"Can't see any other way of 'andling fings," agreed Charlie.

"Will it work?" Mo wondered.

Frankie shrugged. "'Ow do we know?" she asked. "As me mum used to say, we won't know unless we tries it!"

And so it was decided.

★ ★ ★

Of course, we only found out later, Malcolm and I, how things worked out for Verity and Lyle. I tried on various pairs of shoes, offered up by Rose, Frankie and Mo, but ended up wearing a pair of boots belonging to Si, stuffed with the bandages I had been wearing since Malcolm wrapped my feet in the shed. Verity and Lyle headed off down the track to the Storhaven road, while Quincy led us up the slope behind the bothy until, in the scudding darkness, we could see Fyrtarn Fjell looming, a black mass, in the distance.

"Ain't never been further than this," Quincy told us. "Me and Mo, we used to wonder what was over there, but we was scared. We was little, and we 'alf believed in monsters."

"Don't worry," Malcolm reassured him. "I think we can find our way from here."

"Right, mate! Good luck!"

The trek across the moorland is a blur to me now. It was a blur then, I think. I suppose it was the early hours of the morning, and I was so weary. Fyrtarn Fjell was always more or less ahead of us, but for a while it didn't seem to get any closer. We didn't talk. Once, I put my foot into a patch of marshland and fell, and Malcolm pulled me to my feet, and we kept going. Another time, Malcolm stopped, clutching his side. "Stitch!" he explained, and then set off again.

Then it seemed, quite suddenly, we were on the fjell slope. Climbing Fyrtarn is easier on the eastern side; the slope is not so steep and there are fewer sheer rocky outcrops. There was a clear path, too, trodden by people from the eastern side of the island at the times of the solstices, or for summer picnics. After seeming to walk for hours without getting anywhere, we were, all at once, on the summit, looking down towards Gamla Hus.

After that it was easier. We started to talk – about how much we needed to explain, about who would go to whom to ask for help. I branched off from Malcolm before we reached the village, to go to the Kullanders', and Malcolm planned to go to the *fi'ilsted* first (Petter is an early riser) and then to Robert, to see if we could use his ponies and cart for the return journey. We agreed to meet, as soon as possible, at the crossroads by the shop. Both Alf and Petter wanted to phone the mainland before setting off, but the phones were down again. "It's all right," I reassured them. "Verity'll do that."

The Kullanders still laugh when they remember me turning up at their place. I thought I was fully in control of myself, but they told me later that my explanation was nearly incoherent. All they understood from my garbled account was that Malcolm and I needed help and that, somehow, I had crossed the island by night, to find them. They were dressed in their storm clothes in no time, and when young Andy came along too, they didn't object.

Down in the village there was quite a stir. Robert was driving his cart up from the northern end of the settlement, where he housed his ponies. The lights were on in the *fi'ilsted* and in the shop, and a small gaggle of people was gathered outside the school. Some, I remember, were still zipping up outdoor jackets and lacing boots, and there was much mirth for years afterwards whenever Sigrid described coming out in her pyjamas and ski clothes – the only time she had appeared in public without a bra

245

since her feminist days! There were more people than could fit on the cart, but to my relief everyone insisted that Malcolm and I had walked enough, and room was made for us in the back, alongside various farming implements that would have to serve, if needed, as armaments!

There was food and drink, too. The coffee Malchi gave us as we set off had whisky in it and, probably for that reason, I was asleep before we came to the pass. I have vague memories of jolting over rocks, of Malcolm explaining what had happened and of exclamations of horror and surprise, of someone moving a garden hoe away from one of my legs to make me more comfortable, and of a jumbled dream in which Granny was saying, "All's well that ends well!"

I probably only slept for three quarters of an hour. When I woke up, we were just driving down into Storhaven. Behind us, the *bondii* who were walking with us were spread out, swinging along the track with the confidence of country people used to the rough outdoors. I saw that a few more people had joined us: Harris, who lived in the bothy close to the ruined chapel, and his uncle, and Jamie MacLoughlan's cousin, and one or two other people I didn't recognise.

The clock on the kirk wall told us it was nearly 9.00am. In the east, the sky was grey; looking back towards the moors, it was dark navy. The streets of the wee town were quiet, although there was a light on in Verity's flat, and several lights on in the little houses on the road out to the airport.

We were making good time. The walkers almost had to jog to keep up with the cart, as we drove along the good road just out of town. When we rounded the bend where the road to the cemetery branches off, we came across a small group of people, men and women, walking along the road.

"Malcolm McDough?" called out one of them, as we drew close.

"*Aja!*"

"The minister said you needed some help!" called the speaker.

"Great!" responded Malcolm, "Just follow us. They'll explain!" he pointed back to the straggling line of walkers, and we continued on our way.

★ ★ ★

By the time we reached the turning up to the *harkrav*'s house, it was light, in a grey, drab sort of way. At the turning there was a patch of mud, with hoof prints in it. "The sergeant's arrived," commented Robert, peering down from the driver's seat. "And several others, I would say."

"Should we leave the pony and trap here?" Petter wondered.

"There's a good place closer to the bothy," Malcolm explained. "But we need to be quiet now."

There was some muttering and nodding up and down the line of walkers. I counted: there were fifteen of us now, and everyone except Malcolm and me looked fresh and bright.

In silence we climbed the steep track. Occasionally one of the ponies' hooves clipped on some rock, but mostly the track was muddy from so much recent rain. The cart creaked a bit, as wooden carts always do, but quietly. I didn't think the sound would be heard from the house. The hoes, spades and forks next to Malcolm and me clanked together a little, until we wedged the food containers from the *fi'ilsted* between them. The walkers, all close together behind us now, were silent, their heads up, their expressions determined.

We were about two-thirds of the way to the house when Verity appeared from behind a rock, her finger to her mouth, shushing us unnecessarily. She came up to the cart and spoke quietly to Malcolm.

"Sergeant Stensen arrived before we got back," she explained. "He's got a couple of other men with him – I don't know them. And they've brought a dog. They're in the house now, getting themselves organised I suppose. Dougie and Ingrid brought five others with them, but I only know Holti. The others aren't kirk people. The Storhaven people are up behind the cottage. We hoped you would bring enough people to help us to surround the *harkrav*. Some of the refugees are on their way over."

"Then what?" Robert wanted to know.

"Well…" Verity looked a bit uncertain. "I phoned the police, in Lerwick and on the mainland, and I tried to explain, but I'm not sure… I think they thought I was some kid, playing a joke. The Lerwick woman told me it was an offence to make hoax calls! And then Dougie tried, on his phone, but they just cut him off. I'm worried that they'll have phoned Sergeant Stensen, and he'll have told them there's no problem… "

Malcolm looked serious. I knew what he was thinking. We couldn't hold the smugglers captive forever, holed up in their luxurious home. We needed officialdom to step in.

We took the cart up to the spot where Malcolm's ponies and trap had been left only two days earlier. Then, walking carefully, gesturing rather than speaking, we spread ourselves out downhill from the house, hidden by the wall.

"Now what?" whispered Malchi, who was next to Malcolm and me.

"We wait," answered Malcolm. "We just don't let them go anywhere. And we hope the police come."

"And if they don't?" Petter was the other side of Malchi.

"I'm not sure," said Malcolm. "I just hope they do!"

We waited like that for about an hour. The sun was up, and bright shafts of light hit the wall in front of us, between the shadows of clouds racing overhead. The wind was cold, blowing from the east still, carrying temperatures from the Norwegian tundra. Shona, from the shop, had lent me a warmer jacket but even so, it was cold waiting there.

At last, we heard voices.

"So, first things first," said a voice – a voice with a *bondi* accent.

"The sergeant, I bet!" whispered Malcolm.

"We find those refugees and shut their mouths for good!" It was the voice of Duncan.

"No!" Fox-Drummin, as always, seemed to be sneering. "The first thing is to get rid of those interfering peasants, the policeman and his friends. They know too much and they're too clever by half! It's a good thing your colleague in Aberdeen phoned you to check the story of whoever it was who phoned in, or we'd have had half of Police Scotland descending upon us!"

"They can't prove anything!" pointed out Duncan. He was only feet away from us, where we crouched behind the wall.

"I won't be happy until I see their bodies floating in the sea!" exclaimed the woman.

I heard Sergeant Stensen laugh. "Well, I'll be much happier then, too!"

"So where do we look first?" It must have gone against the grain for Fox-Drummin to have to ask the sergeant.

"Not down by the road," answered the sergeant. "We came that way, and there was no sign of them. And nothing seemed to bother the dog, except a hare up towards the cemetery."

"So, up on the moors?" asked Duncan. "It's not easy-going, up there."

"Yes, up on the moors," agreed the sergeant. "Bring your rifles. We've got a day's hunting ahead of us!"

I didn't like the sound of that at all. Rifles? Hunting isn't really considered a respectable pastime on En-Somi. There was a time when a group of *harkrav* talked of introducing grouse so that there could be grouse shooting up here, but the terrain is all wrong, and anyhow, it's too difficult for visitors to get here. We don't hunt the hares. Someone did a study years ago and concluded that if we could keep rats and cats off the island, then nature would achieve its own balance. As a result, hardly anyone owns guns of any sort. Even the *nasyonii* are only equipped with tasers, and I had never heard of them being used.

"We can't let them leave here!" hissed Malcolm.

"You're right!" whispered Petter.

Up on the terrace, the dog was barking.

"We need to give him something with their scent on it," remarked the sergeant. "Have you got anything?"

"Must be something in the shed," suggested Duncan.

We could hear them open the door. "Here, boy!" the sergeant said. Then, "I suppose this is where they were resting? So, these old cushions must carry their smell! Here, Fergus, smell this. Good dog!"

There was a short pause.

"All right?" came Fox-Drummin's voice from close to the wall.

"That's odd!" It was the sergeant, still inside the shed. "The dog's interested in your potting compost!"

"Oh, for God's sake!" Fox-Drummin wasn't concerned with the dog exploring his shed. "Let's get going!"

"*Nei*, but wait a minute…" the sergeant's voice was slightly muffled. "Well, bingo!" he suddenly shouted.

"Oh no!" It was Lyle, crouching on the other side of Holti. "They've found my phone!"

250

"Well, I'll be damned!" I had never heard Fox-Drummin sound remotely impressed before. "Was that in my potting compost? How the hell did that peasant cop get it past us?"

"Could he have phoned for help?" Duncan sounded worried.

"*Nei!*" The sergeant was unconcerned. "Not after that first call which we already know about. He couldn't make a call that wasn't logged with me too. That's the way these phones work."

"Right, then!" Fox-Drummin was back in control. "Leave the phone in the house for now, let's get hunting that cop and his friends!"

Frankie had crept up behind us. "Time for action?" she asked Malcolm.

"*Aja* – yes," he agreed.

Then Frankie stood, so that she could be seen from the terrace, and yelled at the top of her voice, "'Old it!"

We all jumped up too. There were islanders and refugees coming from all directions. Those of us who had been hiding behind the wall were climbing over it, Verity and the Frasers surged in from the direction of the track, and some *bondii* I didn't know rushed round from the back of the house. The dog started barking frantically, the *harkrav* woman screamed, and for a moment I thought we had succeeded. All we needed to do was to back the lot of them into the bothy and then we would have them – for the moment.

It might have worked, too. The woman had already retreated inside, and the sergeant was looking wildly all around him, obviously taken entirely off guard. There were two men I didn't know, and one of them followed the woman inside. There were only four men left outside: Fox-Drummin and Duncan, the sergeant and a person he had brought with him.

But then Fox-Drummin took control. He quite simply raised his rifle and aimed it directly at me.

"That's enough!" he drawled. "Stand back, all of you!" Then, to the sergeant, he said, "It looks as if we won't need to go hunting after all! The quarry has come to us!"

We were all standing stock still. I had never had a gun pointed at me before, and it didn't seem real, but at the same time my heart was pounding in my chest. I felt rather than saw Malcolm move towards me.

"Back!" commanded Fox-Drummin as if he were talking to a dog. Then, to the sergeant, "Have your taser ready! Duncan, we need your rifle too."

He was glaring at us. "Right, all of you," he demanded. "Sit on the ground. Every one of you. Hands on your heads! Duncan, if anyone of them so much as moves, shoot them. The knees are often a good target... not you, woman!" He was addressing me now. "You come here!"

Around me, everyone was sitting down. I saw out of the corner of my eye how hard it was for Holti to lower himself to the ground – he was an old man. None of them was prepared to risk my life. Would Fox-Drummin really shoot me? I felt pretty sure he would. I walked over to him, as he had instructed. Fox-Drummin held his gun pointing in my direction, only a few inches from my ribs.

"Now, you listen carefully!" His voice was calm but full of threat. "I need to explain some things to you, and you need to think carefully – very carefully – about what I say. Because your future – the future of all of you – depends on you using your common sense. Which," he added, "there's been very little sign of, recently!"

Nobody said anything.

"Good!" Fox-Drummin sounded like a schoolmaster now, a teacher from some old movie. "Well, I explained to you *sommy klingers*," he was looking in the direction where most of the refugees were sitting, "I told you before how things could be for you. You either stay here and work for us, and we look after you, or you go back to the mainland and take your chances. It's all the same to us. I'm sure there's plenty more where you come from! You haven't changed anything by these ridiculous antics of yours!"

Then he glared around at the rest of the crowd, all seated on the ground, all with their hands on their heads. "I expect you've come here at the suggestion of the cop?" he asked. "But you must have realised already that, whatever tall story he's told you isn't true. Do you think Sergeant Stensen would have brought his dog out here to help us if we were the ones in the wrong? The fact is, these people from the west of the island, they're poor. Much poorer than those of you who live in Storhaven!"

I realised at that point that, of course, Fox-Drummin didn't know that a good number of his captive audience also came from the west. The sergeant knew, of course, and gave an uncomfortable cough, but Fox-Drummin ignored him.

"The truth of the matter is this," he explained, "these peasants broke into our house. I'm sorry, I'm sure you don't like to hear such things about your fellow islanders, but it's true. All we want is to bring them to justice. It has nothing to do with the rest of you. The best thing you can do is to go quietly home and leave it to the good sergeant here to do what's necessary!"

Dougie Fraser did a brave thing, then. He called out, "I don't believe you!"

There was a chorus of agreement. Fox-Drummin went a little pink.

"Well," he answered, "that doesn't really matter at all. Your beliefs are, after all, your own business. But let me just remind you of one or two things. En-Somi is a remote island. Well, of course, we all know that. Our population is small. We have a subsistence economy. The government on the mainland can't support us, out here, without the taxes of the few of us who actually bring in some money. They can't afford to subsidise the ferry, or pay the schoolteachers, or maintain the other services. You know that! But of course, they don't have to worry. And why not? Because we do it! Duncan, here, and my neighbours and even my own good self! We're the ones who pay the island taxes! It's thanks to us that the mast was erected. We subsidise the ferry. And if we stopped – if we just moved away for one year, paid our taxes in Edinburgh or Aberdeen – what do you think would happen? The ferry company would reduce their services. A particularly bad storm would damage the mast and you'd have no more internet access.

"Believe me," his voice was lower now, and had a grim ring to it. "Within years you would all leave. You'd have to. Think what happened to the people of Mingulay, Cara, Liten Stein and Scarba. All those islands were inhabited once; they're all deserted now! You know that's true, and you know it could happen here too!

"The fact is, you need us. You call us *harkrav* and think of us as outsiders, but without us, this island would be nothing. Nothing!

"So, all things considered, don't you think that the wise thing to do – the only practical thing to do, under the circumstances, is to go home, let the sergeant do the work he's paid to do, and mind your own business? There's no reason we can't all live here, on good terms with each other, if only we all mind our own business!"

Fox-Drummin could be very persuasive. As I listened to him, I must admit that, for a fraction of a second, even I could see the advantages of letting the whole matter drop. Would the refugees be any better off if they left the island? At least they were settled on En-Somi. And it was true that, without the taxes paid by the *harkrav*, the island economy would probably collapse. From what Verity had told us, and what we had overheard, it didn't seem as if any help would be coming from anywhere else.

I looked across at the faces of my friends. And I read defeat.

★ ★ ★

254

The wind had dropped. A strange silence fell over the whole scene. The dog, seated at the feet of the sergeant, had his tongue hanging out, and was panting hopefully, waiting for action. Away in the distance we could hear sheep baaing. I thought vaguely that there would be a fresh crop of lambs by Easter, and I wondered, as if I were thinking about a plot in a film, whether I would live to see them. The gull which had landed on the wall before – or one very like it – swooped down to investigate, and then circled away, out over the wide, free ocean. I could feel the point of the rifle against my ribs, and smell garlic from Fox-Drummin's breath as he glared in my direction.

Then, slowly and stiffly, Holti hauled himself up off the ground, using the wall behind him to steady himself.

"Sit down!" demanded Duncan, waving his rifle rather uncertainly in Holti's direction.

The old man did no such thing. "Why?" he asked. "What will you do if I don't? Shoot me? I'm eighty-three years old already! Quite ready to meet my maker!" His voice was surprisingly strong for such an old man. "More than I think you are!"

Fox-Drummin dug the rifle a little harder against my ribcage, at the side, under my arm. "Never mind your worthless old life!" he almost hissed. "It's not you who'll feel my first bullet! It's this one here – interfering bitch!"

Malcolm sprang to his feet. "*Nei!*" he shouted. His face was white. "You leave her alone!"

The sergeant stepped forward and fired his taser at Malcolm. Malcolm let out a scream, and fell to the ground again, writhing.

Holti was still standing. "Oh, so brave!" he taunted the sergeant. "Definitely a proud member of the *nasyonii*, tasering an unarmed man for standing up!"

"Shut up!" said Duncan between gritted teeth. "Just keep your peasant mouth closed!"

But at that point, Ingrid also stood. "Why should he keep his mouth closed?" she demanded. "We're *bondii*, free men and women, *En-Som-in-Fedii*, every one of us! So taser me for standing, if you want to…"

"Or me!" called out Dougie, also standing, putting one arm round his wife, glaring at the sergeant.

"You can taser me while you're at it!" claimed Petter, also standing.

"And me!" It was Malchi calling out now.

All along the line, men and women were taking their hands off their heads, standing up, fixing the armed men with angry eyes, determined eyes.

"Sit down!" shouted Fox-Drummin, red in the face, breathing deeply. "Her life is in your hands! Don't think I won't shoot! Don't think I haven't killed before!"

Then I heard it, in the distance. Not a plane. It was a helicopter – and the only time helicopters ever flew into En-Somi was if there'd been an accident.

I saw Duncan look across at Fox-Drummin. "What's that?" he asked, sounding suddenly uncertain. "Air-sea rescue?"

"*Nei.*" It was the sergeant who answered. His face, which had looked grim ever since he had tasered Malcolm, was looking grimmer still. "I get an automatic notification if air-sea rescue or border patrol are on the way." He patted the phone holster on his belt.

"Police?" asked his sidekick, one of the men whom he must have brought with him.

"*Nei,* impossible!" exclaimed the sergeant, but I heard a note of panic in his voice.

Suddenly, the dog started to growl, and to pull at his lead. Something was attracting his attention, something on the track leading up to the bothy.

"What…!" It was Fox-Drummin, staring open-mouthed beyond his house, in the direction in which the dog was straining. He let the rifle slip, and in that instant, Petter sprang forward and pulled me away from the man.

At almost the same time, we all saw what had shocked Fox-Drummin. Standing at the entrance to the patio, clutching the spades and forks from the back of Robert's cart, was Jean. *Aja*, Jean, from the Copper Kettle, and a small group of people I didn't know.

"What the hell!" Fox-Drummin must have felt completely out of control of the situation by then.

"Not 'ell!" announced Jean, looking surprisingly calm. I believe she even smiled. "Law an' order!"

"Law and order, my foot!" Fox-Drummin was trying to assert his dominance again. "What do you know about law and order! You're no better than the rest of your crowd!"

"Maybe," agreed Jean, and she was still smiling. "But better 'n you, that's for sure!"

"Shut up!" demanded Fox-Drummin.

"Why?" wondered Jean. "I've been shutting up at your say-so for long enough!"

"You keep your stupid mouth closed," hissed Fox-Drummin, "or I'll demand my loan back. Then you'll be homeless! Destitute! No better than that lot!" He nodded angrily to the cluster of refugees.

"I *ain't* no better than them," announced Jean. "But I'm better 'n you, like I said. I ain't no smuggler, and I ain't never bribed no one, and I sure as 'ell ain't never murdered no one!"

Malcolm had staggered to his feet. He stood beside me and gripped my hand.

"So, what's you all going to do now?" demanded Jean. "Shoot the lot of us?"

"It would serve you right if we did!" Duncan was, it seemed, a poor loser.

"And get rid of our bodies... 'ow?" Jean wanted to know. "I sees, what, fifteen – twenty islanders, and them refugees... And you'll explain all these deaths by saying...?"

I could see the rage on Fox-Drummin's face, but beside him, the sergeant and Duncan just looked frightened. The man whom the sergeant had brought with him sidled away, and then gave a sort of jump, so that he had joined the group of refugees. Behind Fox-Drummin, I could see the woman peering out through the window of the house, a look of alarm on her face.

Then came a new sound. It was a steady sound, the sound of marching feet. Not lots of feet, but very regular. A disciplined sound.

"Oh, yeah!" Jean spoke again. "I forgot to mention. I phoned the coastguard in Aberdeen. I 'eard people talking in the street outside my 'ouse. They was saying that the minister wanted 'elp. I guessed what was up. So I phoned. Seemed they 'ad an idea somefing was wrong up 'ere, but they wasn't sure. So they sent an 'elicopter. That'll be them, now!"

And as she spoke, the men turned the corner and came into view.

Well, you probably know the rest, or you can guess it. All the evidence of the smuggling was still on Lyle's phone, and so it was pretty straightforward. Fox-Drummin, Duncan, the woman and a couple of other *harkrav* were arrested and taken off the island before the next storm blew in. Sergeant Stensen's story was headline news for weeks: a corrupt police officer working with arms smugglers. I think they even made a film about it, years later, in the *Bad Cop, Good Cop* series.

It was tough for the refugees. Theirs was not an easy transition. They had been little better than slaves for years, the children had almost no education and most of them, children and adults, were suffering from some degree of trauma. But theirs is a different story.

★ ★ ★

We *En-Som-in-Fedii*, islanders, all made our ways home, to Storhaven or to Gamla Hus, or to our various bothies on the moors. Olaf wrote a song about us, and people still sing it, in the *fi'ilsted*, and when we all get together for Solstice. Life moved on. Things changed, as things always will, but En-Somi remained the same. There are still orcas in the sea and *muckle scarf* in the air, there are still wealthy *harkrav* on Floirean's Cnoc, and a few ruined bothies out on the moors, though fewer now than there used to be. The seasons come and go, wilder than ever, and less predictable, but stunningly beautiful.

And so, as you see, I have grown old on this lonely island.

LOCAL DIALECT

aja	yes
bondi	peasant. Plural *bondii*
Bothan Ros	Rose Cottage
Caldbrae	Cold Hill (from Cauld Brae)
cludgie	loo
domstol	the court of the kirk elders (as in the elders' meeting)
En-Somi	Lonely Island
En-Som-fly-Kninger	refugees
En-Som-in-Fedii	islanders (plural)
fi'ilsted	literally 'fish hearth', best translated as 'pub'. Plural *fi'ilstedi*
Gamla Husmannsplass	'Old Homestead' – the village
Gamla Hus	abbreviation of *Gamla Husmannsplass*
gensi	a pullover jumper. Plural *gensii*
goddi morgoni	good morning. Often abbreviated to *morgoni*
gronnki sengi	kale beds
harkrav	from *har krav pa* – elites (literally 'entitled')
hei	hi or hello
huldufolk	elves (literally 'hidden people')
Hus	abbreviation of *Gamla Husmannsplass*
langspil	zither-like musical instrument
Liten Stein	Little Rock
mam	mum

Mori-mori	grandmother
muckle scarf	cormorants
nasyoni	police officer. Plural *nasyonii*
nei	no
Oyrod	Island Council. Members of the *Oyrod* are *oyrodi*
papa (or paps)	father or dad
pari-pari	grandfather
Paske Ekstrom	Eastern Extreme
pylsa	the island version of hot dogs
solstice-brenni	the fires lit to celebrate the winter solstice. Plural *solstice brennii*
sommy klinger	corrupt and insulting form of *En-Som-fly-Kninger* or refugee
un-fed	outsider. Plural *un-fedii*

262